SAFE AT THE
EDGE OF THE
WORLD

OTHER BOOKS BY THE AUTHOR

So Much Owed

Shadow of a Century

Under Heaven's Shining Stars

Sisters of the Southern Cross

Catriona's War

The Tour Series

The Tour

Safe at the Edge of the World

The Story of Grenville King

The Homecoming of Bubbles O'Leary

Finding Billie Romano

The Robinswood Series

What Once Was True

Return to Robinswood

Trials and Tribulations

The Carmel Sheehan Series

Letters of Freedom

What Will Be

The Future's Not Ours to See

The Star and the Shamrock

The Emerald Horizon

D'an phiobaire, mo fíorghrá, go deo na ndeor.

Where the wave of moonlight glosses
    The dim gray sands with light,
    Far off by furthest Rosses
    We foot it all the night,
    Weaving olden dances
    Mingling hands and mingling glances
    Till the moon has taken flight;
    To and fro we leap
    And chase the frothy bubbles,
    While the world is full of troubles
    And anxious in its sleep.
    Come away, O human child!
    To the waters and the wild
    With a faery, hand in hand,
    For the world's more full of weeping than you can understand.
W.B. Yeats

CHAPTER 1

*D*eclan and Lucia held hands as the luxury tour bus trundled and bounced along the narrow, winding Irish roads. Declan glanced around as she laid her head on his shoulder, still a little uncomfortable with this type of public display of affection. Beside him, lost in her own world, Lucia gazed out of the window. She was such a sweet girl, not at all the spoiled princess she could be given her background. He felt such a strong surge of love and sense of needing to protect her. Sitting here, the sun shining in the window of the bus as the green fields sped by beside them, he almost found it hard to believe that they were in danger, but they were, and to forget it, even for a second, would be a very grave mistake.

The past forty-eight hours kept running around in his head. It was inconceivable to him how much his life had changed, and yet here he was, on a bus tour of Ireland, sitting beside Lucia, thousands of miles away from home and, well, everything. He wondered, did they look like a normal couple on vacation? He hoped so. This was difficult enough without anyone else on the tour asking awkward questions. It felt right, the two of them together, but in so many ways and for a myriad of reasons, it was wrong. His head hurt from trying to analyse this whole situation. The tour guide and bus driver, Conor, was a highly entertaining guy, and if he weren't so caught up in his own thoughts, Declan knew he'd enjoy the commentary. The atmosphere on the bus was jovial and everyone seemed to be having a good time. He laughed when they did, though he'd missed the joke, and even took pictures when told to, but the land of his ancestors was passing him by in a blur.

As he'd told Lucia several times since they left the states, worrying solved nothing, so he tried to focus on the endless emerald fields and stony farms of the Irish countryside. His reflection in the glass showed the face of a man much older than he was just a few short months ago.

His black hair was grey at the temples and his face had gotten thinner. At six foot two he couldn't really afford to lose weight, but the stress of recent weeks meant he just couldn't eat. Despite his best efforts to blend in as a happy-go-lucky tourist, his piercing green eyes seemed to him to betray him; he thought he looked hunted. He wondered if people noticed. One or two of the ladies on the coach had been friendly, maybe a little too friendly for an initial meeting, but he was used to that. Lucia often teased him about the admiring glances he received from the ladies of the parish every Sunday, but he explained it was because they didn't see him as a man as such; that's why they confided in him and sought him out. She wasn't convinced though, pointing out that old Father Orstello, who was in his eighties and had very bad rheumatoid arthritis, didn't get the same treatment. He smiled; all these feelings were so new, to have a woman love him as Lucia did, to find him attractive, for him to reciprocate. It was all so amazing, and under any other circumstances but these, it would be wonderful.

If times were normal, and this were a normal vacation, it would have been just fantastic, though possibly they would book into a little hotel somewhere and explore on their own, but a bus tour was safer. Someone had confessed to him a few years ago that he was having an affair and that he had taken his mistress on a bus tour simply because there was no paper trail. You didn't need to rent a car, or check into a hotel using your details. You just booked the tour and the tour company made all the reservations for you so it was much more difficult to be caught out. At the time Declan had been appalled at such duplicitous behavior but the information had proved useful. They'd had to get out immediately and with a minimum of fuss, and a bus tour was the first thing he thought of. Ironically, this one was called Irish Escape. That's precisely what he and Lucia needed so he made the reservation in New York at ten pm and flew to Ireland at seven am the next morning. Thank goodness for lastminute.com.

He'd always wanted to visit Ireland. He knew he'd love it; he planned to one day visit the places his great-grandparents came from, maybe even find a cousin or two, but they certainly weren't here to relax and take in the gorgeous scenery. He was surprised to notice how Irish he looked, now that he was here. He'd expected there to be lots of red-haired people, but Conor had explained that the more typical Irish look was exactly Declan's combination of coloring: pale skin, dark hair, and blue or green eyes. Lucia looked so Italian by comparison. Declan's skin never tanned while she was olive-skinned, with dark brown hair that fell over her shoulders and eyes the colour of melted chocolate. He felt his stomach lurch as he thought of her beauty. No woman had ever had the effect on him that she did. She didn't dress provocatively, quite the opposite, and unlike the other female members of her family, she wasn't one for tons of makeup, but she had a natural beauty that was breathtaking. He was unsure about so many things, but his feelings for her were never in doubt. He loved her, heart and soul, and no matter what happened next, he would be by her side, protecting her.

Lucia told him that she was sure their fellow passengers thought she was a little unhinged, so jumpy and nervous, but Declan assured her that nobody on the tour thought anything about them. They were just folks on vacation who wanted to see Ireland, drink a pint of Guinness, and take some pictures. He told her she was being paranoid. She sighed, replying that maybe he was right, but how on earth were they supposed to just act normal, seriously? He asked himself the same question, but he had to make Lucia feel like he was in control, that she was safe, so he kept his concerns to himself.

'Fake it till you make it,' Declan repeated to himself several times a day, so he stood in for pictures, and acted like the enthusiastic tourist as best he could. It was torture initially, but as time went by he began to let the sense of tranquility on this island seep into his bones, and take in the splendour and peacefulness of the land. He felt curiously at home, even though it was his first trip to Ireland. It felt like nothing bad could happen here. It didn't stop him scanning every newspaper headline and checking the news channels the moment they got back to the room, but as the sun shone through the glass of the window, warming his face, he took a deep breath. Maybe it was all going to work out ok. He just had to keep it together for a bit longer; he could do that.

He thought about his ancestors who came from Ireland, who left their home and everything they knew and understood, for the excitement and uncertainty of life in the United States. If they could show such resilience, then so could he. He had Sullivan blood in his veins, and Sullivans were made of tough stuff.

A cousin of Declan's, Patti, was into genealogy and so she had presented each branch of the clan with a beautiful family tree a few Christmases ago, showing how Daniel and Hannah O'Sullivan, both aged seventeen, got married in the church at Queenstown, County Cork, a mere two hours before sailing from the dock there for Ellis Island. They came in to the United States through the new Immigrant Inspection Station in 1938. He recalled his grandmother telling him about the trauma of getting to the states, sailing by the Statue of Liberty and seeing the Manhattan skyline, tantalizingly close, but the immigration station had to be endured first. The inspection officers boarded the ships and processed first- and second-class passengers there and then, allowing them off the boats almost immediately, but the third class, which Dan and Annie, as they were known, were, had to wait on the ship for two days because so many immigrants were awaiting processing. Declan would hang on his granny's every word as she told him about the button hook, which the doctors used to check under eyelids for some awful disease. He couldn't quite remember now what it was, but his grandma was determined that both she and Dan would be found in perfect health. They exercised on the ship every day and only drank rainwater, they brought their own food and doled it out daily; they were determined from the start to pass any inspection, get into the United States, and make a new life.

When he was a student, he'd visited the museum there and was moved to tears as he thought about brave young Dan and Annie standing in separate lines in that huge hall, every language of the world ringing in their ears, their hearts filled with trepidation and hope. She had some dollars sewn into her skirt, sent by her older brother Declan—he was named after his grand-uncle, who was killed on the railroad two weeks before Dan and Annie landed. She loved him, and often talked of her first days in New York when a neighbour and friend from home had to break the news to her. She was tough though, and with Dan they forged ahead. She said she considered for one minute the possibility of going back home, so heartbroken was she, but she realised that the fare and the few dollars were Declan's legacy to her; to return would be to dishonour him, so they stayed. They settled first in Hell's Kitchen, where they had some contacts, but they were quick learners and hard workers. Dan soon got his foot on the ladder of a building firm and worked his way up, eventually setting up his own firm in Brooklyn.

They lived to see Declan grow up and he had lots of memories of them, surrounded by the extended family. Dan and Annie went home to God within months of each other in their eightieth year, and their send-offs were fitting tributes to two brave, hardworking, kind people who took on the world and won. They died surrounded by their children, grandchildren, and even a few great-grandchildren. The extended Sullivan family were deeply proud of their Irish heritage. They took all the things about Ireland they liked, admired, and could identify with and celebrated their culture with gusto. Declan smiled at the memory of his dad, Dan and Annie's youngest son, singing "Mother Mo Chroí" every St. Patrick's Day, and his rendition of "Danny Boy" at the funerals of their many friends and relations left few eyes dry. His mother, Bridget, a good Irish-Catholic girl herself, played her part when the family kept the tradition first started by Annie, entertaining the neighbourhood each March 17 with music, songs, and enough corned beef and cabbage to feed a nation. Declan thought about his parents, how they'd have loved it here. It was hard to believe they were gone too, killed instantly together in a car accident five years ago. They had planned to visit Ireland for the first time the summer after they were killed. His dad had been so excited at the prospect of visiting Ireland; he'd been researching the trip for months, working out where they could visit to establish the link between his generation and those that went before. He fought back the stinging tears behind his eyes as he gazed out the window.

He missed his parents desperately, but at least their untimely death meant they didn't have to endure the last few months. He couldn't begin to imagine how they would have felt at seeing everything they worked so hard for destroyed. It had embarrassed him as a young man how proud they were of him.

For fourteen years it looked like they would be childless, when suddenly at the age of forty-four, Bridget and Tom Sullivan found out they were going to have a baby. His mom was delighted if a little embarrassed, she later confided to him; it wasn't seemly to be pregnant so late in life. But he was born fit and healthy and the whole family was thrilled. Tom wanted to name his son after his mother's brother, the reason they were all in the states. He remembered vividly his mother recounting the first time baby Declan was placed in Annie's arms; she said the connection between them was instant and so strong it was palpable. She and Dan were proud of all their grandchildren, but Declan had a special place in Annie's heart. He used to love visiting his granny and granda (though all the other kids in his class had different names for their grandparents, his were called what grandparents were called back in Ireland). They loved his visits and always had treats for him. He was an only child but was never lonely; he had so many cousins and aunts and uncles around. It was all one big happy family, and his childhood was punctuated by birthdays, communions, confirmations, and weddings. Those carefree days seem like a lifetime ago now.

His parents worked so hard so that he could be well educated, sending him off to the Jesuits when he was seven. Looking back, he probably seemed like a deeply thoughtful child, and he was always very devout. All his life, God was not just a notion, someone to be kept in a church, but more a real living presence in his life. He remembered the day he told his parents he was going to the seminary. They were so happy. He had a vocation, he'd always known it, since he was a little boy, that he wanted to be a priest and they couldn't have been more pleased. Annie and Dan sat in the front pew of the cathedral beside Tom and Bridget and even though his grandparents were elderly and very frail, Declan remembered thinking the four of them might burst with pride. They were good Catholics, went to Mass every Sunday without fail, and observed feast days, Lent, and Advent. To have a priest in the family was a dream many Irish Catholic families harboured but few realised. They weren't the kind of family to be boastful, they worked hard for everything they had, but that day, well, it was a high point and he knew it.

Once ordained, he baptised the babies, married the couples, and buried the dead of the Sullivan family. He loved New York and New Jersey and felt he was at his best there. Bishop Rameros and he were good friends, and Declan always made a great case for staying. He visited his parents in Brooklyn often, only a short drive away from where he lived in Hoboken, New Jersey.

So many of his fellow priests had to deal with the care of elderly or infirm parents but he was lucky: Tom and Bridget were fit and healthy and were really enjoying their retirement; they loved to travel all over the East Coast in their RV. Declan used to joke that he needed to make an appointment to see his parents. After the accident, he fell apart for a while. He just missed them so much, and not having any siblings, he found it hard to explain just how huge their loss was for him. One of the first real conversations he'd ever had with Lucia was about them. He didn't usually let his parishioners into his personal life, but she was different, in every way imaginable. The only time he'd ever cried for his mother and father with another person was with her. He'd spoken about it at the time to Fr Orstello, with whom he ran the parish, and he was kind and understanding, and felt bad that his illness prevented him from being much help to young Father Sullivan, especially when he was grieving. Fr Orstello had a large extended family, lots of nieces and nephews, and he was very close to them, so he rarely needed to confide in Declan. Though the two men were fond of each other, they weren't that close.

Declan was very raw for a long time, frequently picking up the phone to call his mother only to realize she was gone. Not that he needed mothering, but just that his childhood home was gone, and with it a large part of him. Slowly, he came to terms with the loss and life resumed.

Lucia watched the Irish landscape go by and knew she should be enjoying the scenery, but all she could do was concentrate on not vomiting. Declan's idea to go on a bus tour, something about being less detectible, seemed like a good idea at the time, when her whole world was crashing around her ears, but now, as the little coach lurched over the impossibly bumpy roads, she just tried to focus on the horizon and control the nausea. She was a bad traveler at the best of times, but this was torture. She'd hardly eaten a thing, even water, but still she swallowed constantly, praying she didn't get sick.

Declan had been amazing and it was entirely her fault that they were in this mess. Lucia squeezed his hand and gave him a gentle smile. She could be in a much worse position now if he hadn't acted so decisively, so bravely. He squeezed hers back, as she tried to focus on what the driver was saying. Conor was telling a very funny story about an old Irish king called Cornelius O'Brien, who was caught in the wrong place with the wrong lady by his quick-tempered wife. He was in the process of building a tower at the time apparently, and was taking one of the ladies of the court to view the progress of the new castle among other activities. The wife caught them and was so incensed with rage at his unfaithfulness she murdered him there and then. Conor explained that forever after the castle was known as 'the last erection of Cornelius O'Brien'. Lucia and Declan managed a smile. The entire bus was giggling and got off to take a photo of the castle and the breathtaking vistas of green patchwork fields bordered by tiny stone walls. They were in County Clare on the west coast of Ireland, and the expanse of the crashing Atlantic was laid out before them, a glittering azure blue. Huge seabirds circled and cawed over-head as they went back and forth to their nests on the high cliffs, the pounding surf relentless below.

This was the second day of the tour, and though she was still jumpy, the gentle Irish landscape was soothing her troubled mind. Last night she'd slept in his arms for the entire night for the very first time. They'd been together before, but never for a whole night, and to wake up to him beside her was such a lovely feeling. At least until the nausea set in, that was. He'd never seen it before and had no idea what to do as she retched and retched and eventually crawled back into bed. She had to explain to him that it was normal, that, in fact, it was the sign of a perfectly healthy pregnancy and that he needn't worry.

Today was Saturday. If she'd not run away, if she would have stayed and done what was expected of her, she'd be married now. She thought about Antonio, wondered how he was. She felt awful, such crushing guilt, at humiliating him and breaking his heart like she had. He wasn't at fault at all, but she couldn't lie anymore. Declan was the one for her, he always had been, and to marry Antonio would have been a terrible lie. She knew that if she'd gone ahead with it she would have ended up hurting everyone in the end but still, it felt so horribly cruel. Her father's face replaced Antonio's. Where was he now? What was he thinking?

9

CHAPTER 2

*D*eclan squeezed Lucia's hand. 'You're thinking about it again,' he murmured gently. 'I always know. It's done now. Let's just try to look like we're enjoying our vacation and put it out of our minds, ok? You're doing great.'

The bus went over a particularly bad bump. Lucia bolted to the front of the bus and gestured to Conor that he should stop. He pulled in at the side of the road and Lucia retched violently into the bushes.

Declan followed her and stood by helplessly as she threw up the few sips of water she'd managed to swallow.

'I'm sorry,' he began to Conor, who appeared with wet wipes and a bottle of water.

'Don't be one bit sorry, Declan. If anyone should be sorry it's those fat cat politicians of ours who don't give a hoot about the condition of the roads!' He handed Lucia some wipes and offered her the water. Declan had never seen anyone look so ill; she was pale and almost green in her complexion, and her hair hung limply around her face.

'I am so sorry, I'm so embarrassed...' Lucia tried to not look up at all the people on the coach watching her sympathetically. She was trying not to cry, but she felt horrible and her sweater was covered in vomit.

'It's these roads, I'm telling you—' Conor was reassuring.

'Well, actually, I'm pregnant,' she interrupted.

'Oh I see, my wife was exactly the same when she was expecting our twins, it was awful. I used to feel so guilty, knowing that only for me, she wouldn't be in that position.' He smiled and patted her on the back.

Declan felt useless. He'd only ever taken care of people in a pastoral way, never as a man in a relationship, and certainly never as a father.

'Here, wear this, at least it's warm and…'

'Not covered in vomit,' she finished for him.

He took off his own sweatshirt and gave it to Lucia. Conor handed her a small plastic bag and helped her to place her soiled sweater inside. Gratefully she drew on Declan's warm hoodie, which was miles too big but comforting.

'I'm so mortified, Declan.' She turned to him and he wrapped his arms around her, soothing her and kissing the top of her head.

'Don't be silly, no harm done…everyone will understand once they know…they're nice people. It's fine, try to take a little water, I'm afraid you'll get dehydrated.' As he opened the bottle and offered it to her, the rain began to fall softly. 'I'm not sure dehydration is something they've ever heard of here.' She managed to joke, glad of the refreshing soft rain on her face.

Debbie, a young red-haired woman travelling alone, came out of the bus with some hard candy.

'I don't know if you needed one of these, to suck?'

'Thanks, that would be great,' said Declan, taking it from her.

'Are you ok? Can we do anything?'

'I think we're ok now, thank you though for the candy.' He knew Lucia would hate all the fuss, but their fellow passengers were just being kind.

'Do you think you can get back on the bus?' he asked Lucia gently, wiping her tears with his thumbs.

She nodded. 'I think so.'

'It's not far to our next stop, five or ten minutes, and maybe you could get some fresh air then or maybe even an herbal tea or something,' Conor suggested as he took the bag with the soiled sweater and placed it in the luggage compartment below the bus.

'That would be great, thanks,' she said as she climbed the steps once more. He was such a lovely man, and she knew he was trying to make it seem as though passengers throwing up in the hedgerows was a normal occurrence just to make her feel at ease.

Conor didn't look Irish at all, and on the first day she wondered where he came from, but as soon as he spoke there was no mistaking that Irish lilt. He was in his late forties, maybe fifty at the most, tall and muscular, with tanned skin, piercing blue eyes, and silver hair. He dressed impeccably in crisp shirts and tailored dark trousers, and Lucia noticed she wasn't the only woman on the tour to cast an admiring glance in his direction. One or two had tried flirting, but no dice. A gold band on his left hand told them he was taken, and was not going to succumb to anyone's advances. Despite his obvious good looks though, he seemed totally unaware of his attractiveness. He chatted with everyone, and seemed to be having as good a time as his passengers. He told them fascinating stories of Ireland, and his knowledge of the country was encyclopedic; it seemed no matter what he was asked, he knew the answer.

He told them he used to do this job full time until he met his wife, and now he did more management and arranging of tours, but on this occasion, as it was the height of the season and they were stuck for a driver guide, he stepped in. The group discussed over breakfast that morning how they'd lucked out to get him. Declan and Lucia were quiet during these conversations, but they smiled and added a word here and there. Conor was the glue that bound the disparate group together, and within twenty-four hours of landing he had the whole group eating out of his hand.

The night before they had been talking about the many interesting people who had joined the tour. One woman, Valentina, was very glamorous, dripping in gold and designer clothes, on vacation with her husband Tony, a loud, bombastic bore. She seemed to take everything in but she barely spoke. There was a cute elderly couple, Irene and Ken, who had no house at all it seemed and spent their entire life on vacation, either on tours or on cruises. They fascinated the group with tales of their extravagant lifestyle, but over dinner last night they'd explained how they'd sold their house in Miami and were determined to spend every bit of the money before they died. One of the other people, a slightly earthy lady with a faint German accent called Elke who was travelling with her daughter, asked them directly what they'd do if they ran out of money before they died and were left homeless.

They looked at each other for a moment then Ken said quite calmly, 'Irene here has cancer, we've opted not to treat it. We just want to enjoy what time we have left and then, well, I won't be hanging around without her, so we won't run out.' He patted his wife's hand and smiled.

Then she spoke, 'We've had forty-nine years together, almost fifty, so we're one of the lucky ones. Whatever time is left we're going to enjoy; it's all good, as they say.'

Their revelation bonded the little group and even though they were all strangers, they felt somehow connected. There were others on the tour as well, but they seemed to be happy to be left to themselves. Conor took extra-special care of Irene and Ken and nobody minded that they always sat in the front or that he got them into their rooms in hotels first. Conor just had that way of making everything look effortless.

He spoke about his wife and his boys sometimes, telling the tourists cute stories about them to fill the hours as he drove fearlessly along tiny roads above crashing ocean. The bumpy roads were so narrow, Lucia was nervous sitting at the window, fearful the bus would go careering off the side into the pounding Atlantic below. Declan loved it though, and was happily snapping away on his Nikon every chance he got. He loved taking photos, and even in this most stressful and peculiar of situations, he was able to immerse himself in the moment when he was shooting. Also it made them look more like tourists and less like fugitives, which was what they were.

CHAPTER 3

*D*eclan noticed some of the men on the trip admiring Lucia; despite her wan complexion, she was a beauty by anyone's standards. In particular that Tony seemed to be particularly lecherous. It was a strange sensation, jealousy, possessiveness. Though one or two of his friends had questioned his lack of interest in women over the years, he could always answer truthfully and say it wasn't anything he considered. He was a priest, and he was celibate and that was that, a done deal. It didn't bother him at all, and certainly not as much as his lay friends thought it must. But with Lucia, everything was different. He loved her and wanted her in a way that he had never felt before. He also found himself both liking and disliking the experience of other men admiring her; he was proud that she was with him, but the thought of anyone else feeling about her the way he did made him feel ill. Immediately the image of Antonio Dias appeared in his mind. It was the right thing to do, for him as well as for Lucia, to leave it all, but that didn't stop the guilt. Antonio and Lucia weren't suited; sure, they came from similar backgrounds but she wasn't really like them. She was different, had a different moral compass for one thing.

She was his soul mate, he was sure of it, and just as God had called him to the church all those years ago, now that he was thirty-five, God had called him to Lucia. While he realized he was definitely the more outgoing of the two, they both tread lightly on the earth, serene and quiet, contemplative people. In another world, things could have been perfect for them. Looking over at her now, he found it hard to imagine any positive outcome. He wished she'd eat, even if she did get sick afterward. It couldn't be good retching on an empty stomach, but she couldn't face anything.

Conor pulled into the car park of the Cliffs of Moher, a place so wild and remote you really felt you were teetering on the edge of the world. There was a gift shop of course and a nice sunny café. Maybe he'd even convince her to eat some bread or toast. That Irish soda bread was so good, dark and dense and slathered with creamy yellow butter. He found himself really enjoying the food here, and he was regaining the weight he'd lost in recent weeks due to stress. Sea birds circled noisily overhead, and the salty wind from the ocean whipped around their faces as they walked from the coach. It had cleared to be a beautiful day, bright and sunny. Conor then took them on a walk through an old ruined famine village that morning and Declan thought again of Dan and Annie and the land they'd left behind.

'Excuse me, I hope you don't mind me interfering, but are you pregnant by any chance?' Declan and Lucia looked at Elke, the German-American lady travelling with her daughter. She'd just caught up with them as they approached the café. Her daughter was behind talking to Debbie and another young girl travelling with her grandparents. Elke had a funky short haircut but with a very long skinny narrow braid over her shoulder, wrapped in colourful threads. She was in her late forties and dressed in a bohemian way—Birkenstock sandals and wide-leg trousers—and Lucia had seen her do yoga on the lawn of the hotel just after dawn when she got up to go to the bathroom. The three of them walked to the café.

'Ah...yes,' Lucia answered warily. This was only the third time she'd said it out loud. The first time was when she told Declan, the night before her planned wedding to Antonio, then to Conor on the roadside, and now to this woman.

'Well, I just wanted to let you know I'm a midwife and I specialize in homeopathy and natural childbirth, but if I can help you at all, I'd be happy to.'

Declan smiled at her kindness, glad she wasn't just being nosy. 'Thank you, that's great to know we have someone who knows about this because I haven't a clue. I'm worried because she doesn't eat...she feels nauseous all the time—'

'I am here, Declan,' Lucia interjected with a weak smile.

Elke smiled and gave Lucia a conspiratorial glance. 'Let's go in out of this wind. I probably have something in my bag that might help.' Elke walked alongside Lucia, leaving Declan to hold the door open for the rest of the group.

'She was right?' Zoe asked him as they followed Lucia and Elke to the cafe. 'She can spot pregnant women at fifty paces. So it's your first baby?'

She was very attractive, Declan noticed, in a Nordic way, with white blonde hair, blue eyes, and a tan, fit, athletic body. She wore all sorts of leather and silver bangles on her wrist and had a tiny sparkly stud in her nose. She looked like an ad you'd see in a glossy travel brochure for California. As a priest, he wouldn't have felt in any way intimidated, but now that he wasn't he found himself nervous. Lucia was different, he knew her so well, but women as women was a whole new world to him.

'Yes, my first, Lucia's first as well, we...we are a bit clueless to be honest,' Declan admitted.

'Well, you're probably doing ok, just being there for her and all that, that's what they say, isn't it? I don't know, but my mom is the baby whisperer so she'll be in good hands. Cool country, huh?'

'Yes, it's amazing. So beautiful and the people are so friendly, at least they have been to us anyway.'

'Yeah, I like it here. I've got a girlfriend back home, but if I hadn't, I'd love to study here, do some post-grad research or something. But I guess I've got to go back, make some money to pay off my student debt.'

Declan noticed how differently people spoke to him when he was dressed in civilian clothes. He'd had to buy clothes at the airport, so he was dressed in dark jeans and a ferociously overpriced Ralph Lauren t-shirt. He knew he'd need a sweater as well and the only one he could find was in the tourist shop at JFK so he was stuck between choosing an I Love NY or an NYPD hoodie. He'd settled on the NYPD one but felt utterly ridiculous in it. At least now Lucia was wearing it. As soon as they got a chance he'd need to go clothes shopping, but right now he had other things on his mind. Zoe was chatting beside him about her girlfriend Gabriella from Chile, who sounded like a lot of work, but Zoe was clearly in love with her. As a priest, people spoke to him about personal matters frequently, most often in the darkness and anonymity of the confession box, so it felt strange to be part of normal human interaction. This girl in her twenties felt no reticence in discussing her lesbian love life with him, and why should she? He was fascinated; it was as if he was coming into a world that always existed but he was seeing it with new eyes.

He never realized it, but he was treated differently as a priest. Now, the men on the tour talked about American football; the awful Tony had even made a ribald comment to Declan about an Irish dancer they saw in the street, something men never did when he had his collar on.

He'd never wear the collar again now, he supposed; that phase was over. He hoped that he and Lucia didn't look too odd. He was thirty-five and she only twenty-three but he wanted people to consider them unremarkable.

They all sat at a large table and people tucked into creamy root vegetable soup or oval-shaped dishes of shepherd's pie, which smelled divine. Elke and Lucia ordered ginger tea and some sweet cookies and he smiled encouragingly at her as she tried to nibble them.

He would have loved the fish pie but ordered a salad in case the smell of fish was too much for her.

Conor joined them as they ate lunch, and the conversation came round to genealogy. Debbie's great-grandmother came from County Galway, and Ken was sure there was some Irish in his family, but he had no idea where. Lucia, Valentina, and Tony were sure they had no Irish in them at all, but Declan stole the show when he told them all about his parents and even got a little choked telling them about his dad singing "Danny Boy." Irene's eyes were suspiciously bright as she said that it was her father's party piece as well. Conor put his hand on Irene's shoulder. 'Ah sure, Irene, you'd want to be made of granite not to cry at that song. It's an Irish-American song more than Irish, per se, but it's sung everywhere now. There's a melancholy in our nature here, I always think, that's the flip side of the vivacious part of our collective personalities. G.K. Chesterton, the poet, had it right y'know: "The great Gaels of Ireland are the men that God made mad, for all their wars are merry and all their songs are sad."'

They smiled, and the sadness passed.

'So, Conor, is it tough being away from home so much in your job?' Elke asked as they all sat in the bright Irish sunshine that shone through the huge windows, offering an uninterrupted view of the stunning vista before them.

'Yes, it really is, though I do a lot less of it these days. There was a time in my life when I toured constantly from March to November and then I'd take off to Spain for the worst of the winter and then back again. I lived in a hotel and all of that, but then I met my wife and that all changed. She domesticated me.' His eyes twinkled and Lucia thought what a lucky woman she was to have finally gotten the handsome Conor O'Shea to settle down. He went on, 'So it would be unfair of me to say it's hard on me. It's much worse for Ana, stuck at home with twin boys who wreck her head and heart and house simultaneously.' He grinned as he sipped his coffee. 'They're a right pair of divils so she's looking forward to me coming home so she can get a break.'

'Divils?' Lucia asked, perplexed. Declan smiled; it was a word he'd often heard his granny use to describe the little ones. Valentina looked a little shocked as well but then she always did; Lucia had explained the effects of Botox to him when they first met her and Tony. They had never heard her speak, but then Tony did enough loud talking for both of them.

Conor explained, 'Oh, it's an Irishism, it's a more benevolent word than devil, though looking at our pair, I'm not too sure that the original word isn't more fitting! They're right tearaways and seem to be just bursting with energy. They only need about five hours sleep and then it's mayhem again. They're total charmers but the mischief they get up to is nobody's business. The trouble is neither of us can stay cross with them, they're so cute. I try, and Ana does the whole "wait till your father gets home" thing, but sure, they've eejits made of the pair of us. They do something bold, then they look up at you with these eyes like butter wouldn't melt and they've won again.' He laughed. 'Yesterday they put makeup on the neighbour's cat, though the same cat sat still through the entire ordeal. Ana was worried about animal cruelty but I told her if the cat didn't like it he'd have scarpered.'

'They sound adorable.' Lucia smiled. 'Do you have a picture of them?'

Conor took out his phone, scrolled to his pictures, and handed her the phone. Lucia, Elke, and Zoe smiled at the picture of the two identical boys, who looked just like their father, and then passed it to Declan. Same blue eyes, tanned skin, and big mops of white blond hair. They looked more Scandinavian than Irish. They were dressed in matching shirts, green on one side and yellow on the other. They were grinning happily and Declan could see how they would be impossible to reprimand.

'There they are, those are their favourite football shirts; one half is an Ireland jersey the other half is Ukrainian. The one on the right is Joe, named after a man who was very good to me when I was a young fella, and the one on the left is Artur, named after Ana's dad, but we call him Artie.' He swiped sideways to get to the next picture. It was of Conor with his arm around a tiny blonde woman who was smiling up at him. She was very striking looking, almost boyish, but different from what she imagined his wife would be. She was dressed unusually, like something from Woodstock, all wooden beads, silver rings, and tie-dye. Lucia had pictured a tall, elegant Irish woman with red hair; this girl looked like a student. 'That's my wife Anastasia.'

'What a beautiful family. How old are your boys?' Lucia noticed how much younger than Conor his wife looked.

'They'll be four next month. We're trying to keep it under wraps for a few more weeks though because they'll be hyper if they think it's soon. My wife is Ukrainian so her parents are coming over for the birthday and they spoil them rotten, but to be honest we all do.' He grinned. 'As you can probably see, I've a good few years on my wife. I don't know what she was thinking to be honest, but she took me on, and now this pair of rascals are just the icing on the cake.'

Lucia could see exactly why she took him on but just smiled.

Declan gave the phone to Irene and Ken to see the pictures, while Tony wolfed his pie and the bottle of craft beer he'd bought. Valentina moved a few lettuce leaves round the plate, eating nothing, but Declan noticed how she couldn't take her eyes off the warm apple crumble with thick whipped cream Tony had waiting.

Ken scrolled through the photos. 'They're so cute. You're lucky. That's what it's all about, Conor, in my opinion anyway. Looking back, I think we were happiest when our kids were small. Not that we're not happy now, and sure, you have more stuff, and a bit more cash when you're older and they're grown up and gone, but when they go, well, it's a big change. The house seems so quiet and clean all of a sudden. I just wish I'd taken more time with our kids when they were younger, but there were bills to pay and all that. Now they're grown up and moved away, living their own lives. It seems it was over in the blink of an eye.' He smiled sadly.

Tony finished his beer and was digging into the crumble when he asked, 'So, Conor, you got much of a problem with illegal aliens here?'

Conor looked unfazed though the others at the table were a little uncomfortable at what he might say next. Tony had already shocked the group with some of his attitudes to women, and he seemed to be determined to explain to anyone who would listen just how wealthy and successful he was.

'Well, Tony, this is certainly a very different Ireland in terms of the demographics to the one I grew up in, and we definitely need to do more to help those coming to our shores in search of asylum, but in general the immigrants have added a huge amount to our culture and to our economy so—'

'Huge mistake,' Tony interrupted rudely. 'If you guys are letting in all these, I dunno, where do your Mexicans come from?' He guffawed at his own wittiness. 'Then you're dumb. You gotta keep 'em out. They're like rats, they'll breed and all of a sudden what seemed like a cute idea, helping the guys in the sheets or old commies or whatever, turns into a huge problem. Thieves, rapists, drug dealers, that's all immigrants are able to do. They don't get what it is to live in a civilized country, y'know, believe me, I know this, I've seen it with my own eyes.'

Before any one of his countrymen could try to fix this mortifying situation, Conor jumped in.

'Well, Tony, my gorgeous wife is Ukrainian, my kids are half Ukrainian, and as you can see, there's nothing ratty about them, so we'll have to agree to differ on that one. Now, folks, I was thinking, how would you like to go hear some traditional music tonight? I've some friends in town and they'll blow your minds. One of them is a young Uileann piper from the states actually; he came on a tour with me a few years back, with his mother. Both of them stayed. His mam, Corlene, is a gas woman altogether. She actually set up a kind of agency for women whose men are inclined to stray. She trains them to keep a tighter leash on them or something. I'm a bit hazy on the details of how it actually works, but it does work apparently. It's mad but she's booked out. The irony is she was here looking for another husband.'

Delighted the conversation had moved away from racism, Zoe grinned. 'Were you her target, Conor?'

He chuckled. 'God no, I'd be much too poor for Corlene's tastes; she likes the high life. But now she's vowed to stay single. She's making a fortune and she has a great friend, a guy she met on the tour called Bert from Texas, and they go on holidays together a couple of times a year. They're not romantic or anything but great mates, and they get on so well you'd swear they were married. Her son Dylan fell in love with Irish music and an Irish musician as well, and they're doing great. They played at the Electric Picnic this year, it's a huge festival in the summer, and they got rave reviews. Myself and Ana went; her folks came over to mind the lads so we had a fantastic weekend. Covered in muck and camping and all that. I'm a bit long in the tooth for that but when you've a beautiful young wife sometimes you have to man up, isn't that right, Declan?' He winked.

'I'm sure trying, Conor, but I'm a bit out of my depth here.' He grinned.

'How far along are you, Lucia?' Irene asked.

'Oh it's very early days, seven or eight weeks, but yes, it's a steep learning curve.'

'You'll feel better in around a month, usually once women enter the second trimester they feel much better.' Elke was reassuring.

'In hindsight, maybe a bus tour wasn't my best idea,' Declan admitted ruefully, and Lucia smiled and placed her hand on his.

'It's great, I'm loving the scenery and Conor's stories. Thanks for taking me.'

Declan grinned and winked at her, giving her hand a squeeze.

'Well, we don't mind a bit,' Ken interjected, 'if it's us you're concerned about. I think it's great, a new life starting, and in a small way we all get to be a part of it.'

They all smiled and agreed except Tony.

'Don't you puke on me, lady, that's all I'm sayin'. This jacket is Armani.' And just in case there was any doubt about it, he took off the coat and showed everyone the label. Valentina had the grace to look embarrassed.

CHAPTER 4

*A*fter a thankfully uneventful day in terms of illness, they arrived back at the hotel. Lucia went for a nap, promising that when she woke she'd get some room service if he wasn't there. He needed some time alone and she sensed that. To go from being a priest, albeit a very busy one in a huge parish, to a full-time partner, boyfriend—even the words jarred him.

Leaving the hotel and walking up the street in the lovely market town of Ennis, he felt he could actually think for the first time since everything blew up. The stores were still busy and lots of people milled about. He thought how nice it was in Ireland that the people still shopped in local stores rather than at huge malls or online.

He walked, lost in his thoughts, until he came to a church. It wasn't his intention to go there but he found himself at the door, and the familiar smells, the silence, the peace were so inviting, they were drawing him in. He pushed the heavy oak doors and entered the silent chapel. The floor of the aisle was tiled in a beautiful Celtic script and flowers adorned every second pew. There must have been a wedding earlier, he thought. The altar was decorated in lilies and irises, and the aroma of them combined with incense soothed his battered soul.

He knelt in a pew halfway down the church and tried to pray.

Where to start? He'd never had a problem connecting with God before; it was less of a prayer for him and more of a constant internal monologue. God was a real live presence in his life, not a notional being but such a substantial part of his consciousness that he could never question His existence. Now, alone in an Irish Catholic church, he was so confused, so conflicted. He got up and sat in a pew, gazing at the image of the crucified Christ behind the altar. The tabernacle hung above it and the sanctuary lamp glowed red. All the familiar accoutrements of the mass were there and he knew that if he were invited to, he could don his vestments and say mass there effortlessly. He would know where everything was, despite the fact he'd never been in this church before. This was his world, but now he felt like an imposter. He'd done the only thing he could: He loved her, and Catholicism demanded celibacy from its clergy. There was no way of coexistence—it was one thing or the other, and for him, it had to be her.

Despair overtook him and he dropped his head to his hands and let out a shuddering sigh.

'A cup of tea often helps.'

Declan sat up, startled, as he'd heard nobody enter the church. Before him stood an old priest carrying a huge stack of battered-looking prayer books that were threatening to topple.

'Em...I just...'

'No problem if you'd rather not, but if you wanted to, I'm making one in the back now in a minute anyway. Sometimes it helps to talk, that's all.'

Maybe that was what he needed—to talk to someone who understood, though how anyone could even begin to understand the mess he was in he couldn't possibly imagine.

'Thanks, I'd like that,' he managed.

'American, are you? Here, grab a few of these, the choir need them for the mass tomorrow but we loaned them to the primary school next door so they need to go back to the gallery,' the priest said, handing him half of the books.

'Ah yes, American, well, Irish American actually.'

'Sure, aren't ye all?' The priest chuckled. 'Forty-four million at the last count I think.' Noting Declan's look of confusion, he explained, 'Forty-four million Irish Americans.'

'Oh right, yeah, there's a lot for sure.'

He followed the old man up the stairs and deposited the books beside a huge pipe organ. There was a battered stool that was bulging with sheet music and several hymnals scattered about the gallery.

'You've got a big choir here it looks like,' Declan remarked.

'We do indeed. Our choir mistress is a tough cookie, as you say in America. Takes no nonsense but somehow she has half the parish belting out "Amazing Grace" every Sunday. Truth be told there's often more up in the gallery singing than there is below in the church, but sure 'tis that way everywhere nowadays I suppose, not that every place has a big choir, but that people don't go to mass in the numbers they used to. You can't blame them considering everything, but there you have it. We just have to soldier on.'

Declan followed him back down the stairs and up the aisle to the altar. Both men stood before the altar and bowed their heads before proceeding through a small door into the sacristy. He was drawn to the old man in the way that he often was with older clergy. He had a shock of white hair that stuck up at peculiar angles from his head and was only around five foot three in height. His belly showed years of being well fed by a likely combination of nuns and well-meaning ladies of the parish, but despite the fact that he must be in his seventies, he was agile and seemed to exude energy. Declan liked him instantly.

The sacristy was warm and crowded with vestments and books, newsletters, and inexplicably, footballs and the hurling sticks Conor had pointed out. Long sticks, like hockey sticks but thicker, that the Irish use to play their national sport.

'Father Eddie Shanahan,' the priest said, extending his hand.

Declan took it. 'Father Declan Sullivan.'

Eddie raised his eyebrows in surprise and nodded. 'You're young to be a priest. All diocesan meetings of clergy over here look like an old folks home outing.' He chuckled.

'Thirty-five. There are two of us in the parish but Fr Orstello isn't well, arthritis, so I'm on my own really.'

'Where's your parish?'

'New Jersey.'

'I was never there. My brother was in The Bronx for a while; I visited him back in the fifties. He's dead now of course. So, what ails you?'

Declan was a bit taken aback by his direct questioning. 'Ah... Nothing, I'm fine, I just...'

'If you don't mind me saying, Father Sullivan, you don't look one bit fine, but it's up to you. Tea? Coffee?'

'Coffee please.' He deliberated for a moment; , he seemed like a straight-up guy, and God knows he'd had enough lies and pretending. He felt like he could trust him. 'Can I make a confession?'

'By all means, anything you say to me here will be under the seal.'

'I'm in big trouble.'

Eddie stopped what he was doing and stared intently at Declan.

'Are you a pedophile? Because if you are, then I must tell you that I will report anything I hear to the authorities. I'm not saying I won't hear your confession, but I won't protect you and allow others to be put in danger. I want you to understand that before you say anything, all right?' Declan could see the zeal burning in the old man's eyes; he clearly felt very strongly about this.

'No, no I'm not, it's nothing like that.' Declan was quick to clarify.

'Go ahead so.'

Where to begin? Declan inhaled and tried to use his breath to steady himself. Eventually he began, 'Well, I'm here with a woman, someone I love, a parishioner, and she's pregnant with my child.'

Eddie looked relieved; it could have been much worse. 'Ok, tell me the story.'

'Well, as I said, my parish is in New Jersey and one of the prominent families in the parish is the Saccos. I don't know if you've heard of them, but they are a mob family, organized crime, you know, mafia?'

'I'm familiar with the concept, but I don't know of them. Go on.'

'Well, the boss, Paulie Sacco, and I...Well, we weren't friends or anything, but he used to come to me and I tried as much as I could to steer him on the right path. He was, is, a devout Catholic despite his crimes, and he came to me for absolution. I used the limited power I had to withhold absolution until he atoned in some way for his crimes. It sounds dumb, I'm sure, he wasn't going to change, but if I could get him to do some good, or if I knew his plans ahead of time, to avert wrongdoing, then I just did what I could. He trusted me, he believed I had the power to grant him forgiveness... I don't know why, but it was what I did.'

'Ok, but what's he got to do with this woman?' Eddie handed him a cup of coffee and a buttered scone.

'Thanks. Well, the woman is his daughter.'

'Right, and I take it he's not thrilled about the match?'

'No, he's furious. He trusted me. I've known Lucia since she was sixteen, she's twenty-three now, but we only started—' Declan could feel himself reddening with embarrassment. '...started our relationship last year.'

'And she feels the same way about you? This Lucia?'

'Yes, she does, but it wasn't like she seduced me or anything, or I pursued her; it happened despite both of us. She was so torn, just as I was. She believed, still does, deeply in the sanctity of the priesthood and tried very hard to fight her feelings for me, just as I did, harder even. She was actually in a relationship with this man, Antonio Dias, son of another gangster, a guy called Fabio Dias, and she was engaged to be married to him. But we just couldn't stop it. We started...well, a relationship then, in every way, but in secret.'

Eddie considered what he'd heard and then asked.

'Ok, but how in God's name did you wind up here?'

'A parishioner of mine once confessed to an extramarital affair; he said he researched the best way to hide, and a tour or a cruise were the only way to travel with minimum paper trail. You book the tour through a third party in the states but your name doesn't appear on any hotel reservation, car rental reservation, nothing. So I remembered that and just booked a tour of Ireland, in a panic I guess. Once she didn't show up at the wedding, neither of us actually, as I was the celebrant, then Sacco would guess. He knew we were close but only as priest and parishioner. On top of that the guy she was supposed to be marrying, Antonio Dias, is the son of another criminal, so he'll be out for my blood just as much as Paulie will, I've no doubt. I couldn't have picked two more dangerous enemies if I tried. So here we are.'

'That's some story.' Eddie sighed. 'If you weren't sitting in front of me, I'd say it's like a plot of a film or something, but I can see by your face that it's real, all right. So what's your plan?'

'I wish I knew,' Declan replied despondently. 'We love each other. There are a million reasons why we shouldn't be together, I know that, but I just can't be without her nor she me. And then, when we discovered she was pregnant, well, I have to look after her. I just don't know what to do next. Sacco doesn't know where we are, at least I don't think he does, not yet, so we're relatively safe, but he'll find us, he has people everywhere, and once he does...either that or Dias finds us...'

There was no arrogance in his voice, no sense of triumph that a beautiful girl, thirteen years his junior, was in love with him; there was nothing but a profound sense of despair.

'You're in a pickle, all right, you weren't joking about that.'

'What will I do though? We can't travel around on a bus tour forever, and poor Lucia is so sick, it's taking everything she has just to keep going. I don't want to burden her, she's stressed enough. I just don't know about anything anymore...not my vocation, my faith... I feel like I've let everyone down, my parents, my Irish grandparents, they were all so proud of me. But even dealing with Sacco, such evil, I don't know how God can even exist alongside such horror... He told me things, things I can't unknow, and I feel filthy because of it, because I know what he is. I never condoned his actions, but just by being with him, I feel like I was complicit. And he is a complex man. I can't really describe him, he's so charming and funny and on one level almost benevolent. Animal cruelty can move him to genuine tears, a documentary about kids in Syria will see him sending a million dollars to the Red Cross. He doesn't cheat on his wife, he has never

28

had a mistress, which is unheard of in that world, he doesn't use drugs or go with hookers. But then, in the same breath, he'll send his henchmen out to rape the wives of men he wants to threaten, or he'll murder a sixteen-year-old kid for talking back to him. I know too much, and it's eating away at me inside. I love Lucia, that's the only thing I'm sure about anymore, but she was a young vulnerable girl, from a dysfunctional family. I should have been her confessor, a moral guide, not...not what I became. I've made such a mess of everything. This is all my fault, I should have resisted, I should never have got involved with that family...' He put his head in his hands, the crushing waves of despair dragging him ever downwards.

Eddie patted him gently on the back and spoke. 'Look, I don't know you but you strike me as a decent man. This Sacco fella, well, I don't know. From where I'm standing, you were doing your best, playing the hand you were dealt. As regards the girl, I'm not going to say it was nothing, that God forgives you, because, Declan, whether He does or not, or whether you believe in Him or not, you cannot live your life if you cannot forgive yourself. And more importantly you're no use to her. You asked me earlier if you could make a confession and we both know for the sacrament of absolution to work as it were, the penitent has to be truly sorry, and you are. Sitting in front of me I see a man torn apart by grief and pain, a misery he believes to have been self-inflicted, and by his actions, inflicted on those closest to him as well.'

'But that's the thing, Eddie, I allowed it to happen. I should have stopped it. I knew where it was going but I was, I don't know, I wasn't strong enough to resist, and I don't think if I was faced with the same set of circumstances again, I would act any differently, so therefore I'm not sorry. I would do it again.'

Eddie went to his jacket pocket and extracted a pipe and began to fill it with tobacco. Declan had only seen those things in movies, but somehow the sure way he cleaned the pipe and filled it again was soothing to watch. Eddie spoke as he worked.

'The end events maybe, the relationship with Lucia, certainly, but you served the Lord by ministering to the Sacco family. Many others would have refused, others still would have tried to do it but have been so appalled by what they witnessed they would have been at the bishop's office pleading to be reassigned, but you did it. And from what you've told me you ministered to them with the same compassion and kindness you would anyone.' Eddie's voice was kind.

'You tried to influence him, tried to get him to follow God's will. He didn't, but not for want of trying on your part. We are all victims of our upbringing. These men of violence and crime are following a path set out for them. And you tried in as much as anyone could to steer them onto a better one.

'Now, on the subject of Lucia Sacco, she is not a young girl; she is twenty-three. I'm sure she knows her own mind; she is by all accounts a decent, kind person who is disgusted at the behaviour of her father. She fell in love with you and you with her. It happens. So you're not the first and you won't be the last. I know plenty of them here too. They tried to fight it, they did everything they could to resist their feelings, but in the end the emotion proved too strong. Who do you think sent Lucia Sacco to you, Declan? You may not believe it now, but I'll tell you who I think sent her, shall I? God. There is nothing wrong in a man and woman falling in love and expressing that love in the manner in which the Lord intended. The church has made rules, most of them in order to stabilize society, some of them self-serving, around this whole issue, but those are the church's rules, not God's rules. I think in the fullness of time, when we meet Him in the eternal life, it will all be clear. Right now, it is less so. But I don't think you're a predator, using your position of trust for your own nefarious ends. You are simply a man, and she is a woman, and you love each other. And you will love this child and rear him or her to be a good person, and hopefully without the influence of the Sacco family. Just as the Lord called you to be a priest, he now has a different calling for you. Look, I don't know you nor the sky above you, but I get the feeling that you are a good man, Declan Sullivan, I know it doesn't feel like it today, but I think you are. Lucia saw that in you, even Paulie Sacco could see it, and it was why he trusted you when he trusted virtually nobody else. In a strange way it was your inherent goodness that led you into this whole thing.'

His words washed over Declan like a soothing balm. Maybe he was right, maybe he wasn't evil.

'Have you spoken to your bishop?'

'No, there wasn't time. We had to go. I booked the trip online, a last-minute thing, and seven hours later we were flying. We were halfway across the Atlantic before either the Sacco or Dias families knew anything was wrong.'

'Maybe you should ring him at least. They'll be worried.'

'Yes, I should, but I'm terrified to make contact in case it leads him to us, Sacco I mean, not the bishop. He and Dias are both big-time drug dealers. This wedding was like an alliance of two big crime families. Lucia doesn't actually even know the full extent of it. I should have said something probably, but I figured what was the point of further blackening her father in her mind, you know? Dias is Costa Rican, Paulie Italian; together they flood the East Coast but they hate each other. On the face of it they're friendly, they work together, but underneath they don't trust each other at all. Dias will see this as a slight. The wedding was going to be a seriously flashy event, both showing off their wealth; they will both have been humiliated now and will either blame each other or blame me, either way... The only hope is that Sacco is being pursued fairly vigorously by the FBI. They are gathering evidence and it's freaking him out, because usually his victims are either too intimidated or dead to testify, but this time the feds are determined,so maybe they'll get enough to lock him up. I don't know...'

'Maybe I could contact your bishop on your behalf? Would that help?'

Declan thought for a second. 'Maybe, thank you, but not yet. I need to get my head straight. Thanks for listening though, I really appreciate it. I was going out of my mind.'

'As I see it, Declan, keeping yourself and that girl safe is the priority for now. Here's my card, call in or ring me anytime. If I can help you I will.'

'Thanks, Eddie.' Declan took the card and shook the older man's hand.

'Thank God for her, Declan, stop beating yourself up. It is what it is, and He sent her to you. Now, kneel down while I give you absolution.'

Declan knelt and Eddie spoke the words that Declan himself had said so many times before.

'God, the father of mercies, through the death and resurrection of his son has reconciled the world to himself and sent the Holy Spirit among us for the forgiveness of sins; through the ministry of the church may God give you pardon and peace, and I absolve you of your sins, in the name of the father, son and holy spirit.'

Declan felt a weight lift from him. Though nothing had changed, in his heart and in his head he felt clearer. 'Amen,' he replied.

Eddie walked him to the door of the sacristy and bade him farewell, with the assurance that he was at Declan's disposal should he need anything.

Declan smiled and nodded his thanks. Walking back down the street, he felt better. His problems weren't gone, but he felt less oppressed by them. A parishioner once told him that for her confession was like free therapy, it unburdened you. He hadn't ever really understood what she meant until now.

The man who had watched him leave the hotel had waited the entire time he spoke to Eddie, and now followed at a distance of fifteen yards as Declan returned to the hotel.

CHAPTER 5

*L*ucia was sleeping soundly when he went back to the room so he decided not to wake her. He stood at the side of the bed watching her sleep, her long dark hair contrasting with the white pillow. She was covered only with a sheet as the room was warm and he could see the outline of her body clearly. He tried to imagine the little person growing inside her, a baby that in a few months would be born. It was hard to imagine. Would he or she look like Lucia or him? Would they have traits of his parents, his grandparents? Lucia's wrists were so thin, like she could snap with even the slightest pressure. She needed him to be strong now. A rush of love for her and the baby surged through him. He kissed her gently on the head and left her to rest.

He noticed that the hotel had a spa attached and decided a swim would be good for him. He was fit and muscular and enjoyed exercise, but the pressures of recent days meant he'd had no opportunity to do anything physical. He didn't have swimming trunks but he assumed he could get some there.

The girl on reception, who was wearing far too much makeup and had hair dyed an unnatural shade of white, showed him the selection of swimwear. Her lascivious gaze was something he found disconcerting.

'Y'know, you could get away with the Speedos. They're tiny but you'd look good in them. Though you should see the state of some of the yokes that come in wanting them, big fat fellas, I always steer them to the baggy type but no, you could definitely pull it off.'

She gave a raucous laugh at her own double entendre.

Declan could feel himself redden under her scrutiny; he felt like she was eating him up with her eyes.

'So you here on holidays?' She obviously wanted to chat; the spa was almost empty.

'Yes, I am.'

'I love the American accent, it's so cool sounding. Like, your man out of *Fifty Shades of Grey*, he's Irish, y'know, but they made him speak in an American accent for the film. No harm too, can you imagine what it would have been like and him trying to do all sorts to yer wan and him with a big thick Paddy accent up on him! Are you here on your own?' She was very direct.

'Er...no. My, ah, my girlfriend is with me.' He tried to sound casual.

'Lucky girlfriend,' the cheeky young Irish girl replied with a wink. 'If you were my fella, I wouldn't have you wandering around on your own. Anything could happen.'

Declan had no idea how to handle this, the collar had protected him from flirtatious females usually, though one or two tried anyway but never as blatantly as this.

'I'll just take these,' he said, choosing a pair of black swimming shorts. 'Can you put them on my room please? 322.'

'Sure.' She made a note in the book and handed him two fluffy towels. 'Do you need goggles? We wouldn't want those nice green eyes to get stung from the chlorine, now would we?'

'Oh yes, goggles would be good too, thanks.' Declan couldn't wait to get away. Thankfully an elderly American people arrived and distracted her so he was free to go on into the changing area.

As he swam up and down, he was lost in his own thoughts. His life had changed unrecognizably and he wondered what advice he'd give if one of his parishioners found themselves in a similar situation.

He'd spent a lot of time counseling families after affairs, unplanned pregnancies, or coming to terms with homosexuality. More often than not, it was just simply a matter of helping people to tap into their own humanity, to try to relinquish their prejudices and see the human side of the story. He knew people found him easy to talk to, though his brother priests joked that the ladies seemed to gravitate to Fr Declan a bit more than Fr Orstello. He took the teasing he got from them in a good-natured way; he was younger and kept himself in good shape, but he never saw himself in terms of a man whom women would look at. He had always been faithful to his vow of celibacy and believed in the need for such a vow in order to keep priests of God focused on the job at hand. He argued with conviction for celibacy when people raised the issue over the years. The basis for his belief was not theological, he said, but practical. How could he, he would say, care for his congregation to the extent that he did if he had all the pressures and concerns of regular family life? For Declan, his role as a priest was paramount and he would not allow anything to get in the way of his pastoral duties.

Now, all of that seemed like a lifetime ago. Now, he was a man who was responsible for the safety and happiness of the woman he loved and for their unborn child, and it was a responsibility he wouldn't shirk.

Fifty pool lengths later, he felt calmer. He stopped and rested and noticed he wasn't alone in the pool any longer. Conor was swimming lengths as well. When he got to the end of the pool, he stopped.

'Hi, Declan, I saw you when I came in but you were clearly going for some Olympic record so I let you off.'

'Hi, Conor, you're pretty fast yourself. I guess it gets tough sitting on the bus all the time, you need to expend some energy, right?'

'Exactly. I like swimming, nobody talks to you, and you can think your thoughts in peace. How's Lucia feeling? Any better?'

'She's sleeping now, so I left her. I went for a walk around town. I met the local priest, Fr Shanahan?'

'Eddie? Ah that's good; he's a bit of a character actually. I live quite near here, and when we were getting married, he went off and learned some of the wedding prayers in Ukrainian so Ana's parents and family would be part of it. He's a family friend. Did you tell him you were travelling with me?'

'No, I just said I was on a bus. He seemed like a nice guy. I guess it didn't occur to me that you might know him but then this is Ireland, not New York. Everyone knows everyone here, I guess.' Declan smiled.

'Well, not everyone, there are five million of us, but you'd know the people in your own area. This place, Ennis, is a big market town by Irish standards, but we live in a village about half an hour away, out on the ocean, and there I'd know everyone pretty much. I'm from Cork, but we settled up here. Ana loves it, and it's great for the boys, playing on the beach every day and all that.'

'The whole country is so beautiful I can't imagine an ugly part, I think—'

A piercing scream interrupted their conversation.

Both men turned to the Jacuzzi where an elderly couple neither of them had seen before were sitting.

'Someone, please help, my husband...' Conor and Declan jumped out of the pool and ran over. The man, in his eighties, was gasping for breath and was gone blue in the face, clutching his chest. 'He has a heart condition, please do something.'

Conor suggested they get them out of the water while he called an ambulance.

Declan helped the woman out and got her a robe that was hanging on the side of the pool and sat her down. By now the young recep-tionist had arrived and was comforting her. Leaving her in the younger woman's care, he and Conor between them lifted the man out and laid him on a towel Conor had placed on the tiled floor beside the pool. Within moments hotel staff, and a lifeguard came running.

'Does he have any medication?' Conor asked the man's wife.

'Yes, nitroglycerin, it's in the room, he took it this morning but I'm not sure which bag...' She was too upset to be rational. 'Room 415.'

'Send someone to the room, 415, and bring all the meds you can find, quickly,' Conor instructed the manager who'd just arrived.

'I'll go myself,' he responded and ran off.

The young lifeguard brought a pillow and a blanket and they tried to make the man comfortable. 'The ambulance is on the way,' he said, taking in the gravity of the situation and began CPR

The receptionist managed to shepherd his wife away to a comfortable chair in reception.

Conor and Declan exchanged glances. This wasn't looking good; despite the lifeguard's efforts his breathing was becoming even more laboured, and the pain in his chest was evident by his contorted facial features. He had a sallow complexion and dark features, bald and very overweight. A gold cross hung around his neck, the precious metal glinting in the man's grey chest hair.

Declan made a split-second decision: the man was most likely Christian so despite the fact that he was blowing his cover in doing so, Declan knelt beside the man, while still allowing the lifeguard to continue with the chest compressions, and made the sign of the cross on his forehead. He leaned close to the man's ear and said, 'Through this holy anointing may the Lord in his love and mercy help you with the grace of the Holy Spirit. May the Lord who frees you from sin save you and raise you up. May the Lord Jesus protect you and lead you to eternal life.'

As he said the words, the man opened his eyes and turned to Declan. He was incapable of speech, but his eyes registered that emotion Declan had seen so many times in this life, that of resignation and relief. The man seemed to relax, the pain seemed to ease, and he breathed his last breath.

As he did the ambulance crew entered the pool area and Declan and the lifeguard stood aside, allowing them to assess the situation. Within moments they were working on the man, attaching wires to his chest and performing CPR. They watched from a distance as the paramedics explained to the man's wife what they were doing. They worked on the body for quite a while but eventually confirmed his death.

The howls of grief could be heard all around the tiled pool area as the paramedic delivered the bad news to the man's widow. Luckily they were travelling with friends so they were called and arrived within moments.

They led her away, and Declan and Conor went to get dressed as the paramedics seemed to have everything in hand. They both got dressed in silence until Conor eventually spoke.

'I think I need a drink. Join me?'

'Sure. I'll just check on Lucia first. I'll meet you in the bar.' Conor left and Declan finished dressing. He'd have to tell Conor the truth; there was no other possible explanation why a lay person would perform the Sacrament of Extreme Unction, the last rites.

Lucia was still sleeping soundly so he wrote her a note to say where he was and joined Conor in a secluded booth at the far corner of the bar away from the door.

A creamy pint of Guinness was in front of the spare seat.

Declan drank deeply; though not a big drinker ordinarily, he did enjoy the taste. It was bitter yet satisfying, not fizzy like beer; it was much smoother.

'So are you going to tell me what's going on or are we going to pretend you're not a priest?' Conor asked, setting his own pint on the table. He fixed Declan with a stare, his blue eyes never leaving his face. 'You can tell me to mind my own business if you like, I'm just here to drive the bus, but going through something like that, witnessing someone die, well, it focuses the mind, doesn't it? Also, and this is where I do need to know, there seems to be a guy following this tour, and I'm wondering if it's something to do with you.'

Declan's heart thumped so audibly he was sure Conor must have heard it. Someone following them? How? He thought quickly. He knew he could refuse to discuss it; Conor wouldn't push it nor would he reveal what happened to anyone else, but instinctively Declan knew he was to be trusted. And if someone was following them, he was putting the entire group in danger.

'What makes you think we're being followed?' Declan asked,

sipping his drink to buy some time until he could get the story straight in his head.

'Well, it's strange, since yesterday several times I've spotted this guy, in a shirt and tie, and the only people who dress like that in the tourist spots are drivers and guides, but I pretty much know all of them so he's not one of us. Then in Bunratty Castle, I noticed him taking photos, not of the castle or of the scenery like most people do, but of yourself and Lucia. So I wondered, but I didn't like to say anything, but now, after that episode in the pool, well, something isn't as it seems. I've never seen a lay person administer last rites before, so I just thought I'd ask. If she's someone that maybe you shouldn't be with, then it wouldn't be the first time, and to be honest it's not my business, but just so you know, whoever is watching ye is onto ye.'

Declan realized Conor assumed he and Lucia were having an illicit affair, that the man was sent by a disgruntled spouse to find evidence of infidelity. If only it were as simple as that.

'Conor, I know that this must look, well, to be honest about it, I can't imagine how it looks. You're right, I'm not a lay person. I am, or at least I was, a priest.'

Declan allowed his words to register with Conor, who remained poker faced.

'And Lucia, well, she and I have fallen in love and she's pregnant with my child, but you knew that part.' Declan was trying not to sound idiotic; for some reason he wanted Conor's approval. 'And so, we had to leave the states, not just because she's pregnant, but also because her father is Paulie Sacco, a mob boss, in fact *the* mob boss of the East Coast, and to top it all, she was supposed to be marrying another criminal's son last Saturday. We ran away the night before the wedding. A parishioner told me years ago that tours were good for hiding on, less of a paper trail or something. Anyway, I booked it and here we are. That man following us might well be sent by Sacco or Dias—that's Lucia's fiancé's father—though how they knew to look for us here, I've no idea.'

Conor put his pint down and rubbed his hand over his slightly stubbled jaw.

'And you're not having me on, are you? I mean this all seems a bit far-fetched, Declan, if I'm to be truthful.'

'I wish I was. No, unfortunately it's all true. Sacco is after us, or Dias is. Either one won't be looking for a nice chat with me. I know how they operate. I betrayed them, Sacco especially; I was his confessor, his confidante I guess, and I stole his daughter. That's how he'll see it anyway. He'll kill me if he can.'

The silence hung heavily between the two men.

Conor sighed and sat back on the chair.

'Well, I've been doing this job for more years than I'd like to admit to, and I thought I'd heard it all, but this is a new one on me. So, you're telling me that this clown that's following my bus around the west coast of Ireland is actually some kind of extra out of *The Godfather* and he's trying to do away with a man pretending not to be a priest and his pregnant girlfriend who are hiding out on my tour.'

'In a nutshell, yeah,' Declan admitted with a heavy sigh.

'Well, you'll have to go to the guards, get them to take this fella in and question him and see what the hell he's doing here.'

Declan looked confused. 'The who?'

'Guards, *Garda Siochana*, the Irish police, they'll have to be brought in—'

'I don't know. I mean we're in enough danger and we're not even sure. I've never even seen this guy; maybe if I saw him, I'd recognize him as one of the Saccos—'

'And do what exactly? Look, I'm not trying to make things more difficult for you, but I've the safety of all those people to consider as well. There's no way we can just carry on as normal, not now, knowing what I know. I'm sorry, Declan, but we're going to the guards. In fact, I'll ring the sergeant here now. I play golf with him.' Conor took out his phone and scrolled through his contacts.

Declan was becoming less surprised with each new contact established; everyone in Ireland did really seem to know each other. In any other circumstances it would have been a cute story about this little country, but Declan felt only worry. If he drew the Irish cops on a member of the Saccos, well, they wouldn't know what they were dealing with; he doubted if organized crime was much of a thing here. Anyway, Conor was waiting for someone to pick up now so they were being brought in either way. He knew Conor was right: if they were being followed, then it did put the others in danger and that wasn't acceptable, but he just hoped he wasn't making the situation worse. He recalled reading somewhere that the Irish police were unarmed; that recollection sent a chill through him. The Saccos and Dias families never went anywhere without weapons, and human life was to them an easily expendable commodity. He hoped the Irish cops knew what they were dealing with.

'Charlie? How're you doing? Listen, I need to talk to you, urgently. I can't go into it, but I'm at the Old Ground, can you call in?'

Conor listened while the other man responded, then replied, 'No, not really, it needs to be now.'

Another pause.

'Grand, see you in a quarter of an hour so, thanks.' He hung up and looked at Declan.

'He's on the way.'

'Ok, you're right, sorry, I just panicked, I'm … Sorry, I'm just all over the place.'

Moments later Conor kicked Declan's foot under the table and gestured with his eyes to a man ordering a drink at the bar. He wasn't anyone Declan recognized, and he looked neither Italian nor Costa Rican, not that that meant much, but generally they kept their operations within the family. This man was tall and powerfully built, with grey hair in an almost military haircut. He was wearing dark trousers and a pale green shirt, open at the neck, and sat at the bar, sipping coffee and scrolling through his phone. He never looked in their direction.

Without warning, Conor got up and went to the bar.

The barman called from the other end, 'Same again, Conor?'

'No thanks, just a coffee for me but a pint for my friend.' Indicating Declan with a tilt of his head.

As the barman went to fill the pint, Conor addressed the guy with the coffee as Declan watched in horror.

'Nice today, wasn't it, though they say t'will probably rain later. Are you golfing?' Conor was light and conversational, nothing giving away that he might have suspected all was not right.

The man fixed Conor with a look for a moment before replying. 'No, no I'm not.' His accent was American.

'That's a Boston accent anyway.' Conor smiled.

'Yeah, I'm from Boston.' The man was saying as little as possible but his eyes were fixed at a point straight ahead of him.

'So are you on holiday or is it business?' Conor deliberately kept his voice friendly, but neither man was in doubt what was going on.

'Business.'

Conor moved in beside him as the barman placed the drinks on the bar and went to deal with another customer.

'That's interesting, because I was wondering what kind of business you might be in that involves following me and my tour around the country?' He spoke quietly.

The man looked directly at him before returning to the point in the distance straight ahead.

'We'd better talk.' The man stood up and walked in Declan's direction, Conor following quickly. Declan thought for a split second the man would pull a gun and shoot him there and then in broad daylight, but he just sat down in the booth opposite him, Conor standing between the two men. Nobody said anything and the tension was palpable. The man reached into his trouser pocket and extracted a well-worn brown leather wallet, opened it, and took out a credit-card-size identification.

CHAPTER 6

*G*eorge Winooski was a senior FBI agent. He flashed his badge discreetly and offered his hand for Declan to shake, which he did, albeit reluctantly.

'What do you want?' The time for social niceties was long gone.

Winooski glanced for a split second in Conor's direction. 'Are you sure you want to do this now? Here?'

Declan looked at Conor, who was still standing. 'Conor knows the whole story.'

'Ok. Your friend here correctly figured out that I've been following you. My instructions were to just follow and observe, but since you know I'm here now, I might as well level with you.'

Waves of relief washed over Declan; at least this guy was a cop, not one of Sacco's men sent to kill him.

"Ok,' Declan managed to speak. 'How did you know where to find me?'

'Father Sullivan, you've been on our radar for quite some time; we are building a case against Sacco and all members of the family, and those they associate with have been under close surveillance. You, and of course Lucia Sacco, have been subject to that scrutiny.'

'So you knew about Lucia and I...' Declan swallowed. If the FBI knew, then there was no reason to think Sacco didn't know too.

'Yes, but I don't think either the Diases nor the Saccos do.' He spoke quietly, as if reading Declan's mind. 'At least they didn't, but now, since the wedding, well...'

Declan sat back and ran his hands through his hair. He was sure nobody had suspected a thing before, but now that the secret was out they were in even more danger.

The agent went on. 'So as you're no doubt aware, there are two high-profile criminals in New York and Philadelphia respectively who are not exactly happy with you. So, I'm following you first of all to make sure they don't get to you and hurt or even kill you, and second of all to see if you can help us.'

'Help you with what?' Declan was confused.

'Well, the case against Paulie Sacco has been going on for three years and we are almost there, but we need your help.' George was pulling no punches. 'We think you might have evidence, given the nature of your relationship with Sacco himself and with his daughter, that might help us secure a conviction.'

'Leave Lucia out of this. She's not like him, she's got nothing to do with any of this.' Declan took a breath to calm himself. 'Look, Mr. Winooski, I've enough problems right now without giving Sacco any more reasons to want me dead, so I don't think I can help you.' Declan's instinct told him to stay away from law enforcement where Sacco was concerned.

'That's where you're wrong, *Father* Sullivan. You most definitely can help us. Think of it this way: you help us to put Sacco away for good, then you and Lucia get to live happily ever after. If you don't, well then that depends, but I suspect that Sacco means business. He wouldn't take something like what you did lying down. He probably doesn't know where you are just yet, but he will. He's got an uncanny knack for gathering information. I don't want to do or say anything right now that could jeopardize any ongoing investigation. I can't go into details, but everyone knows that we've been after Sacco for years but he's smart, and he's surrounded by loyal people so it's difficult. It's virtually impossible to get people to testify against him, whether out of loyalty or fear, either way it's why we can't make anything stick. You could be a very useful witness for the state in nailing Sacco, and then, once we get a conviction, we can make sure he's out of harm's way.'

'You seem to be labouring under somewhat of a misapprehension here. I don't know anything about—' Declan began, trying to sound convincing.

'I said we can't make it stick, not that we don't know every detail about him, who he sees, what he says. We know you know, Declan, it's not a matter of conjecture on our part, so don't bother with this charade.'

Declan wasn't fooled by this man's outwardly friendly manner. He meant business.

'Well, if I did know something... And if I don't, you know, tell you anything...? What then?' Declan asked. He wasn't at all sure that testifying against Sacco was a good idea whatever the positives from the point of view of a conviction.

George held his gaze. 'I don't know. You wait, live your life on the run, and someday...Sacco gets lucky. You withdrew money from a Chase Manhattan account your parents left you on the day before you left. Lucia Sacco did the same, but that won't last forever. You can't stay on this tour. You'll have to find someplace to live, you'll need a bank account, an address, references, and once you do, well, Dias has technology even the FBI hasn't heard of; he will find you. As I believe the IRA said of their attempts to kill Prime Minister Thatcher back in the '80s, they only need to get lucky once, she needs to be lucky every day.' Winooski was circumspect. 'We both know he won't just forgive and forget; it's not in his nature. Besides, it's the right thing to do.'

Conor watched the cop as he spoke. He could tell he was a straight talker but a cop to his marrow; he wouldn't have any patience for anyone shielding the likes of this Sacco character, priest or not. Still, Declan actively testifying against someone as bad as Lucia's father seemed to be, and him with a pregnant girlfriend, might not be the wisest course of action. Conor could see Declan was traumatized by everything that had happened so he felt kind of protective of him.

'Does he have to do it now? Go back and testify now?'

'Well, Conor, I'll put it to you this way: we don't have a court date because we can't raise enough material witnesses. If Declan here were to testify, then yes, with relative speed we could get him back to testify.'

He turned back to Declan. 'If you decided to tell us what you know about Paulie Sacco and his dealings, then we can protect you, but if you decide your loyalty lies elsewhere, then...' George shrugged. He didn't have to go on.

'What do you know so far? Where's he at now?' Declan had imagined the scene in his head so often. The packed church, decorated with such extravagance as would have only befitted the Saccos, Fabio Dias standing beside his son at the altar, Paulie in the porch waiting for Lucia, the entire congregation, a who's who of American crime, waiting for the priest to come out onto the altar and then the dawning realization that the wedding wasn't going to happen. No priest, no bride—it wouldn't have taken long for them to put two and two together.

'We know that he's fuming. Dias wasn't convinced Sacco didn't know in advance, an elaborate attempt at humiliation, they hate each other as you know, but he soon realized, probably because of Sacco's reaction that he knew nothing, suspected nothing. You covered your tracks, I'll give you that much. We also know that he blames you completely. We have a lot of surveillance on him but he's not a straightforward criminal. He's a very complicated man. Our psychological profilers tell me he is tough to understand. He's a sociopath, but not like they've often encountered. He can be quite charming, very sociable, and can even at times seem empathetic. He gives a lot of money to charities, and he can show incredible generosity to individuals and causes that move him. He cries at sad movies, at opera, at animal cruelty, and yet when he commits the most brutal horrific crimes, he feels no remorse, none. He also fixates on things, and in this case I'm afraid you have become a fixation. He will stop at nothing to get revenge. He saw Lucia as his property, and you stole it. Sometimes he sees things quite simply for a very complex man.'

Declan waited for words of comfort, assurances that everything was going to be fine, but they were unforthcoming.

'So what now?' Declan asked.

'You decide what you want to do.' He took out a sim card pack and placed it on the table. 'Here's a new number. Take out your old card in case he tracks it to you. I'll call you in a minute, that way you'll have my number; let me know as soon as you decide.' As he stood up to leave, he spoke directly to both of them, but locked eyes with Conor for a moment. 'Be on your guard. He wants to find Declan and he is used to getting what he wants. Declan and the people around him are in very real danger. Don't be fooled into thinking that you can hide out here indefinitely. He'll find you, it's just a matter of time. We think at the moment that Sacco is under the impression that Declan is in the care of the church, holed up somewhere, but he's looking for him and he has connections everywhere, in the most unlikely places. Sooner or later he'll figure out that the church doesn't have him. Call me immediately if you see anything out of the ordinary, ok? I don't want to freak you out here, but this is one of the most dangerous men in America and he is on a mission to find you. You can't be too careful.'

Agent Winooski left the bar and Conor sat opposite Declan, mulling over what he'd just heard. His primary concern had to be for the safety of the entire group, and having Declan and Lucia on the coach certainly seemed to be putting the others at risk. He hated to be the one to tell him that he had to go, but he felt like he'd no choice. He wished Ana was there; she was a great listener and always came up with solutions. He'd come to rely so heavily on her in the years they'd been married. She'd changed him, made him more secure and safe in his world. He was more open with people now. Before Ana, he was friendly and all of that, but he'd kept himself closed off. That's what happens when you're badly hurt and he had been badly hurt by his first love. He never imagined he'd ever allow himself to be that vulnerable again, but Ana broke down every one of the walls he's built around himself. Declan looked exhausted and confused.

47

'Look, Declan, I hate to say this...' he began, but as he did Lucia appeared beside them.

'Hi,' she said. 'Hope I'm not interrupting, I got your note so I came down.' Declan moved in and Conor saw the tenderness in his face for this girl. She was so thin and pale-looking, the dark violet circles under her eyes were clear through her almost translucent skin. Her jet-black hair hung in waves around her heart-shaped face, and her big brown eyes were innocent and trusting. She no more looked like a mob boss's daughter than he did himself, Conor thought.

Declan put his arm protectively around her shoulders. It was the first time Conor saw him initiate a public display of affection; it had been all her up to then. Years in the tour business had taught Conor to recognize those things. Now that he knew the truth about Declan, he could see why: all of this relationship stuff was new to him. He was a grown man but in some ways he was as awkward as a teenager at his first disco.

'Not at all, Lucia, can I get you something to drink?' Conor smiled.

'Em...sure... Do you think they'd make me some tea? I never used to drink it but I've had it here a few times. Coffee makes me nauseous these days. But maybe if this is a bar, they don't do that?' She was as unsure of herself as Declan was. Conor felt a wave of affection for them and knew he couldn't abandon them to their fate. She was so ill and he was doing his best, but the pressure was getting to him as well. He'd speak to Charlie in a while, fill him in, and see what he said, but cutting this pair loose would be wrong. They were barely coping as it was.

'That's no problem. If there's one thing you'll always be able to get in any establishment in Ireland, it's a cup of tea.' The young barman was cleaning a table recently vacated by customers a few feet away.

'A pot of tea when you're ready, Brendan, please, for three.'

'Coming up, Conor. Do ye want biscuits?'

'Sure, why not? We'll need to keep our energy levels up somehow.' Conor smiled, and Lucia and Declan managed weak grins. 'I'll give you a hand.' Conor got up to give the couple a bit of space. From his location at the bar, he knew Declan was filling Lucia in on the encounter with Agent Winooski. When he returned to the booth, they looked even worse than when he left.

'Conor, we've been talking and we're going to leave the tour. Thanks for everything but—'

Conor held up his hand. 'Hang on, I know what you're going to say, but if I've my way, ye're not going anywhere. Ye're safer by far on a tour. No paper trail, nobody even knows who ye are. Everything is booked under the tour name and ye're not going by ye're real names even so this is the safest place for ye to be.'

'But the others...' Lucia began.

'I'm meeting the local sergeant here in a bit, he's a friend of mine anyway, and I'll fill him in on the story so far, see what he recommends.'

They both looked doubtful.

'Look, I know you are worried, and the FBI agent certainly left us under no illusions as to how dangerous this Sacco man is.' Conor paused, realizing he'd forgotten for a moment that this man was Lucia's father. 'But where the Irish guards have the advantage over the FBI is they know this place, they notice people acting suspiciously, and they know a lot of the locals by name. Our country gained its independence simply by knowing the country better than the British, and we can use the same tactics. You're worried, I know, but honestly, I notice a lot and I'd spot it if someone was following us. I spotted your man the FBI fella almost straight away. In this business, it might look like there are loads of people, but I've been around for so long I know everyone pretty much, and those I don't know are tourists and you all have a look; it's hard to describe but I can tell by body language or something, I don't know, just the way people are, if something's not right. Ask my wife, she thinks it's weird.' He grinned, trying to diffuse the tension and relax these two people in front of him who were so stressed out. 'Look, if you two leave and book into a hotel, you'll need to show credit cards, passports. The same if you rent a car. With technology nowadays he'll find ye much quicker on ye're own. We've no reason to think he's got a clue where you are, so why not just stay put? For now at least? That way, ye remain under cover.'

Conor smiled at his choice of phrase; he must be watching too many TV programmes.

Declan thought for a second. What Conor was suggesting was definitely the safer option for Lucia and for himself, but he still felt he was putting the others in danger. He glanced at Lucia; a need to protect her and the life growing inside her surged within him. Conor was right, and he had proved himself to be perceptive, so they should probably follow his advice.

'What do you think, Lucia?' Declan asked.

Lucia knew and understood Declan's concerns for the others in the group, but she felt safe with Conor and wanted to stay, for now at least. 'I think Conor's right, we're safer here. My father is only after us. He won't want to draw attention to himself. He's got enough problems with the FBI without involving Irish police or Interpol or whatever. He's fuming, I get that, but I don't think he'd risk doing something that would impact anyone else, only us. And let's face it, if he's after us, then wherever we go there's going to be other people, so they're at risk by just being near us. I'm not taking the safety of the others in the group lightly, I just... I know he's mad, but I'm still his daughter. He won't kill me so staying close to me is the safest thing you can do.'

Conor stood up. 'Ok, that's settled. Tomorrow we move on to Killarney, and the roads are a bit better from here to there than they were out around West Clare, Lucia, so hopefully you'll not be so ill. In the meantime why don't you two just try to relax, have some dinner; even if you don't feel like eating, Lucia, you might be better after it. You need to get some nourishment into you, for yourself and for that little boy or girl you're carrying. Declan, the local sergeant sent me a text there, he'll need a statement from both of us about the poor man in the pool so I'll fill him in about the rest of it then. Don't go outside of the hotel though. I'll come and find you when he gets here. When an American dies here, the Embassy takes over so it can be a long process, but we'll just give our statements and move on with the tour.'

'Of course, and, Conor, thank you. For everything.'

Conor smiled and ran his hand through his short silver hair. 'I would normally say, all in a day's work, but that wouldn't be true in this case. But look, we'll be grand. Now if you'll excuse me, I'm going to see if Ana can come over to the hotel with the boys. I need a bit of simplicity in my life after today.'

'You do that. Enjoy your family time.' Lucia stood on her tiptoes and kissed him on the cheek. 'We are so lucky to have met you.'

Conor smiled and his eyes seemed to twinkle. 'See ye later.' And with a wave he was gone.

CHAPTER 7

*D*eclan lay on the bed thinking as Lucia was emerging from the bathroom wearing a robe, her hair wrapped in a towel. She looked at him and said, 'What? Has something happened?' She was on edge again.

'No, nothing's happened. Let's turn on the TV and see if there's anything on the news.'

He pressed the remote and the TV sprang to life on the CNN channel. Nothing. Lots of stuff about the president, some story about a guy in Georgia who found gold on his land, and the sports roundup for the day. Not a word about the upcoming trial, the biggest mob trial in decades. Declan turned it off and Lucia picked up her iPad, typing 'Paulie Sacco' into the search bar. The usual stuff came up: news, a Wikipedia entry, some newspaper reports from previous years, and then a breaking news video piece. She beckoned Declan over and pressed play. The clip showed Sacco emerging from the church where Lucia was due to marry Antonio, face like thunder. The clip only lasted a few seconds and the headline screamed, 'Mob boss Sacco's daughter is a no-show for her wedding to Antonio Dias, son of Costa Rican millionaire Fabio Dias.' There was no substance to the story as of yet but no doubt the media would love this, and once the connection was made to a priest... Well, that's news gold. They searched for other reports but found nothing.

Agent Winooski had explained Sacco's discovery that his twenty-three-year-old daughter had run off with the priest sent ripples of fear through the entire mob family. Other families had heard about it, and Sacco was humiliated in the eyes of his peers. Dias was also furious; nobody made him look like a fool and got away with it. Once he established that Paulie Sacco was as mystified as anyone, he left with his family, back to their mansion in Philadelphia. Paulie knew that as far as Dias was concerned it didn't end there. Sacco had to find Declan, not just to save face but to show Dias they were on the same page. Sacco was a feared criminal on the East Coast, it was true, but he was a small fry compared to Dias.

Apparently Sacco believed that some people must have known about the affair between Lucia and Declan and thought they were laughing behind his back. He would stop at nothing to show the world that nobody crosses Paulie Sacco and gets away with it. It was always accepted that one day Paulie would pick the son of one of the satellite families for her to marry, but in the meantime she was completely out of bounds to everyone.

They clicked the iPad off instantly and jumped as a knock came to the door.

Declan held Lucia's hand. 'It's ok, I ordered room service while you were in the shower, thought it might be better than going to the restaurant downstairs. Is that ok?'

Lucia just nodded.

Declan went to the door but didn't open it.

'Who is it?" he called.

'Room service.' The reply came from a young female with a strong Irish accent. Relieved, he opened the door.

The waitress rolled in the trolley and placed the tray of smoked chicken salad with dark brown Irish soda bread for Lucia and a steak and French fries with onions and mushrooms for him on the table. Declan had ordered tea for Lucia and coffee for himself, and because it sounded so good, he'd also ordered a sticky toffee pudding with vanilla ice cream.

Declan tipped her as she left and he saw Lucia pale as she looked at the salad.

He squatted in front of her and held her hands. 'Lucia my love, I know you feel so bad, but can you please at least try to eat something? I'm getting worried about you, you can't keep vomiting and eating nothing at all. You're fading in front of my eyes. I've no idea about pregnancy or women's health, but I do know you need to eat.'

Lucia looked into the kind, gentle eyes of the man she loved and nodded. 'I'll try.'

He smiled and his face transformed. His pale freckled skin was so soft and she gazed deeply into his sea green eyes. Leaning forward, she kissed him softly on the lips.

'I expected there to be more in the news. Is that good or bad, do you think?' Lucia asked.

'Good, I'd say. The FBI are probably ensuring the media keep quiet, not wanting to prejudice a jury and all of that.'

Lucia smiled indulgently. 'You've seen too many movies, Declan Sullivan. I'm not sure the cops have the power to do that.'

'Well, maybe not, but either way the less news about Paulie Sacco or us the better. I mean, at least if it's not splashed all over the papers, then we're safer, and that has got to be good, right?'

Conor texted to say that the sergeant had arrived but they had enough on the death in the pool so a statement from Declan wasn't necessary, and that he'd made him aware of the rest of the story and for them not to worry. He was glad; the thought of going through the whole thing again tonight wasn't a pleasant one. He just wanted to stay in this room with Lucia.

Conor waited in the car park; Ana was on her way. He loved so many things about her, but one was how united they were. If either one needed the other, then they were there. They were each other's number one priority, and he felt more happiness in the years he'd been married than at any time before in his life. Ana just knew before he said a word almost that he needed her tonight. She'd thrown pyjamas for the boys in a bag and she was on the way. There were two double beds in his room so the boys could watch a film in bed before falling asleep, and he and Ana could sit and chat, maybe have a glass of wine. He liked being a tour guide but he hated sleeping alone now. It struck him as strange considering he'd been single for so many years before Ana, through choice. He had been hurt badly as a young man and vowed to never allow anyone that close again, and for many years he hadn't. He had lots of women friends, some with whom he had a physical relationship, but never love, never what he felt for Anastasia. It had kind of crept up on him. She was a waitress in a hotel where he stayed frequently and for a long time they were just friends. She was much younger than him, and in the end she had to be the one to make the first move. He still remembered the night vividly; she'd cooked him dinner in her tiny flat that she shared with another Eastern European friend and declared her love for him. He shuddered now thinking how close he'd come to rejecting her. Not because he didn't feel the same way but because he was scared, but she allayed all his fears and he held her in his arms that night and now, any night he spent alone was a long one.

The events of the day had exhausted him, between seeing that man in the pool just die in front of him and, as if that wasn't enough to contend with, the crazy story of the priest and the mob boss's daughter. He could see how terrified they were, so he tried to be cheerful and positive, but inside he was still appalled at the whole thing, not because of the affair or romance or whatever it was between Declan and this girl—Conor never understood how priests could stay celibate in the first place—but the fact that of all the women in the world he chose this Paulie Sacco's daughter. He seemed such a capable and intelligent guy on one level, but he just found the whole thing so incredibly stupid and naive of Declan. What the hell was the guy thinking? He was fairly sure she wasn't the first woman to show interest; he was a good-looking man, Conor could see that, and he imagined that under normal circumstances he probably had a magnetic personality. Conor guessed that people just liked him, men and women. There was something about him, like when he had seen him in action at the pool. He hadn't panicked; he just did what he needed to do, and Conor had marveled at the ease with which he did it. Even Janice on reception was giving him her hungry stare, as the other drivers called it, but he was oblivious. Janice was on friendly terms with a lot of the guys on the regular tour circuit, many of whom had wives and kids at home. She tried her luck with Conor once, a few years earlier when she'd first started working at the hotel and Ana was pregnant with the twins, but he had been very firm. He would never cheat on his wife, but that didn't stop Janice trying every chance she got. He wasn't surprised to see her reaction to Declan. It stood to reason women must have tried to seduce him over the years, priest or not, but this girl had gotten under his skin.

His reverie was interrupted by the sight of their silver SUV rounding the corner into the car park. Ana stopped near where he was standing to let the boys out before she parked; he knew they'd have been driving her crazy to get out to their father once they'd seen him. Two little figures bolted into his arms as she drove into a space.

'Daddy!' They threw their little arms around his neck as they both vied loudly for his attention. Conor carried them effortlessly to where Ana was extracting a bag from the trunk of the car.

'Hi, gorgeous.' He grinned and kissed her.

'Gorgeous? I don't think so, this one maked the magic potion he says with everything he can find in the kitchen when I was talking with you on the phone and he get a big fright when I come back in kitchen he spilled it everywhere, and on me too. Grrr.' Ana waved her fist at Joe in mock anger, but he and Artie just giggled. Conor smiled at her lovely Ukrainian-accented English. Despite being in Ireland many years, she still formed sentences in the most peculiar way sometimes. She was always on him to correct her, but he never did; he thought it was cute. He held her hand and had Artie on his shoulders and Joe in his other arm as he walked into the hotel.

CHAPTER 8

*L*ucia woke with a start. It was still dark and Declan was sleeping peacefully beside her. She waited for the inevitable wave of nausea that began every day now. Maybe if she lay completely still, her mutinous body would not realize she was awake and the endless exhausting cycle would be delayed. Unbidden, the image of her father from the video clip came to mind. He'd looked so full of hate and rage. Had he always had that potential? Could she really have been so blind all those years to not see what kind of man he really was?

The knowledge that her father was a criminal made her feel sick. She felt her heart begin to pound as she was gripped with a familiar sense of foreboding. She thought back to her childhood. How could she not have known what her family was? It all made sense now, of course. The police raids on the house, the occasional sight of guns, the stopped conversations whenever she entered a room. She remembered finding a cooler in the garage when she was a child; she'd wanted to take a picnic, and when she'd opened the cooler it was stuffed with money. Her nanny had closed it quickly and told her it was to pay the pool men who were working there, and she'd just accepted it. It never occurred to her why her father didn't go to work in an office or a store, but kept irregular hours. He told her the gun he carried was to shoot at foxes around the waste management facility he allegedly ran. Because she was home tutored, she had no contact with other children, except occasionally her cousins, but even they seemed to avoid her. She was too religious and studious for them; they were into boys, hairstyles and makeup, and things about which Lucia neither knew nor cared. Her cousin PJ, Paulie Junior, had been seeing a girl called Adrianna who, though an absolute Barbie doll in appearance, was nice to Lucia when they met. She seemed to find Lucia fascinating, and while they had literally nothing in common, they did chat a bit at family functions. She was the only one of the family of her own age who gave Lucia more than a passing glance.

She berated herself for not noticing how peculiar it was that her uncles and her father's friends were constantly milling around the house, not working regular jobs either, but yet they seemed to enjoy the best of everything. They all drove Italian sports cars and wore lots of heavy gold jewellery. Her father was always buying her expensive things, things she neither wanted nor used, until eventually the diamonds and shoes and dresses disappeared from her closets. She guessed the maids took them; either way, she didn't care. The trappings of wealth didn't interest her, and she dressed and behaved conservatively. It was really only when she got to Felician College in Rutherford, a short drive from her home in Hoboken, New Jersey, and began to meet people unapproved by her family that she was shocked to learn of her father's criminal life. She loved her father, and finding out the reality was devastating.

There was nowhere to turn; everyone, her whole extended family, were in on it. Uncles and cousins who she would have sworn were in legitimate businesses were to a man, members of the family and therefore criminals. With mounting horror and despair she'd scrolled through the court reports in the newspaper archives, disgusted with herself that she remained ignorant for so long. She longed for someone to turn to, someone who could help her make sense of it all.

All the years she was growing up, her mother was useless, beautiful but cold as the marble statues that lined the atrium of their house, who showed no interest whatever in her only daughter. She forbade Lucia to call her Mama or Mom, insisting on Emmanualla. She relinquished all decisions regarding her daughter to her husband and was little more than a mannequin in the enormous mansion the Sacco family called home. She spoke on the phone to her relatives back in Sicily but hardly ever to anyone in the Sacco house. She dressed impeccably in Italian designer clothes, spent hours in the gym attached to the pool and in the beauty salon of a very exclusive day spa, but Lucia often wondered what it was all for. Certainly not to please her husband, that was for sure. She never understood her parents' marriage; they seemed so unsuited. Her dad was handsome and funny and charming while her mother was silent and remote. She was Sicilian, brought over when she was in her early twenties as a bride for the up-and-coming Paulie Sacco. She spoke English perfectly but used only Siculu, a language distinct enough from standard Italian to make her unintelligible to even those family members who could speak Italian. Lucia remembered hearing the melodic language when her mother spoke on the phone to her family back in Sicily. She spoke to Lucia in English when she absolutely had to but Lucia always got the impression her mother was anxious to get the conversation over as quickly as possible.

Lucia recalled asking her mother when she was seven if she would teach her Siculu and she would never forget her reaction.

'No. You will never go to Sicily, so you will never need it.'

The idea that Lucia could use it to communicate with her mother didn't seem to register with Emmanualla Sacco.

As she learned about her family and what they really were, Lucia discovered her parents' marriage had been a strategic one, to unite two families. Her very existence had been based on a deal. It made her feel sick to think of it. Emmanualla's brothers, Pietro and Marco Favone, ran the city of Palermo; she was a way of tying the Favone and Sacco families together. Paulie and Emmanualla had never even met before the wedding. Lucia had tried often as a child to build a bond between her mother and herself, but it was no good; it was as if her mother had no interest in getting close to her own daughter; now she knew why. Emmanualla obviously hated Paulie and the fact that she was practically sold into marriage. Her sole purpose was to produce an heir, and Lucia was the manifestation of that contract. She wondered if her mother had wanted a boy; she thought her father probably did though he said he was happy with his princess. She wondered at her only child status: was it by accident or design? She would never know.

Her dad had been the one to show her affection. When she was little, he would put her on his shoulders and gallop around the house, pretending to be a pony, her squeals of delight urging him on. They played catch in the pool, he taught her to swim, and she had so many memories of sitting on the rug in his office, playing with her toys while he worked. Had he discussed details of his crimes while she played there, an innocent child? At night, he would read her stories of the Romans, and old Italian folk tales, often falling asleep beside her. She loved him dearly and he loved her.

She just could not come to terms with the fact that this man, this monster, who was wanted by the police for so many dreadful crimes, was the same man. Disillusioned, and an isolated freshman in college, she'd turned to the only thing she felt she could trust: her faith.

She'd constantly berated herself for being so stupid, for believing all the lies about the waste disposal business. She would take to her grave the faces of her fellow students when they'd realized who she was. Some showed revulsion, others grudging admiration, imagining how they could boast they knew Paulie Sacco's daughter, but in the eyes of most of them there was nothing but naked fear. She recalled with burning shame the moment she went on her first day to register for some societies. There were so many to choose from but she loved art and there was a Renaissance Society so she decided to join. Milling about the large hall were thousands of students, and she eventually located the table she wanted. The guy and girl manning the desk were smiling and friendly, talking animatedly with others as she approached.

She wasn't used to these situations and wished, not for the first time, that she'd gone to normal school. She willed herself forward and tried to sound confident.

'Hi, I'd like to join please,' she'd managed. Several of the boys stopped what they were doing and looked at her, making her squirm.

'Absolutely, no problemo!' A confident-looking guy in his early twenties smiled and thrust a clipboard with a registration form attached into her hands. 'Just fill out your details, don't forget your phone number, that's vital,' he winked at her to show he was just harmlessly flirting, 'and we'll have you signed up in no time. I'm Wes by the way.' He stuck his hand out to shake hers.

'I'm Lucia.' She smiled, shaking his hand. 'Lucia Sacco.'

His face changed and suddenly the hubbub of conversation at the desk stopped abruptly. All eyes were on her.

'You're Lucia Sacco, like of Paulie Sacco?' Wes asked, the only one with anything to say.

'Yes, he's my dad.'

She cringed now at her innocence. No wonder they were horrified. Every single person on the East Coast knew who and what her father was, everyone except her it seemed.

The awkwardness was palpable.

'Ok...right...well, em... If you just fill out the form, we'll let you know. We've a lot of people wanting to join so...' All flirting and joking were gone. Wes clearly wanted her to go away.

'Ok...sure.' She knew something had gone wrong and it was at the mention of her father. Other kids had iPhones and access to the internet, but there was no internet in their house—her dad said it was something to do with the phone line being too old or something—and she hadn't any friends so there was no need to have a smartphone. Her cousins and their girlfriends were told by her father to put their screens away when they were in the Sacco house and his word was law. He had effectively cut her off from the real world, and she never even knew it. It was as if there was this huge secret and everyone was involved in keeping it from her. She remembered watching a movie years ago, with her dad, called *The Truman Show* starring Jim Carrey about this guy whose whole life was a TV show and his whole world a set and he never knew it. It was an entertaining movie at the time, but now she realized she was Truman. Everything was presented as perfect and real and all of it, every single bit, was totally fake. He had tried to talk her out of college, did everything he could to convince her to go travelling, accompanied of course, or to just stay living in their mansion, but in the end she'd insisted and he ran out of reasons why it wasn't a good idea. Short of forbidding her, and he never refused her anything, he had to let her go. He must have known it was only a matter of time before she figured out what he really was.

She had always been a spiritual child and loved being in the church. Her tutors were always strict Catholics, and her formative years were punctuated by religious events and observances, so for Lucia the church was as comfortable and familiar as her own home. Her father attended regular mass and was a believer, so it was another thing they shared. She recalled sitting for hours before a beautiful statue of Our Lady that her father had brought her from Rome, one of the only gifts from him that she truly loved. The Blessed Mother's beautiful face transfixed her and she prayed for forgiveness when she realized she loved that statue more than her own mother. For all of her life before college, she lived between the Sacco mansion and the parish church of Our Lady of Grace, three blocks away.

The church was a beautifully simple one, dark and quiet, with the

Stations of the Cross carved lovingly on the walls. The marble altar was decorated in the most vibrant of colours by the local parish flower arranging committee, who took their task very seriously. They would nod at her when she entered and knelt in prayer as they worked. She would have loved to help, the Sacco garden was magnificent and she knew her father wouldn't mind donating some flowers, but even before she understood what her family was, she knew she wouldn't be welcome. She wasn't sure why, but she knew people kept her at arm's length; now it was patently obvious why.

When the old parish priest, Fr Sanchez, died ten years ago, he was replaced with a much younger man, Fr Declan Sullivan, who was to prove a constant in the family's life. Fr Orstello was there as well, but he didn't approve of the Saccos and was very cold towards them; he barely acknowledged Lucia and her father each Sunday. Italians generally like to have Italian clergy, but Orstello ignored them and there was something in the demeanor of the young Irish priest that Paulie admired. Lucia always liked him as well, and they chatted frequently about matters of doctrine and faith. He treated her like a normal person and didn't seem to share other parishioners' mistrust. He asked her when she was seventeen if she'd like to play the organ sometimes for mass and she jumped at the chance. Even the regular organist warmed to her eventually, sharing sheet music and allowing Lucia to suggest hymns they could play. She had studied piano since she was three and loved it; to be asked to play in the church was a great honour. Because of Fr Declan, the parish people seemed to trust her a little bit more than they had previously. She was still a Sacco and to be treated with extreme caution, but they were fairly friendly, and she felt that she belonged there.

Paulie had been pleased to see Lucia getting out of the house and was relieved it was to the church she was drawn. Like a lot of the men she knew, her father saw women as things to be objectified and sexualized, except for mothers and daughters. They were to be revered and adored. The fact that she was spiritual meant, to him, that she was pure, which was how he wanted her to stay, so he took a great interest in her church life. So much so that he became quite the benefactor to the parish, supporting Fr Declan's efforts with those less well off in the area. Through this, they became friendly, and eventually the young Irish priest was invited to dinner in the Sacco home. He became a regular face at the dinner table, and even Emmanualla seemed to come alive in his company. He managed somehow to raise the tone of conversation, and everyone seemed to want to be their best when he was there. Her Uncle Joey liked to talk to him about the Vatican, and he surprised the family by his in-depth knowledge of Catholic history. Uncle Sal was tougher to win round, but Declan did in the end, causing Sal to announce that maybe not every Irish was all bad—praise indeed.

As she got older and became more and more interested in the church, she and Fr Declan often had spirited conversations on aspects of canon law, which left everyone else at the table in awe.

That first semester at college, when she discovered what kind of people her family were, she was plagued with wondering how a good priest could minister for so long to such evil people. In the absence of anyone else to talk to, she confronted him. They met and spoke at length, and he was open and discussed the matter in detail. He explained his position, which was that everyone, even the worst sinner, can come to God at any time and seek His help and forgiveness. It was not up to priests or bishops, or anyone else for that matter, to decide who was worthy of the grace of God; his job was to minister to the congregation wherever he was sent and that was what he was doing to the best of his ability. God had sent him to New Jersey, to the Sacco family, Declan truly believed that, and so he had to do his best. Of course, he didn't condone the activities of the mafia and their connected families, but he was there to grant absolution to those who were truly sorry and to guide, as much as possible, those people onto the path of goodness. He explained, without going into specific details, that some courses of action her father and others intended to take were averted through his intervention. Fr Declan never claimed it was his powers of persuasion that stopped a particular crime from taking place, but it was the Lord, working through him, who might have brought about a rethink, and that was surely a good thing.

Lucia began to see that Declan believed that he was doing some good, and that without him, the Saccos would have been even worse. Declan explained how Paulie Sacco gave a lot of money to charity, paid for academic scholarships for kids from the many disadvantaged areas of the city, and funded drug rehab programmes in the city's projects, and when Lucia railed that he was also the one dealing those drugs, employing these criminals, Declan explained that yes, that was true, but wasn't it better that he did some good as well rather than just doing bad? He explained that he tried in every way he could to express his revulsion for the kinds of activities the Saccos engaged in, but in the end he had to accept that he could do more good if he stayed within the family. If he lectured and preached to Paulie, then the whole thing would collapse. This way, while he never condoned it, he was in a position to sometimes lessen the violence, and he felt that was his calling. It was an impossible argument, endlessly going round in circles, but in the end, she saw he was right. One person, even one priest, couldn't steer the family away from a life of crime, one that bizarrely they saw as their heritage, but he could shine an occasional light of hope or goodness into the abyss, and wasn't that worth something?

She began to confide more and more in Father Declan, trying to make sense of the life she thought she knew but now seemed to her built on a lie. They talked for hours, prayed together, and slowly she began to find a path through the realization of who and what she was. The one aspect of her learning to cope with her family, where they disagreed, was on how she should deal with her father, confronting him with the accusations she had heard. Declan knew Paulie better than most, and he warned her repeatedly that he would not take it well, but she was still in some way clinging to the memory of the father she thought she had—the kind, loving one who would give her anything she wanted. Declan had seen first-hand what happened to those who challenged Paulie, but she was determined. They argued, and she told him that he only thought he knew her father, that underneath the tough exterior was a kind, gentle man. She was convinced that Paulie didn't really want to live that kind of life; he had been born into it and saw no way out. She thought back to how innocent her nineteen-year-old self had been, believing if she could help him, show him a path out of the dark, murky world he inhabited into one of redemption and repentance, then she would do it. He just needed to be given the chance, to have someone believe in him.

She would take to her grave the conversation in his study that day. He was delighted to see her as usual, stopped the meeting he was having with Uncle Sal and PJ, and sent them on their way. He suggested they take a walk in the garden and went to take her arm, but she said she wanted to talk to him about something important. He agreed easily and sat back down in his huge leather seat behind the antique walnut desk. She sat opposite, on the much smaller chair, deliberately placed there to make the visitor feel inferior to him, she now realized. She told him that she knew everything, and that while she hated what he was, that there was hope, if he changed his ways. Her father's normally relaxed and happy face clouded over, first with what looked like rage but instantly converted to contrition. Lucia thought back often to that day; even now, she was staggered at her own stupidity. He just gave her one of his signature Sacco performances and she fell for it. Her father was a chameleon; he adapted to his surroundings and thus survived. He stood up, came out from behind his desk, and led her by the hand to the huge calfskin sofa and sat beside her, holding her hands in his, sincerity oozing out of him as he appeared to struggle to find the words to explain.

'Lucia, my darling, what can I say to you? I love you with all my heart, you know I do. I wanted to keep this thing, our thing, from you for as long as possible. Maybe that was wrong of me but you're such a precious innocent flower, I never wanted the dark realities of life to touch you. It's bad sometimes, and some of the things you've read or heard, well, there is probably a grain of truth in them, though of course, the media love to exaggerate. I won't lie to you, but you need to understand, it's our legacy, for right or wrong, it's what's been handed down to us, from those who went before, who landed here from the old country and were spat on and kicked by drunken Irish and conniving Jews and the rest of them. We needed to make our space here, and we have, but it's a struggle all the time. We're just protecting our own, that's what everyone does, right? The Irish, the Russians, the Mexicans, they're all just the same, looking out for their own. Even in the animal kingdom, lions can't be worried about the antelope and how they feel, right? They've got to look after their own pride. Well, it's the same with us. The media portray us in a certain way, but they don't get it, they don't want to get it, they want to have someone to hate, someone to blame for the mess, but we're not the cause, never have been.'

Lucia looked deeply into her father's eyes and desperately wanted him to see that there was another way.

'But, Daddy, I know that, I know you got this from Grandpa and his brothers, but it's wrong, it's a sinful life. And you can walk away, you can do good. We don't need all of this.' She waved her hand expansively around the beautifully decorated opulence. 'We can live a simpler life, a life close to God, seek His forgiveness and He will answer. You are a good man, I know you are, but you've been caught up in this thing for so long you don't see any other way. But there is, I promise you, there is a way out of the darkness of crime and sin and misery into the light of God's love.'

'You really believe that, don't you?' he asked, tears in his eyes.

'Of course, God loves you, Daddy, he does, but you must repent.'

'And you think I can just stop, and you and God can help me to do that, huh?'

'I can, God can.' She nodded. 'But only if you stop this, all of it, right now. You're a smart man, you could make money doing anything. We have enough money anyway, we don't need to live like this. You can, honestly you can, you can turn your back on everything, maybe even go to the police and tell them. I would go with you, tell them what I know; it will be good for you to confess and start again...'

He let her hands go and walked to the ornate glass doors that led to the verdant green lawns, his hands in his pockets. He waited for a few moments before speaking, his back to her all the time.

'Lucia, listen to yourself. Go to the cops? Even if I wanted to, which I don't, how long do you think I'd survive if I suddenly started shooting my mouth off? Huh?'

He turned and gazed at her, unmoving. His eyes glittered bright, but dark as flint, all traces of trying to placate her gone. 'You will never speak to the police, do you hear me?'

It frightened her; she'd never seen him like this; she'd only seen the confident, in-control man she thought he was before.

She nodded, unable to speak. She couldn't meet his gaze, focusing instead on the priceless Italian masters' oil paintings adorning the walls, and expansive lawns and glittering pool beyond the French doors.

The walnut grandfather clock chimed incongruously in the stillness of the room. Lucia felt a cold grip of fear. It was as if she had never seen this man before. Eventually he spoke, in cold measured tones, all the remorse and love gone.

'Lucia, you don't understand. This is who we are, it's who you are, like it or not. You've got to understand. We got this…this thing…our thing, from our fathers and their fathers. Like I've tried to explain to you, they were suppressed, downtrodden for centuries, but they rose up, they fought back to become powerful so nobody could ever hurt them or do them wrong ever again. What do you think would happen if I just stopped? Shall I tell you? Gone.' He clicked his fingers. 'All of this, everything we stand for, family, loyalty, respect. All of it gone, just like that. You think if I stop engaging in certain activities then vice will disappear from society, no more drugs, no more hookers? C'mon, Lucia, you're not that naive. Someone else will do it—the Irish, the Russians, the Costa Ricans—nothing would change. Only us, everything we've worked hard to build, over generations, gone forever, and nothing would change except for us.'

Lucia looked at her father for the first time, really looked at him, and saw what he was. The small part of her that was sure she could change him, that bit of her that thought losing her respect would be too much for him to bear, died in that moment. He didn't love her, not really, not how she thought he did.

Declan was right. He would never change.

In an instant, the coldness was gone and he was her loving father again. It was remarkable how he could turn it on and off. Lucia was reminded of a snake shedding its skin and wriggling away. He crossed the room once more and sat down beside her again.

'Sweetheart.' He held her hand and she longed to recoil in horror. She didn't want him to touch her. 'This is how it is, but you don't need to have anything to do with it. You just stay out of it all and enjoy the benefits. I'm so proud of how you've turned out. You're smart, and beautiful and someday you'll marry and give me grandchildren and we'll be so happy, just like we are now.' He stroked her face and smiled.

'I love you, principessa, I always did from the moment I laid eyes on you. I didn't even mind that you were a girl, though some men would wish for a son. And you were the only one God sent us, and that's ok; you're enough for me. All I've ever done is love you and provide for you, so let's just keep it that way, ok?' All traces of tears were gone, and Lucia realized they were all a part of the act. He probably had the moment planned; he knew she couldn't stay ignorant forever. She knew what he expected and Declan's words echoed in her mind.

'He doesn't forgive and he doesn't forget.'

'Ok, Daddy.' She smiled a fake smile and as he hugged her, she felt revulsion and fear.

The following weekend she met Antonio. Her father invited him and his father for a barbeque, and it seemed like it was expected that the two young people would get along while Paulie and Dias talked business. Lucia had never had a boyfriend and had no romantic interest in Antonio, but she was friendly and he was kind. They actually got along well, and that night as he and his father left, he asked if he could take her to the movies some night. Antonio was nothing like his father; he was sensitive and quietly spoken. He loved to read and they discussed books and plays and art. Lucia glanced at her father and saw his smiling approval so she agreed. Looking back now, she wished she hadn't, as this was complicated enough, but she was lonely and he was a nice guy. She never thought they'd end up engaged.

Lying in the dark of an Irish hotel room in the early hours of the morning with Declan sleeping beside her, she wished that the world would just stop. At this exact point, they were here, cocooned in safety here at the edge of the world, thousands of miles away from everything, but it wasn't possible. Her stomach heaved and she barely made it to the sink as she threw up the little she ate the night before.

CHAPTER 9

*C*reeping back to bed, she felt a little better. She didn't want to wake Declan; he looked so peaceful, and as she gazed down at his sleeping face, she knew that despite everything this was where she should be, with him. She had fought it for so long, but now she was resigned and at peace with her decision. Sleep was gone. She would lie here now, as she did most nights, just thinking, the last few months playing out like a movie in her head.

Though she was a freshman, she didn't live on campus like her classmates as her father insisted she continue to live at home. He said he'd have a driver take her and collect her each day, but she refused. She explained that she wanted to be like a regular student, and she'd never make friends if they thought she was a spoiled little princess. Reluctantly he agreed and bought her a red Corvette Grand Sport. Lucia hated the car, it was so flashy and showy, but her father looked so pleased with himself when he gave it to her, and at least she had more freedom with her own car.

She spent a lot of time at the church. There, and seeing Antonio from time to time. He lived in Philadelphia and was studying to be a veterinarian surgeon. His father was so proud and didn't seem to mind that his son wasn't following him into the family business, which on the face was a legitimate business of international transport but was in fact a drug cartel. On several occasions she considered breaking things up with Antonio, as the months turned into a year and then another, but while she was seeing him, then nobody asked any questions about the time she spent at the church. Antonio was busy with his studies and so if they met once a month for a movie or a pizza, that was manageable. Antonio understood that she wasn't just any ordinary girl so he never pushed for more than a chaste kiss at the end of an evening. Paulie approved and often asked her about him, and complimented her on her choice of man. Lucia wanted to answer that she never recalled choosing him at all but held her tongue.

Antonio was perfect in so many ways, and it suited her. When he wasn't there, which was most of the time, she told her father she was studying or practicing with the choir or playing the organ, but in reality she would sit in the sacristy and talk to Fr Declan. Over time, when there was nothing more to say on the subject of Paulie Sacco, their conversation moved to other things. They both loved nature and took walks along the Blackriver trail together, identifying birds and plants as they went. In her junior year, she managed to convince her father she needed her own space. He seemed anxious to please her after their conversation, and while she hated to think how he paid for everything, she had no other way of supporting herself.

She found a lovely one-bedroom apartment near the campus but not on it. She was anticipating another battle when she brought it up again, but Paulie seemed so happy she had gotten over the realization of what he was, he could refuse her nothing. He even helped her move in, dragging boxes upstairs and taking her out for dinner to Paisanos, the best Italian restaurant in town. He paid her rent in advance, had all her utilities billed to him, and insisted on her taking a gold credit card. The day after she moved in he had a beautiful Steinway piano delivered to her. She felt like Judas taking his money but she couldn't think what else to do.

She agonized over it with Fr Declan, but in the end they both agreed that refusing his generosity would only enrage her father, and cut her off from everyone, including him, so he encouraged her to stay, at least until she graduated. Often she brought up the possibility of just cutting herself off from her father, getting a job and living independently, even changing her name, but he dissuaded her. He believed that both his and Lucia's presence in Paulie's life was a positive thing and they had to do what they could. She got him to invest in so many charities, and she didn't care that it was his need to have her adoration again that motivated him; she was determined to make some retribution for him. If she was honest, she didn't want to leave her family now because it would also mean cutting Declan off. They talked on the phone most days and met up occasionally. For years she told herself all she wanted from him was spiritual guidance and support, but as time wore on she knew she was lying to herself. She was falling in love with him, and while she knew it was wrong, she couldn't help it. She thought about him constantly, she called him every day, and arranged to see him as often as he could. He was always happy to hear from her and agreed to each meet-up she suggested, but she was the one doing all the travelling.

She tried to stop, she even went to Philadelphia every few weeks for weekends with Antonio, but she spent the entire time there wondering what Declan was doing. She made it clear to Antonio that she was so busy with her studies that the arrangement they had was perfect for her. He was very busy as well, studying and going on trips to see various animals in their natural habitat. Like Lucia, money was no object for Antonio either so they were both very happy with the arrangement. When they did meet, they chatted amiably and he held her hand as they walked the streets of Philadelphia. He never pushed for a more intimate relationship with her but was very affectionate so it suited her fine.

She felt bad about using him, but it seemed to suit him as well. He told her one night that he loved her, and she didn't know what to say. It was all so confusing, Antonio loved her, and he was a nice person; he worked hard and had nothing to do with criminality. Their families approved and there was never going to be a future for her and Declan anyway; that was only a silly schoolgirl crush on an older man she couldn't have. To her eternal shame, she told Antonio that she

loved him too. The happiness on his face, the excitement at intro-
ducing her to his friends as his girlfriend as time went on, made her
feel like maybe she could do this. Forget Declan and invest in her and
Antonio. Months went on and he texted and FaceTimed her every few
days. He made infrequent trips to visit her, and she always made sure
her father provided lunch or supper when Antonio was there so she
was hardly ever alone with him.

The proposal came out of the blue, and in front of the entire
family at her father's birthday celebrations. Declan had been invited
as well as all the extended family. Antonio had asked Paulie's permission and Sacco had graciously agreed; the idea that Lucia would be
anything other than thrilled didn't occur to either of them. He slipped
the gigantic rock on her finger, and Lucia caught Declan's eye. She
swore she saw pain there, but she nailed on a smile and pretended she
was thrilled. For the first time in her life, she had something to talk to
her cousins about as the wedding of the century was planned. She told
her father and Antonio that she didn't want to wear the ring to college
because it attracted too much attention, and they were fine about it so
she worked hard and got good grades, replied to Antonio's texts, and
daydreamed about Declan. She saw him every chance she got,
confided in him that she didn't love Antonio but that she felt trapped,
and he counseled her, let her rant and cry, and was her friend. The
problem was, with every passing day, that was not enough.

One day, she skipped classes and drove back to Hoboken. She
didn't know what she was going to say to him, but she had to see him.
She spent longer than usual on her appearance. She normally never
bothered with makeup or anything like that and her outfit was the

same jeans and sweatshirt most of the time. Today though, she braided her long dark hair in a plait that she brought over her shoulder, and wore a red silk dress that showed off her golden brown skin. Her father had bought it for her last summer in Rome, and he always said she looked beautiful in it. Whenever they went out together he would always say, 'Wear the Roma dress,' and even though she rarely dressed up, she loved to see the adoration in his eyes when she wore it.

She texted Declan.

'Columbus Park, near the west gate. 1 hr?'

'You ok?' came the reply immediately.

'Yes. Just want to see you,' she replied.

'At meeting. Done by 2. Can you drop by apt?'

'Sure.'

She could feel her heart thumping. This was crazy, she knew that; maybe he didn't even feel that way about her, though something told her that he did. Why else would he keep in touch? There was nothing more to be said about her father, things were as they were, but the contact remained as strong as it was when she first found out, stronger maybe. When they were together, she almost forgot he was a priest. He wore his collar only when on church business; usually he was dressed in casual clothes, and though he was thirty-four, he looked younger. She wondered if people thought they were just an ordinary couple. She often had to fight the urge to hold his hand, or sit too close to him.

She drove around, mind racing. This was so wrong. God would punish her. As if being Paulie Sacco's daughter, driving around in a fancy car paid for out of people's misery, every stitch of clothes on her back, every bit of food in her mouth, all bought with the pain of others weren't enough, now she was going to ask a priest to break his vow of celibacy. Not to mention Antonio—this was such a mess.

The realization struck her again; there was no point in sugar-coating it, that was exactly what she was going to do. To try to lure a priest of God away from the church with the promise of...of what? Sex? Marriage, a family?

Stop this, she admonished herself, leave now. Book a flight and just go, anywhere. Away from her family, away from Declan. She had access to money, she could withdraw cash so he'd never know where she went, and start again, a new name, a new country even. Declan would stay a priest, doing good, and she would never contact anyone in her family ever again. She wondered if they'd even notice or care. Her father would, but mainly because he'd lose face in front of the family, because his daughter took off. Her mother definitely wouldn't, and her extended family, well, they looked at her like she was from another planet most of the time. As for Antonio, he deserved better anyway, someone who truly loved him.

As she drove around trying to kill time until Declan was free, she came to the Dominican Convent of the Sacred Heart. She pulled up outside and watched the activity inside the big gates. Nuns and lay people milled around; it was an old people's home as well as a convent so she assumed they were medical staff as well as patients. She noticed a youngish-looking nun deep in chat with another older woman when suddenly the young nun threw back her head and laughed. The sound was carried on the still air, and it reminded Lucia of a fountain, bubbling and gurgling. The nun's life was clear, uncomplicated. Serve God and do good in the world. She looked so carefree and happy. An idea struck her: she could be a nun, she could go into one of the enclosed orders, spend her days praying and singing and trying to atone for her sins and those of her father. She could dedicate her life to God and everything else would just fade away. The solitude, the peace would be exactly what she needed to soothe her troubled mind.

Her phone beeped; it was 1.45. Declan.

'Home now. Here all afternoon, see you soon? D.'

She looked at his text. She'd speak to him, ask his opinion on her idea, and see what he said.

'10 mins.,' she replied. She parked in an underground car park two blocks up the street from Declan's apartment; her car was so ostentatious it attracted attention. Her father had even gotten her personalized number plates so there was a chance one of the family would see it if she parked it outside, and she didn't want to have to answer any questions from them about why she was visiting the priest in the middle of the week when she should be in class.

When he buzzed her in to the apartment, she saw a flash of something in his eyes as he took in her appearance. He had never seen her dressed like that before. She felt a surge of satisfaction followed instantly with shame for her vanity. His apartment was the second floor of an old brownstone walk-up and it was all open plan apart from the bedroom and bathroom. She'd been there a few times before, but only to drop off things for the church. She looked around her now as he busied himself in the kitchenette making coffee and small talk as he worked. She got the impression he was deliberately putting his back to her.

He walked back to the lounge area carrying a tray with coffee and cookies on it, and she thought he never looked more handsome. He was wearing black jeans and a light blue shirt open at the neck, where he had recently removed his Roman collar. His dark hair was longer than usual, flopping down over his forehead and curling over his collar, and his pale skin was gradually becoming slightly tanned as the summer months approached.

'Have you been baking?' She smiled.

'No, just a kind parishioner. If I ate all the cookies and cakes I get, I'd be the size of a house. Usually I take them to St Seraphina's; the kids there are happy to devour them.' He placed the tray on the coffee table and stood beside the fireplace.

'So, shouldn't you be at college?' he asked.

'I'm thinking of becoming a nun,' she blurted.

He paused. 'Ok… Are you not engaged to Antonio Dias?' She thought she detected a sharpness in his voice.

'You know how I feel about him. He's a nice guy, and I know I shouldn't… I don't know…but I don't love him, I never have, you know that.'

'But yet you agree to marry him? Lucia, you need to start taking responsibility here. You're not a kid anymore, you're a grown-up. You say you like Antonio but not enough to marry him, then I'm not the person you need to be having this conversation with. He doesn't deserve this, it's not right, and now you're telling me you want to be a nun? Do you think you have a vocation?' he asked, not sounding at all sure that it was the greatest idea he ever heard. Lucia heard frustration in his voice. He always spoke directly to her, never talked down to her, but this time she could hear the aggravation he felt.

'Yes...maybe. I'm not sure. I just know I can't live this life anymore.' She walked to the window and stood with her back to him, afraid that if he saw her face, he'd see the truth written there.

The silence hung heavily between them.

'Look, Lucia, I'm not trying to talk you out of it, only you know what's truly in your heart. But you'd only be joining to run away in that case, not because the religious life is what you really want.' His voice was reasonable again. He had moved and was standing right behind her, not touching, but she thought she could feel his breath on the back of her neck. It sent a shiver down her spine.

'Maybe I would, but is that so awful? Loads of religious people chose that life for reasons other than a bolt from the blue that called them surely. And it worked out for them. I mean have *you* never doubted your vocation? Never thought that maybe you should do something else? Something different?' She turned around, head down.

The question hung in the air, heavy with meaning. They stood a foot apart.

'This is not about me, it's about you and what you want. Is that what you really want from life, Lucia?' he asked, his voice huskier than usual. Her eyes were level with the buttons on his shirt.

'No,' she whispered, trying to swallow the lump in her throat.

'So what *do* you want?' His voice was soft, gentle.

She looked up into his face, the face that haunted all her hours, day and night. The laughter lines around his green eyes, his pale skin, with the freckles across the bridge of his nose, his cupid-shaped lips, the way his dark hair was grey at the temples. She ached to touch his face, to run her fingers through his hair. He was twelve years older than her, and a Catholic priest. Everything about it was wrong, but to her he was perfect.

'I can't have what I want,' she said quietly, all pretence gone.

'To get away from here? Away from your father? From Antonio?' he asked.

'That, yes. But that's not what keeps me awake at night, what I've been fighting for years...' Her gaze raked his face for a clue as to what he was thinking.

They stood facing each other, neither daring to move for what seemed like minutes. He placed his hands on her shoulders and looked intently into her eyes. There was nobody else in the world, just the two of them. She knew then he felt as she did. She heard him groan, as if he were in pain, and then suddenly they were kissing, hungrily exploring each other's bodies with their hands. She could feel the muscles of his broad back, feel the beating of his heart as he pressed himself to her body. On and on they kissed, Lucia knowing for sure that he was the only man she would ever love, could ever love. She expected him to pull away, to realize what he was doing, to beg her not to read anything into it, but he didn't. His lips moved from hers to her forehead, and he held her tightly to him while she cried.

'It's ok, it's going to be ok...' he soothed her, rubbing her hair. As they kissed again, she opened her eyes and looked directly into the eyes of the Blessed Virgin in a painting hanging on his wall. It felt as if the mother of Jesus was watching her and was exuding despair and disappointment. She pulled away from him.

'How can it be ok? How? You're a priest and I'm Paulie Sacco's daughter. I'm so sorry, I never meant to fall in love with you, I tried to fight it, I did, but now—'

'I never meant to fall in love with you either, Lucia, you're all I think about. I tried to pretend I was just your confessor, your friend, but the feelings I have for you are not that of a priest and a parishioner. I love you, Lucia, I really do.'

'But we can't...' she began. The enormity of her actions crashed over her like icy waves. She felt as if God Himself was watching them, appalled at their behaviour.

'No, you're right. We can't.' He sighed as if the weight of the world was on his shoulders.

'I should go,' she whispered.

'I don't want you to,' he replied, his arms tightening around her.

'Declan, we can't do this. It's my fault, I should never have come here, you took a vow…'

'I know I did. I do, but why did God send you into my life, give me these feelings for you, only to take you away from me again? It's not right, maybe this is the life I should be living…'

Lucia remembered feeling such weight of guilt. He was not hers, and he never could be. He was a priest and belonged to God. Her family were responsible for enough evil in the world without her making a priest renege on his most sacred vow. If she didn't go right now, this second, she doubted she'd have the strength. It broke her heart but she removed herself from his arms and managed to say, 'I'm going to go, Declan, I should never have done this, I'm sorry.' She ran out the door and back to her car, bumping into pedestrians in her haste to get away. She got into her car and drove before she had a chance to think any further, only stopping when her vision was so blurred with tears she could no longer see the road in front of her. She couldn't remember anything about the drive back to her apartment.

She knew she would probably never see him again. The church would move him away, across the country, maybe even abroad. That's what they usually did when a priest needed to be removed for whatever reason. So often on their long walks they had spoken about the horrors that had emerged in recent years. There had been so much scandal in the church about pedophile priests; it had cut Declan to the core, that his beloved church could be so calculating, so cruel, moving those criminals from one parish to another where they could abuse more innocent children. Fr Orstello had chosen just to block it all out at his age, and living in chronic pain, he just couldn't take any more suffering. Declan could see the effect each new revelation was having on his fellow clergy, the innocent ones who were afraid to wear the collar now in public. The hierarchy of the church provided no support, no directive even on how to handle this, and priests felt abandoned by their once trusting congregations and by their bishops and cardinals. It was a horrible situation. She had been there for him as he raged and prayed and wondered what to do. But like with the Sacco family, he felt God had called him to the priesthood, and only He would tell him it was time to leave it. He was vocal at mass about how appalled he was, and was instrumental in setting up support groups for victims in the diocese. His sudden departure would cast a horrible shadow over him, people thinking the worst of him, and it was all her fault. If he says he's being moved, she decided as she drove, she would insist on being the one to go. He would give up too much. She'd leave him in peace, to do the work God set out for him, even if it killed her.

He texted her the next day, and she stared at the screen. 'Can we talk? Please? I need to see you D x'

She knew if she saw him she'd lose all her resolve. She ached for him, but she just couldn't do it. She was already wracked with guilt at the actions of her family, the fact that she lived as she did because of others' misery, as well as her deceiving Antonio, and so to take Declan from the church would be a mortal sin, nothing less, and to continue in a relationship with him, no matter how much she craved just that, would be to fly in the face of God.

'Please don't contact me. We have to end this, it's wrong, I can't do it. Please.'

She had to almost force her finger to tap send. She knew he wasn't going to pursue her against her will; if she said back off, then he would. This really was the end. She tapped the green send icon. And lay on her bed, crying as though her heart would break.

'Ok. As you wish. I do love you though and nothing you or anyone else can say or do will change that. Dx' came the instant reply.

She tried in the weeks that followed to go to classes, to visit her father, to get excited about the wedding, which was spiraling out of control in terms of lavishness, get on with her life, but it was impossible.

She was miserable. Every night in bed she resolved to call it all off with Antonio, and every day she thought better of it. Her father would demand to know why, and then she'd have to tell him about Declan, and that just didn't bear thinking about. All of the blame would be placed firmly at Declan's door; she couldn't do that to him. She felt like she was sleepwalking through her days, tossing and turning all night. Antonio was deep in his final exams so he didn't notice her being distracted. Not that he would have anyway; Antonio didn't know her, not on anything but the most superficial of levels. She drove to Hoboken one Sunday, sat outside the church, just to get a glimpse of him, knowing she was torturing herself, but she felt like she just had to see him. He came out after mass as usual, shaking hands with parishioners and sharing a chat and a laugh with them. An elderly lady was telling him a story, her hand resting on his arm, and she could see he was trying to focus but he looked distracted. Eventually the crowd thinned out and he went to go back inside the church. Knowing she shouldn't, she picked up her cell.

'I'm outside, I know I shouldn't be but I just can't go on without seeing you. Lx'

Two minutes later he appeared on the church steps again, vestments removed and in his ordinary clothes, looking around frantically.

She drove up to the kerb and he jumped into her car.

'Wow. Nice wheels!' He smiled. He'd seen the stupid car from the outside but he'd never been in it. She felt embarrassed at the cream leather interior and the expensive stereo system. She tried to explain.

'He insisted, I should have refused, but things were so bad between us, I just thought it was easier…'

'Lucia, it's just a nice car, relax, nobody's judging.' He paused and looked at her profile. 'It's so good to see you,' he said softly. 'I wanted to call you, or just show up at your door but I wanted to respect your wishes as well.'

'You look tired,' she said.

'Sleep isn't something I'm getting a lot of these days. I'm busy all day so I can just about function, but at night I can't stop thinking, mulling over everything over and over...' He rubbed the light stubble on his face.

'Me neither. I thought if I just cut you off, then...I don't know...I'd forget or move on or something, but it's not working out that way.'

They drove out of the city along the highway until she saw a sign for a hotel. It was far enough away in an obscure location that it was unlikely they'd meet anyone who might recognize them. She pulled into the car park and switched off the engine. It was one of those lovely old plantation house standalone establishments, not a chain, and the house was covered in red creeper. Families were milling about, going in for Sunday lunch.

Declan's phone rang.

'Oh shoot.' He groaned, tapping the answer button.

'Hello your Grace.'

Pause.

'Yes, that's fine. I'm not sure what time I'll be home though, I've a few matters to arrange before I go. Maybe Fr Orstello could drop by the parish office. Delia will be there and she has a key and can give him all the details.'

Another pause while the bishop spoke.

'Of course, I will. Thanks, and yes... I'll speak to you when I get back. Thanks, your Grace.'

They sat in silence for a moment.

'I'm going away for a while, to a retreat centre, just to try to get my head straight. I'm leaving tomorrow. Your father asked me to do the wedding, but I said I couldn't. He wasn't taking no for an answer. He couldn't understand why I wouldn't perform the mass when you and I were such good friends. I eventually agreed to do it just to avoid him getting suspicious. But, Lucia, you know that I couldn't marry you to someone else, someone you don't even love. While I'm gone, can you say you don't want me to do it or something?' He stared out the window as he spoke.

'I should break it off with Antonio, I know that, but I'm afraid my father will suspect something between us. I should have never let it start in the first place, but it was so easy. He was in Philadelphia, he seemed to need so little of me, and I could spend all the time I wanted with you... But, no matter how much I want it, or even you do, we can't be together, we just can't, so maybe Antonio is the best thing for me. He's a good guy, and he wants to leave, go to work in Asia or something, maybe we'll do that and...' was all she could manage.

'I told Bishop Rameros, about you, and how I felt, and how you felt... It was his idea that I go away for a while. He thought it might do me some good, a bit of time off.'

'I suppose it would be good.' She forced herself to agree but inside she wanted to scream, 'Don't go, don't let them talk you out of us... stay with me, let's just take off, both of us now, not a word to anyone.' But she held it back.

'The purpose of the retreat is not to try to talk me out of it,' he said, as if he could read her mind. 'It's more just to give me time and space to rest, to talk it over with someone professional, just to help me I guess.'

'I'm glad,' was all she could say.

'It won't change a thing, Lucia. I know you're adamant that we can't be together, and that's your right, but I can't change how I feel. I love you, I have for ages even if I couldn't admit it, even to myself.'

He turned to face her. She was conscious of his nearness, she could smell the spicy male smell of him, and she could feel his breath on the side of her face as he spoke. She stared straight ahead, not trusting herself to look at his face. She knew that whatever the outcome at this moment, that was her future.

'Lucia, if you tell me, here right now, that you don't love me, that you don't want me, then I'll have to accept that and try to find a way to live my life without you. But if you love me, please tell me. I'm twelve years older than you, I'm a Catholic priest, you are Paulie

Sacco's daughter, none of these things are in our favour, but if you love me too, then we can make it work. *I* will make it work, no matter what anyone says, but if it's not what you want, then I'll stay away from you. For good, I promise.'

She turned to face him. Declan was an honourable man. If she told him to leave her alone, then he would.

As she looked into his face, the turmoil of the past months seemed to grind to a shuddering halt. She felt a mental clarity that had evaded her up to that point. God had placed her on this earth, into the Sacco family, and He had put Declan into her life as well. What she felt wasn't wrong or sinful; it was love. The purest, deepest, and most honest love she could ever imagine between two people. She believed with all her heart in a loving God, a God who was Himself, love. What she felt for Declan was good, not bad, a blessing, not a sin.

He mistook her silence for indecision.

'Just tell me to go and I'll go, if it's really what you want.'

'It's not. It's the opposite of what I want...'

'But?'

She smiled slowly as tears formed in her eyes.

'No buts. None.'

CHAPTER 10

They stayed and chatted in the car for over two hours that day, making plans, talking everything out, holding hands, kissing. In that brief window of time, everything felt right, like it wasn't going to blow up in their faces. How stupid they were. Despite the decision to be together, they agreed that he should still go on the six-week-long retreat, away upstate somewhere, to an enclosed order that specialized in priests in crisis. He was completely sure he wanted to be laicized, but in order for that to happen, the church would want him to talk to someone; this just expedited the process. On top of that, Declan explained how the bishop had been so kind and understanding in organizing it; it would have been wrong to refuse to go at the last minute. As the sun set on the hotel car park, she heard his stomach rumble.

'You must be starving.' She smiled.

'I know at times of great emotional upheaval I shouldn't be thinking of my stomach, but I didn't sleep at all last night, finally dozed off at around seven, then the alarm went for morning mass at eight so I've not eaten in...' He looked at his watch. 'Around twenty-nine hours.'

'Well, the owners of this hotel must have given up on us ordering anything a while ago, so let's at least grab a sandwich to justify sitting in the car park for three hours.'

'Good idea.' He grinned and they got out of the car. He had removed his collar but was still in his black pants and shirt. She went over and opened the first two buttons on the shirt.

'Now at least you look more like an off-duty waiter than an off-duty priest.' She smiled, a little sadly.

As she turned to walk towards the hotel, he stopped beside her. She turned back, enquiring, to see his hand outstretched, a shy smile on his face.

She took his hand and together they walked into the restaurant.

Over a delicious meal, they chatted and laughed, and for Lucia it was the best day of her life.

'I wish we didn't have to go back, face everyone. It seems so simple here, just us. I know they'll try to talk you out of it, and even if they don't, my father will go crazy, and the parishioners, I can't imagine ever facing any of them again…and there's Antonio to think about too.' The magic of the afternoon and evening evaporated as the reality of the challenges they faced dawned.

'I've been thinking about that. Maybe you shouldn't say anything to Antonio, or anyone just yet. I don't want you to have to deal with all of that on your own. You said Antonio is away for the next two months in California?'

She nodded. 'Yes, he's taking some kind of course at UCLA. He leaves tomorrow and he's not back until a few days before the wedding.'

Declan thought for a moment. 'Look, this is unfair to him, it really is, but would it make it any worse if you held off telling him until he came back? If you say something now, and I'm not around, then everything will erupt with your father and Fabio Dias, and I just don't want you having to cope with all of than on your own. I know what Paulie's like; he won't accept you just don't want to marry Antonio. He'll interrogate you and he'll put two and two together; we can't risk that. It has to be done carefully. I know you feel bad about Antonio, but my primary concern is protecting you.'

Lucia smiled. 'I know you think he'd hurt me, and I'm under no illusion as to what my father is, but I don't think I'm in danger. He's my dad, for better or worse.'

Declan's face revealed that he didn't share her confidence.

'I hope you're right, but let's not take any chances, ok? Just do nothing until I get back, please?' He held her hand across the table and looked deeply into her eyes. She could refuse him nothing.

'Ok, I won't. Though six weeks of picking out flowers and choosing readings for a wedding that's never going to happen is going to be torture.'

'I know. Maybe you can tone it all down, tell them you've exams coming up and you want to focus on those, that's true, isn't it? And then maybe they'll put on less pressure.'

'My father wants all of this, not me or Antonio. He just wants to show off, and he can do all of that on his own. He's apparently hired some wedding planner who's done weddings for celebrities, I don't know, I kind of tune out when he's telling me about it. He just doesn't get it, that even if I did want to marry Antonio, then I'd just want something small, a spiritual experience that would mean something. But he'd never understand that, so it's easier to let him do it his way.'

'What about Emmanualla? Is she involved at all?'

'You're kidding, right? She'll show up on the day and be stunning but as for having anything to do with me, no. She made that clear when I was a kid; she gave birth to me but that's where it ends. I've tried several times over the years, but she sees me as my father's daughter and therefore not hers. It's hard to explain. She lives in the house but she was never my mother, not in any real sense. She has her own rooms, at the other side of the house from mine and my father's. They haven't shared a room or a bed in as long as I can remember. She does her own thing, stays out of the way, shows up when he needs her on his arm and smiles a bit, not very much. They never speak, never interact in any way. He pays the bills and she can have whatever she wants so long as she doesn't do anything to suggest they are anything but a perfectly happily married couple, and that's it. In our culture, marriage doesn't need to be about love. Most of my aunts and cousins are married to people chosen by the senior members of the family. I guess that's why women's relationships are so tight, or at least the others are. I've never fit in but I can see how close my aunts are; it's a clear demarcation between women and men. The men earn money, the women beautify themselves with it and ask no questions. I could never have that kind of relationship.'

He smiled slowly, melting her heart. 'I don't think that's something you'll need to worry about. I'm not sure how we'll manage but we will. I'm trained as a priest, not exactly a very transferable skill set, so I'll have to retrain as something else. In the meantime, designer hand-bags and sports cars might be off the menu.'

'I'll live.' She grinned.

Eventually they realized the staff were looking restless as they were the last people in the restaurant. They got up, apologizing for keeping them, and left a generous tip when they settled the bill. As they walked across the lobby hand in hand, she looked at him, knowing he was thinking exactly what she was.

'Lucia, please say so if you don't want to but we could put off the inevitable...for a while at least...if you wanted to...' He sounded so unsure of himself, she loved him even more.

'Stay? I'd love to.'

Taking the initiative, she walked boldly to the front desk and asked to book a double room for the night. If the receptionist thought it was odd that they had no luggage or that it was a spur-of-the-moment decision, then she gave no indication of it. Lucia opened her pocket-book and was grateful she inherited her father's mistrust of plastic. She had withdrawn cash yesterday and paid for the room, registering as Lucy and Declan Edwards, the only last name that occurred to her.

They went wordlessly to the room, both nervous and also filled with anticipation.

When they closed the door, he immediately said, 'I wasn't suggest-ing... Well, if you want to just talk or just be together, whatever you want is fine with me.' He wasn't his usual confident self.

Suddenly it occurred to her that maybe he wasn't ready to break his vow of celibacy yet. She wanted to reassure him.

'If you're not ready, I understand, it's such a big thing... I've never either...'

He smiled and drew her into his arms.

'I'm ready. There's nothing I want more,' he whispered into her hair.

He kissed her deeply and ran his hands over her back, drawing her close to him, feeling the contours of her body against his. He'd wondered, fantasized about this moment, and immediately felt ashamed, but now there was no sense of guilt or shame. They loved each other; surely a love so pure and good couldn't be wrong. She responded to him so fully that as they tumbled onto the bed together, it was not the fumbling, clumsy encounter he had feared but something joyful and exhilarating. He'd never been closer to another person and he never wanted to leave her side for the rest of his life. As she clung to him, he moved in her, and she cried, not from pain or fear, she assured him, but from relief. She could stop lying to him and to herself.

He left for the retreat the next day and she dropped him at the corner of his street very early in the morning. She threw herself into her studies, telling her father she was too busy with assignments to come home on the weekends to discuss wedding plans and that she trusted his judgment and that of the planner completely. She felt awful lying, but Declan was right: they needed to have a plan. She stayed away from everyone, especially her father, fearing he'd see right through her if they met. He accepted her explanation easily. He seemed preoccupied; the FBI were on his case and so he was spending a lot of time with Joey and Sal trying to outwit them.

Her mood fluctuated wildly; she felt so alone without Declan, so scared for the future, but she didn't dare confide in anyone. In bed at night she tortured herself with worry about what was going on at the retreat centre. What if they convinced him that it was all a terrible mistake? She couldn't bear to lose him. She longed for someone to talk to, a close friend, but she had none.

She knew a lot of people but she kept her distance; she didn't join any societies on campus, and the very few friends she had soon gave up inviting her to things. The name Sacco alone was enough to keep her isolated. All she wanted was Declan. She fantasized about a life for both of them, far away from New Jersey, maybe even far away from the United States, where neither she nor Declan would be anything but themselves, not a Catholic priest, not a mobster's daughter.

She heard nothing from him, but he had warned her that he wouldn't be able to contact her. The order was enclosed, which meant no contact with the outside world. Antonio texted a few times but with the time difference they rarely managed to speak in person. He tried to FaceTime her a few times but she always missed his calls, texting back soon after with a lie about lectures or tutorials. Antonio was a studious young man and understood and admired her academic zeal, so he never suspected a thing. The planner emailed her samples of invitations, table settings, and guest favours, and she agreed to everything. The weeks without Declan were dragging; she longed to get even a text from him but knew it was impossible. On top of the stress of the fake wedding preparations, she tried to focus on her upcoming exams, but she was tired all the time. She slept for hours, even during the day, often missing lectures. She didn't want to eat, so her refrigerator was totally empty of anything remotely edible; she hadn't gone to a grocery store in days. She knew she should pull herself together, but she was just so crushingly tired. She thought the emotional exhaustion of the previous months was catching up to her.

One evening, just as she was dozing on the sofa, her buzzer went. Nobody ever visited, except the odd lost pizza delivery guy, so she ignored it, trying to go back to sleep.

The buzzing became more insistent until eventually she had no choice but to answer it.

'Yes,' she said groggily into the intercom.

'Lucia? Open up, willya? I'm getting soaked.'

Lucia woke up instantly. It sounded like her cousin PJ's girlfriend Adrianna. What on earth was she doing there?

'Adrianna?' she asked tentatively.

'Yeah yeah, it's me, open up!'

Lucia knew she had no choice but to buzz her up.

She opened the door, bewildered as to what Adrianna might want. She hadn't seen her in over two months. Had something happened to her father? In his line of work danger was inevitable, but who would have sent her? Adrianna was the only one of the women in the family who gave her the time of day but they most definitely were not friends.

'Hi Adrianna, what a surprise.' She tried to sound friendly.

'Hey, Lucia, how you doin?' Adrianna exclaimed.

'Er fine, fine, thanks. Busy…' She indicated the pile of papers on her desk, untouched for days, as she looked in a closet for a hair dryer.

'Oh yeah, what you studyin' again? I know you told me but I ain't got no head for stuff like that. PJ says some people are here to do stuff in the world but I'm just here to decorate it!' She laughed self-deprecatingly.

'Business, international trade that sort of thing… It's pretty boring actually.' Lucia was bewildered. Surely Adrianna didn't just turn up out of the blue to discuss her studies.

'Oh yeah, that's right. What you plannin' on doin' with all of that, y'know, when you're done your degree or whatever?'

Lucia handed her the hair dryer and immediately Adrianna was absorbed in repairing the damage the rain had done to her usually perfect mane. She prattled on as she worked, telling some story about PJ buying new pants that were too tight for him and he took them back for a bigger size and the other guys were teasing him about getting fat and he went crazy and punched someone or something.

Lucia found it hard to hear her over the noise of the dryer, plus she couldn't care less about the squabbling of the Saccos.

Once her hair was returned to its former glory, Adrianna set about applying even more makeup taken from her gigantic Versace handbag. On and on she talked, about the new car Uncle Joey got. The beauty salon that all the Sacco women attend, one owned by Paulie's sister, having to close for three days because of a leak in the roof and the women complaining so much about it the guys put the builders on double shifts to get it finished sooner. About Sal's wife's new diet that, according to Adrianna, sounded disgusting, something to do with grapefruit and olive oil, but was working great. Lucia barely got a word in, apart from an odd yes or no, and twenty minutes into the visit, she still had no idea what the other girl wanted.

'So what brings you up here?' she asked, trying to inject brightness into her voice. The strong smell from Adrianna's perfume, which she applied liberally at the end of the cosmetic job, was making her feel nauseous.

'Oh y'know, we were just sayin' we ain't seen you in so long and— Lucia, are you ok, honey? You don't look so good.'

Lucia felt her stomach churn and she bolted for the bathroom, getting there just in time to retch violently into the toilet.

She stood up, made sure she wasn't going to throw up again, and returned to Adrianna.

'Jeez, girl, you look really bad. Like, totally green, y'know? Did you eat somethin' bad? My sister Claretta, you met her, right? She's like, pukin' her guts up day and night but she's pregnant so that's kinda normal, but at least that ain't your problem!' She laughed at her own joke.

'No, I think I ate something, I got some Chinese food last night, maybe it was off,' she said weakly.

A thundering realization hit her. Exhausted, nauseous, she tried to remember when she'd last had a period, was it before she and Declan were together, more than a month ago? Surely not. Mentally she did the math and suddenly it all made sense. How could she have not seen this before? Panic threatened to engulf her.

She needed to get rid of Adrianna, go to the drugstore, and buy a test. This couldn't be happening, there had to be some mistake, another reason for her symptoms, she couldn't be pregnant.

'Maybe I should just go to bed. Look, thanks for stopping by, it was so nice to see you...' She didn't care if it sounded rude, she just needed her to leave.

Adrianna stood her ground.

'Look, Lucia, your pop is worried about you. I'm supposed to drop by all casual like that's normal. I tried to tell him we ain't that sorta friends, but you know what he's like. Anyway PJ said if Paulie asks you just got to do it, so here I am, and now that I seen you, look, I got to be honest here, hon, you look terrible. Ok, so you're not hanging from the lampshade, which is what he was worried about, but, girl, you are *not* good. Why don't you come back with me, we'll get Dr Cappini to give you somethin'. It's probably gastric flu, my mom got that last year. Man, it was gross, comin' out both ends of her day and night, but she did lose like ten pounds so that was good. But, Lucia, seriously, you don't need to lose weight. Maybe you were a bit curvy before, but now you look great, like, so so super skinny, you don't need to lose one more pound.'

If Lucia had the energy she would have smiled. Adrianna was obsessed with weight, it was her favourite topic, and she endlessly read those stupid magazines where thin celebrities got fat or vice versa.

'Thanks, Adrianna, it's so kind of you to worry about me like this, but honestly I'll be fine. I had some prawns last night and come to think of it they did smell a bit strange. I just need to get it out of my system.' She could see Adrianna was reluctant to go, not wanting to go back to Paulie with the news that she left his sick daughter alone, but also not wanting to be around a puking Lucia. 'I'd only vomit in your car if I went with you now.'

That horrific thought sealed the deal, and Adrianna left but made Lucia promise to call her dad that evening.

'Sure, sure, I just got caught up with my exams but I'll call him, I will.' She hustled Adrianna out the door, desperate to be rid of her.

She closed the door and sat down, feeling like her legs could no longer bear her weight. Why had it never occurred to her? Now it all made perfect sense: She couldn't bear the smell of coffee, where before she was a five-espressos-a-day girl, she had no mind for food, she was sleeping all the time, and as she frantically tried to remember, she definitely hadn't had a period since Declan left.

She threw on a hoodie, scraped a comb through her hair, and left. She was sure the kid working the till in the drugstore was smirking as she handed over the money. All the way back to the apartment she prayed, 'Dear Lord, please no, please not now. Things are bad enough, don't let this be happening, Lord.'

She and Declan hadn't used protection. Neither of them had even thought the day would have ended up with them in bed together, but she foolishly thought it would be ok. How could she have been so stupid? Twenty minutes later she stood in her bathroom, afraid to look at the plastic stick resting on the side of the bath.

'Please, God, please please, make it negative, please, I can't be pregnant, this whole situation is hard enough without this, please, God, please,' she begged fervently for the fiftieth time.

With trembling hands she picked the test up. One pink line for negative, two for positive, the box said.

Two strong pink lines in the little window. She slid down the tiled wall, sat on the floor, and cried.

Three days later, she still hadn't left the apartment except to go to the store for oranges, which were the only thing she could bear to eat. Her final exams were coming up and she needed to study. Though *Impediments to International Trade* was just about the furthest thing

SAFE AT THE EDGE OF THE WORLD

from her mind, she tried to focus. She read the chapter heading four times when her phone beeped.

'Am at Felician – can I see you? D x'

Her heart thumped. He was here. The retreat must be over; he had said it was six weeks but only four had passed. It was three weeks to the wedding. Joy soon gave way to dread. What if he was coming to tell her in person that he'd come to his senses, that he was moving away, the bishop would relocate him somewhere across the country, to the foreign missions maybe? Should she tell him about the baby? What was the point if he wasn't going to stay?

'Come to my place, 225b Adams Avenue, just press the bell I'll buzz you up.' She wanted to put an x on her text as well but this was hard enough, so she resisted.

She frantically jumped in the shower and washed her hair for the first time in days. Then she quickly brushed her teeth—she had vomited so much she must smell disgusting—pulled on a skirt and top, dumping the awful sweatpants and t-shirt she lived in into the laundry basket, and brushed her long dark hair. For the first time she wished she had some makeup to make herself look less awful. She got loads of cosmetics as gifts from her many relatives, but she just donated them to thrift stores. She was just about to dry her hair when she heard the buzzer. She quickly tied her wet hair up in a ponytail.

She didn't dare lift the receiver, she didn't know what to say, so she just buzzed him in. Moments later, there was a gentle knock at the door.

She took a deep breath to steady herself. 'Stay strong,' she whispered to herself, 'let him go gracefully. Dear Lord, if that's what he wants, please help me.'

She opened the door and there he was. Dressed in civilian clothes, he looked so different. He had lost weight as well, and there were deep shadows under his eyes. He wore jeans and sneakers and a dark green sweatshirt; there was blood on his cheek where he'd cut himself shaving. She longed to hold him, to kiss him, but she couldn't; she had to be strong.

'Hi.' She smiled, willing away the tears that came unbidden to her eyes.

'Hi,' he said with a smile. 'It's great to see you.'

'You too.' It was no good; tears poured down her face.

'How've you been?' he asked.

'Ok.'

He raised an eyebrow in enquiry.

She smiled ruefully, 'The truth? Miserable.'

'Me too,' he admitted.

She offered him a seat and she flicked on the fire; it was getting chilly in the late evening. 'Can I get you a drink, coffee?' She went into the little kitchenette to fill the coffee machine with water, hoping the smell didn't make her retch again, anxious to be doing something, to put off the inevitable moment of final rejection.

'Maybe later, but for now I just want to talk to you.' The words filled the silence in the small apartment. She dreaded what was coming. She took a deep breath, turned off the tap, and gripped the side of the sink for strength.

He stood up and walked over to her, turning her around to face him. He put his arms around her and held her so close she could feel the beat of his heart.

'Are you leaving?' She hated herself for asking but she had to know.

'Yes, yes I am,' he spoke quietly.

Her heart was breaking. She knew it, they had convinced him, or God had sent him a sign; either way, she had to let him go.

'Then go, please, Declan, just go. I can't do this...' She couldn't stop the tears.

'But I thought... I thought this was what you wanted.' He looked hurt and confused as she pushed him away from her.

'I can't do it, Declan, I can't be your friend. If you're leaving, going to another parish, or another country, if you're leaving me, then you have to just go, right now, because I just can't do this anymore.' She struggled to get the words out.

'Lucia darling, what are you talking about? I'm leaving the priesthood, not you, I'm never leaving you, not unless you want me to,' he whispered, both his hands holding her face, wiping her tears with the pads of his thumbs.

'So they didn't change your mind? I was sure they would...'

'Of course they didn't; they didn't even try. I saw a great guy, a priest, I told him I was in love with a woman and that I'd tried to fight it and so had she. I never mentioned your name. And he helped me confirm what I already knew, that there was no way out of this. God called me to the priesthood, He sent me to your family, and I now believe He's sent me to you. I'm going to leave, to be laicized, but it takes time. We'll have to tread very carefully, not just with the church, but with your father as well. We'll need to be very, very careful, until we work out what's the best thing to do. But I love you, Lucia, and I can't help it, and I want to be with you, if you'll have me.'

She led him by the hand to the sofa and told him about the baby. She'd rehearsed the conversation over and over in her head, but in the end there was no easy way to say it, so she just blurted it out. Initially, he was as shocked as she was but he recovered.

Drawing her head onto his shoulder, he stroked her hair. The setting sun shone through the windows and she leaned back against him, his arms around her, and she felt safe. 'Wow, I'm going to be a father, not Father Sullivan anymore, but an actual father, of a child. I can't believe it; someone is going to call me Dad.' He was mesmerized.

'But what about my father, the wedding, the bishop, all of it?' she asked, worried that he wasn't thinking straight.

'I know. It's a lot to deal with, and it's going to be difficult but, Lucia, just for tonight let's just be glad and enjoy the blessing we've been sent. Can we do that? I'm not stupid, I know it's going to be bad when everyone finds out, but for now, it's just you and me, here with our little baby growing inside you, and honestly, there isn't a happier man on earth.'

She smiled at the memory as the bells clanged for seven o'clock mass at the cathedral beside the hotel. She couldn't believe it; he wanted to leave the priesthood, to give everything up for her. She knew she should have felt like the worst sinner ever, but she just felt deep relief. Declan was going to be hers. They'd thought they understood just how complicated it would get back then, but now they were here in Ireland, thousands of miles away from everyone and everything. It all seemed surreal. The FBI, Conor, the baby, everything seemed so messed up it was hard to imagine any positive outcome. She realized now that they had been stupid to think they could just walk hand in hand into the sunset and it would all be fine. That night though, in her little apartment, nothing else mattered.

CHAPTER 11

*T*hey woke and lay there, looking into each other's eyes for a while. Declan ordered room service because he didn't want to leave her, and the smell of the dining room was too much for her to endure first thing. He ordered toast and peppermint tea for her, and though she felt ill, she resolved to try to eat some of it at least. She could see the worry in his eyes at how thin she was. They talked about the man who'd died yesterday and the FBI agent's question.

'What do you think?' he asked her. 'Should I testify?'

'I don't know, Declan. I'm so conflicted.' She noted his look of confusion. 'Not because of him being my father and me being loyal to him, nothing like that, but more like if you testify that puts you right in his firing line. He'll never forgive that.'

'He'll never forgive this either though.' Declan placed his hand gently on her abdomen. 'Or the fact that you and I ran off together. I don't think another reason to want me dead makes any difference.'

'Maybe not. I don't know. He needs to be brought to justice. I know that, and I guess a tiny part of me hoped he'd see the error of his ways, try to break away from it, but he won't, and he never will. What he does causes such misery to so many, but I'm afraid, Declan, I guess that's the truth.'

'I know. I am too but don't tell anyone.' He grinned and winked at her. 'Look, I have to do what's right and if I can help the cops put him away, then I've done the right thing, and the added bonus is he's out of our lives. But I'll only do it if it's ok with you.'

'But what about the seal of the confessional? Even if you wanted to reveal what he confessed, you couldn't, could you?'

'No, and that is another problem. Anything he told me in confession is inadmissible, but a lawyer could argue that the nature of our relationship was that of priest-penitent so there's a chance that nothing I say would be accepted in court.'

'So does that mean you can't testify anything you know?'

'Yes and no. Technically yes, I can't say anything he told me in confession, it's inadmissible even if I wanted to, but the reality is that he revealed enough to convict himself at other events and occasions where I was present in my capacity as a friend. Some states have allowed that over the years though not New York.

George Winooski said they could get it tried out of state if necessary. He's got crimes all over the East Coast so any one of them could be the one to get the ball rolling. The other issue of course is the fact that I am no longer a member of the clergy, and perhaps a judge would allow me to testify as myself rather than as a priest. It would depend on the state, the judge, and how determined the authorities are to convict. From the church point of view, well, that's even more complex.

They want the seal upheld absolutely, with no exceptions whatsoever, but there are many within the church who disagree, especially in light of the clerical sex abuse scandals. I've spoken and written about this myself. I believe absolutely in mandatory reporting, but the church is, in this, like in everything, slow to change.'

'So where does that leave you?'

'Us. Whatever we do from now on, Lucia, it's the two of us together. I won't do or say anything without discussing it with you and vice versa, agreed?'

'Agreed.' The knock on the door caused them both to jump.

'It's just room service again. We'll have to try to chill out or this baby is going to think its parents are nutcases.' He grinned and kissed her quickly, jumping up and pulling on a robe as he went to the door.

'Who is it?' he asked, still cautious.

'Room service,' the young girl's voice answered.

As he opened the door Conor walked by, accompanied by his wife and kids. They made a lovely family.

'Morning,' he greeted Declan cheerfully.

Declan opened the door farther, and the girl wheeled the trolley in as Conor introduced Declan to his wife and boys.

'Hello, it's nice to meet you, Ana. Conor's told us a lot about you and Artie and Joe.' He shook her hand warmly.

'And you, he told me about the pool last night, so sad. Conor was helping last night his wife, and to getting the embassy, for helping also.'

Declan smiled at the small blonde woman with the silver jewellery and long flowing dress down to her ankles. He'd forgotten that Conor mentioned she was from the Ukraine. Her accent was still very pronounced despite living in Ireland for a good few years now.

'Yes, very sad. I'm glad you could help, Conor.'

'His wife wanted me to convey her gratitude to you as well for everything you did,' Conor said. 'They are gone to Dublin early this morning by taxi to sort out the paperwork. She's lucky that she was travelling with friends so at least they can support her.'

Lucia appeared at Declan's shoulder as the waitress left.

'Ana, this is Lucia, my girlfriend.'

'I'm sorry we're not dressed yet. We'll be on the bus by nine, I promise, Conor. I'm just trying to eat something first.'

'You do that, and don't be worrying about anything, we'll be grand.' He gave her a wink. 'Now I must say good-bye to my people for a few days since we're leaving County Clare and heading south, so I'll let ye finish ye're breakfast and I'll see ye on the bus.'

'Bye, Declan and Lucia, nice to meet you.' Ana smiled and then, noticing Joe had a crayon and was about to do a redecorating job on the hotel wallpaper, she bolted after him. 'Joe, no!'

'It never stops. I hope ye're ready for it!' Conor chuckled and took his remaining son up in his arms while Ana wrestled the crayon from the other one.

'I don't know if we are, but it's happening, so we'd better try.' Declan put his arm around Lucia and gave her a gentle squeeze and kissed her head.

'See you on the bus.'

The morning was beautiful and Lucia managed to focus on the gorgeous landscape and ignore the waves of nausea. Conor was right: these roads, though still tiny by American standards, were smoother. They stopped at Limerick and took a walk around the medieval city with its huge old walls, and Conor entertained them with stories of battles and sieges and treaties that were broken before the ink was dry on the parchment. The way he told the tales had everyone right back there in medieval Ireland as kings and heirs apparent battled it out for supremacy.

As they stood on the banks of the river looking up at the city, Tony suggested a group picture. He demanded everyone give him their phones or cameras to take the photos. Lucia handed hers over too rather than argue. She had taken it out earlier in the day as they drove along, careful not to open any apps, check email, or log in to Facebook. She'd had so many missed calls and texts, but she deleted them all without reading them. She felt bad but they were all from her family and from Antonio, and there was nothing she could say to any of them. As she'd cleared the messages, Tony's big head had appeared in the gap between the seats.

'Hey, an iPhone 7! I got one too, but mine's the seven plus. Nice phone eh? I got mine the first week it came out, cost a thousand dollars but who cares?'

Lucia had tried to ignore him and eventually he'd given up, but he knew she had a phone so now she handed it to him. As they organized themselves into a group, she noticed him fiddling with it.

'Is everything ok there, Tony?' she asked.

'Oh yeah, I'm just fine, just taking a picture of a beautiful lady is all!' He guffawed loudly, and if Lucia wasn't very much mistaken, both his tone and the way he looked at her was nothing short of lecherous.

Deciding she was too tired to argue, she decided she'd delete him once she got her phone back. The photo was taken and Tony gave her back the phone, holding it for a second longer than necessary.

'He came on to me earlier, but I told him that even if I wasn't gay I find him totally repulsive.' Zoe grinned as she whispered to Lucia.

Lucia smiled back at her. She and Zoe were around the same age, and for the first time in her life she felt a connection to someone as a real friend. They'd only spoken a few times, but she was so open and honest and unashamed of who she was. Lucia admired her and wondered if she'd ever have a friend like that.

'I'll have to unfriend him immediately. It's so weird, I mean, I'm pregnant, and clearly with Declan and yet he flirts, and in front of his wife as well. I don't know...'

'I know! What on earth would make anyone marry him? She seems nice, she even has the grace to look embarrassed when he's going on. Do you remember him asking Conor how much he earned and asking him if he picked his wife out of a catalogue?'

'No, thankfully I missed that,' Lucia replied, horrified.

'This morning at breakfast, Conor was eating with his family and we were of course giving him space to be with them, but Tony just walked up to him and asked him straight out in his big boomy voice! I thought Conor was going to thump him. Poor Valentina looked like she wanted the ground to open up and swallow her.'

'Oh no, that's awful. I met Conor's wife briefly this morning, she seems lovely.'

'She certainly does,' Zoe admitted with a grin.

Lucia couldn't help but chuckle at the other girl's mischievous wit.

'Seriously though, he's a jerk, I'd avoid him if I were you.'

'Don't worry, Zoe, I intend to. I've got quite enough to deal with right now without adding him to my list.'

After the tour the group split up. Ken and Irene went to visit the mighty King John's Castle, an imposing edifice on the banks of Ireland's longest river, the Shannon. Others went to the Hunt Museum, which if she were feeling better would have fascinated Lucia. This couple, Conor explained, called the Hunts were art collectors and their entire collection was on display, from Greek and Roman artifacts to Irish archaeology to paintings by Picasso and Renoir. Tony and Valentina wanted to check out the stores, but Lucia was exhausted. She hadn't slept much the night before and found herself struggling to keep her eyes open.

Elke came up beside her as Conor was explaining what time to be back at the bus and murmured, 'I've always maintained women should get maternity leave in the first trimester, the exhaustion is crippling, isn't it?'

'It sure is, and I didn't get much sleep,' Lucia agreed.

'I'm sure if you asked him Conor would let you sit on the bus, maybe take a nap. Should I ask him?' Elke suggested.

'Hey, that's a great idea.' Declan was glad of the other woman's suggestion; Lucia looked dead on her feet.

'I feel bad always making you miss out—' she began but Declan interrupted. 'Enough of that, this is my baby you're carrying, so I want to do everything I can to make this easy for you. Besides, I can go back, settle you in, and if you fall asleep, then I'll run out and shop for some clothes, ok?'

'Great, thanks, Declan.' She leaned against him.

Elke spoke to Conor and within minutes it was arranged. Conor settled her into the bus and showed her how to recline the seat. He even had a fleece blanket in the parcel rack so Declan tucked her up and with the warm Irish sunshine streaming in the window she was soon asleep.

Lucia's sleep was interrupted by the buzzing of her phone. She had forgotten to switch it off after taking the photo. Bleary-eyed, she felt her heart leap in her chest. Adrianna's name flashed on the screen. She was trying to call her. Lucia was instantly awake. She was alone in the bus and just sat there, staring in horror at the screen of her iPhone. She was afraid to touch anything in case she answered it by mistake. Eventually it rang out. Moments later a WhatsApp appeared.

'Am I seeing things? Ireland? What the hell are you doing there? And is that Fr Declan in the picture? And who is Tony Davis? Everyone going crazy here, you better call home. Ax'

The phone was connected to wifi; Tony must have done it some-how. How on earth did Adrianna know where she was? And that Declan was with her?

The screen lit up again. 'Adrianna Vecci and sixteen others commented on your picture.' Lucia tapped on the Facebook app. There it was, the picture Tony had taken an hour ago where he tagged himself and checked into King John's Castle.

Lucia started to panic. She needed to find Declan, but his phone was off and she had no idea where he might be in this city. If Adrianna knew, then the family knew, which meant it was only a matter of time before her father found them. Maybe he knew already.

Her heart was beating so loudly she was sure the passersby on the street could hear it. The photo had been up on Facebook for almost two hours; even if her father dispatched someone right away, he'd only be flying now. They had a few hours. They needed to leave. Where was Declan? What time had Conor told them all to be back? 4pm? 4.30? She couldn't remember. She needed to think rationally. Maybe she should call her father. Maybe she could reason with him, after all. Though she knew what kind of man he could be, he'd never shown her any of that. The closest he'd ever come to being angry with her was the day she'd suggested they go to the police; apart from that one incident he'd always been loving and kind. Maybe she could get through to him.

Something stopped her picking the phone up and calling him. Declan and she had agreed to do nothing without the other's input so she needed just to wait for him.

She looked at her watch, a Cartier one Uncle Sal had given her on her birthday. The delicate gold bracelet hung from her thin wrist. It was 3.50; the others would surely be coming back soon. She started with fright when the bus door opened, but it was just Conor.

'Did you sleep? You look a bit better, I—'

'My father knows we're here,' she interrupted him.

'What? How does he know? The FBI guy said—'

'Tony took a photo with my phone, back at the castle, and he saw the Facebook app on it and friended himself on my account. When he took the picture, he tagged me and it showed up on my newsfeed. Everyone at home saw the picture, with Declan in it as well. My girlfriend's cousin called and texted. I have so many missed calls and text messages but I just switched the phone off again. Conor, I'm so scared, I keep telling myself it's just my dad, he's not going to hurt me and I don't think he would, but the agent from the FBI is right, he's going after Declan and I...' She couldn't go on.

Conor walked down the bus and sat on the seat opposite her.

'Shhh...relax, we'll deal with this, ok? Declan will be back in a few minutes and we can figure this out. We're leaving here now anyway and going about sixty miles away so we're out of immediate danger. Let's call the agent now and tell him what's happened, and maybe he can come and meet us if he's still here.'

Lucia felt safe with the big Irishman and she knew that he was right; nothing was going to happen in the immediate future but she needed Declan to be with her.

'There he is now, he's crossing the road. It's all going to be ok, Lucia, try not to worry. You'll be freaking the baby out!'

She managed a weak smile as Conor gave her hand a quick squeeze. Declan got back on the bus and thankfully none of the others were back yet. She told him the situation as quickly and as calmly as she could.

He took a deep breath; he had to remain calm.

'Ok, let's call Agent Winooski. I told him we'd let him know if anything happened.'

Conor handed him his phone. 'Use this, just in case. There are so many apps nowadays with location services we don't want to take any more chances.' Declan nodded and pressed call.

'I'm so sorry. I should never have given Tony the phone...' Lucia began.

Declan put his arm protectively around her and kissed the top of her head. 'Don't worry, we'll deal with it' he said as he waited for Winooski to pick up.

'Hi, Agent Winooski, it's Declan Sullivan, there's been a development.'

Conor and Lucia watched as he listened to the FBI agent.

'Ok sure, it's the Killarney Lake Resort, I think we'll get there about...' Declan raised his eyebrows at Conor.

'Five thirty,' Conor confirmed.

'Around five thirty pm, yeah, ok...sure...we won't. Ok. See you then.' Declan hung up. 'He's coming to the hotel to meet us. He just said to keep both our phones switched off, I've taken the old sim card out of mine, and to do nothing until we speak to him.' He saw the look of terror on Lucia's face. 'Relax, it's going to be ok. I promise, we just need to wait and see what he's got to say, ok?'

The remaining passengers returned to the bus and they continued on their journey. Declan held Lucia's hand all the way but they spoke little. Occasionally she caught Conor's eye in the rearview mirror and he gave her an almost imperceptible wink. Despite the precariousness of their situation, there was something soothing about having both Declan and Conor on board. They made her feel safe.

The detective was at the hotel before them, and Conor arranged it that they were given their room key first. He texted the number to the agent and a few minutes after Declan and Lucia were in the bedroom, there was a gentle knock at the door.

'Who is it?' Declan asked before opening.

'George,' came the reply, and he opened the door to let him in.

They sat at the table in the bay window of the luxurious room. The entire resort was nestled under the mountains and had direct access to the lake. The hills around blazed with purple rhododendron and there were deer at the lake shore, totally unperturbed at being on show. It was so breathtakingly beautiful, yet all Lucia could think about was how much danger they were in.

'So they know where you are in terms of Ireland but not where specifically you are in the country so that's something. The Facebook post would have indicated you were in Limerick but you are a hundred kilometers from there now. Your names don't appear on any booking forms or car rentals so even if he could access that information, which I doubt he could anyway, he won't find anything so for now, you're safe. What remains to be decided is your next move.'

Lucia glanced at Declan. They had talked around this situation so often but they kept coming back to the same issue. She slipped her hand into his, hoping to give him strength. When he spoke, his voice was full of conviction.

'I'll testify, there's no issue with that whatsoever, we've decided that, but there is an aspect of this you haven't considered: the seal of the confessional. The information I know comes not necessarily from within the confessional itself but from conversations with Paulie, but because of who I was, and what I represented to him, he would have seen it as confessional and therefore in the eyes of the church, that's what it was.'

'So you're afraid of excommunication, is that it? Surely keeping yourself and the mother of your unborn child safe trumps that?' Winooski was not hostile exactly but provocative in his tone.

Declan felt his hackles rise in resentment. 'Agent Winooski, I'm not *afraid* at all, and as far as my relationship with the church goes, well, I'll deal with that myself. My point is that my testimony will be inadmissible because of the priest-penitent nature of the relationship I had with Paulie Sacco.'

'Hmmm… I don't know enough about it. We need to have our legal people look at it. But you're willing to testify everything you know? You're sure? Because there's no going back.'

'Yes, but in return we need FBI protection. I know what he's capable of, better than most I imagine, so I need to know that both Lucia and I are going to be safe, whatever the outcome.'

Winooski thought for a moment. 'Ok, you've got that. Witness protection isn't an option as you are outside of the US now, and in order to set that up, we'd need you to return. That's too dangerous. I think you're actually safest staying here, on this tour, moving as part of a group, and that guy Conor seems like an intelligent man. I'll get another agent out here with me and we'll be around at a distance, but near enough to monitor everything. All Sacco family members are being watched so no one's left the country. Sacco wouldn't outsource this job, he'd only trust the inner circle, so as long as they stay put in the States, you're ok. What do you think?'

Lucia and Declan looked at each other.

'Could you give us a few minutes, Agent Winooski?' Lucia asked. 'I think we just need a few minutes to talk.'

'Sure, and the name's George. I think we can dispense with formalities at this stage, don't you?' He gave a brief smile.

'Ok, George.' She smiled and Declan noticed how even the life-toughened cop melted a little. She had that effect on people. 'Would you mind calling Conor as well? I think he needs to be a part of anything we decide.'

'Sure.' George made for the door. Before opening the bedroom door he turned back. 'I do know how hard this must be for you both, but if you trust us, then we can work this out. I know you both must have reservations, huge ones, and please don't think this is a threat, it's not my intention, but the FBI won't protect you if you decide you won't or can't testify. I'm sorry but that's how it is, and I need you to be fully aware of the facts if you are making a decision.'

Declan absorbed this information. 'We understand, thank you, George. We'll have a chat and if you could go get Conor, then maybe we can see where we are from there.'

George Winooski nodded and left.

'So, now what?' Lucia asked, looking pale and wan, but underneath there was a steely determination.

'What do you think?' Declan led her to the big double bed and lay down. She snuggled up to him, her head on his shoulder as he lay on his back staring at the ceiling.

'I'm not torn, not really, in case that's what's holding you back.

He's my father and I guess on some deep level I still love him, or love what I thought he was, but I love you so much more. You're a good man, Declan, trying to do good in the world, and he's...well...he's not that, so tell the truth about what you know if that's what you think is right.'

Declan sighed. 'It's not just that though, is it? First, staying here, putting everyone in danger, it doesn't seem right, and second, even if the church allowed me to testify and break the seal of the confessional, there's no way of knowing if the judge will allow it, and if he doesn't, we've shown ourselves to Paulie as traitors and he'll be even more murderous than he already is.'

Lucia got up onto one elbow and gazed down at his face. 'I might be different from him, I am, but I have his blood in my veins and I can tell you this: he won't ever forgive us, never, so we can't make this situation worse by testifying.' She paused, then came the question he was dreading. 'I don't really want to know, but how bad is it? Like is it just drugs and girls, or is it worse?'

He'd considered this moment several times in his head over the past week. What to tell her? Should she know the full extent? He decided it would serve no purpose but then they'd agreed to no more lies.

'It's worse, it's as bad as you can imagine, or maybe you can't. I hated hearing about it. I even considered leaving altogether but God sent me to him, and I prayed each night that my presence was ameliorating the worst of his activities. I think it did, to a certain extent...but I don't know...I'll tell you everything if you want me to, but I don't think it would do you any good.'

'I know he trusted you and I do too. Maybe you're right, maybe I'm better off not knowing the details. I can't ever unknow it then and maybe I'll wish that I could. I know that he respected you and thought you were a really good man. He liked having you around because it made him feel less culpable or less evil or something, like he couldn't be all bad if he had a priest as good as you nearby. I know he was involved with drug running, and that he had girls working as topless dancers at his club, but as for the rest of it, I guess I'm too cowardly to want to know the details.'

'Well, if I get to testify, then it will all be in the public domain; you won't be able to avoid it I'd imagine. Also, I want you to understand that I get where you're coming from. To the world, the FBI, everyone, Paulie is a monster, and he is. In many ways he is every bit as bad as he's painted. And I'm not just saying this because he's your father, but I've seen a good side to him too. Not that it wipes out the bad, nothing could ever do that, but he's not all bad. I know it and you know it too.' Declan searched her lovely face for what she really thought.

'Thank you for saying that. I know he needs to be stopped, and I'm under no illusions as to what kind of man he is, but it helps to know you know he's got another side, a side nobody really gets to see. Are you scared?' She leaned up on one elbow, looking down into his face.

'Yes, there's no point in saying I'm not, but I'll do it. As the agent said, it's either that or live our lives looking over our shoulders. There's no other way, and anyway, it's the right thing to do.'

She lay back on his shoulder once more. They lay there, not talking for a while, each lost in their own thoughts and holding each other. Lucia turned onto her back and placed Declan's hand on her still-flat abdomen.

'We need Daddy to protect us and keep us safe, don't we, little one?'

Declan sat up and kissed her belly, his fingers trailing her skin in wonder at the activity going on inside.

'I will, whatever it takes, I'll do it for you, for both of you.'

After a nap in the hotel, Lucia woke and said she needed some fresh air. As they walked down the street, they ran into Ken and Irene, who were looking for a particular pub Conor had recommended. The town was on the edge of the national park, and horses and buggies, cyclists and walkers, filled the streets.

As Declan and Ken struggled with the street map, Irene turned to Lucia.

'You're looking much perkier, my dear, would you like to join us? Conor recommended we go to hear this band, they're friends of his, so we thought we might listen to the music for a while and maybe have a little drink. They don't allow smoking in the bars here, so it will be ok for you and the baby.'

Lucia was about to refuse, but there was something in the old lady's eyes that made her agree. She was terminally ill and yet here she was making the best of life. She wasn't crippled by fear of the unknown, and she gave Lucia courage.

'Sure, why not? It sounds great.'

Declan took her hand and the four of them walked in the direction of the pub. Across the street sitting in a car was George Winooski and another man; Declan gave them an almost imperceptible nod before locating the pub Conor had mentioned.

The place was busy but a group of young lads saw the elderly Irene and Ken and gave up their seats. When Irene protested, one of the boys, with a whole lot of tattoos and a shaved head, said, 'Nah you're grand, sit yourself down there, missus. I'm taller standing anyway! And my nan would murder me if she thought I left you without a seat.' And with a chuckle they moved to the bar area.

Declan went to the bar, checking quickly for anyone acting suspiciously, but it seemed full of tourists and Irish alike, all having a good time. The music was loud but electrifying, and the girl and boy duo held everyone's attention effortlessly.

Lucia, Irene, and Ken sat down and waited for the drinks to come, transfixed by the music. The girl was Irish, judging by her accent when she introduced the songs, very pretty, but with electric blue hair, buzz cut at one side, and a whole sleeve of tattoos. Lucia was impressed that Irene knew it was called a sleeve, but she explained that her niece was watching *American Ink*, a show about tattoos, on their last trip home and insisted her aunt join her, so Irene was a bit of an expert. She confided that sometimes, if Ken was out and about, she often tuned in to the show in the hotel or on the cruise ships. She kind of liked hearing the stories of why people got the most amazing artwork on their bodies. Irene and her niece discussed it when they Skyped every few days.

Declan retuned with the drinks, and as he passed a group of girls, they eyed him appreciatively, Lucia noted. Her face must have given her away because Irene touched her arm and whispered quietly, 'He only has eyes for you, my dear, don't worry.' And gave her a little wink.

The blue-haired girl played the fiddle and harp and sang like an angel. The guy with her played the Uileann pipes, definitely the most complicated instrument they'd ever seen, but when he played, it was haunting. He looked a little tame for her, with a sober shirt and trousers and a slick haircut, but she could tell from the way he looked at her, he adored her.

Conor popped in to the bar to see them, and in between songs he whispered something to the girl. She spoke to the young man on the pipes, and together they did the most amazing rendition of "Danny Boy," so much so that tears flowed down Irene's cheeks. Conor winked at her from the side of the bar where he stood and raised his glass in a toast to the heavens. Ken put his arm around his wife and gave her a squeeze. The duo played a few more tunes—they were mesmerizing and had the crowded put eating out of their hands—and then took a break. Having got them both a drink, Conor brought them over and introduced them.

'These two are friends of mine, Laoise and Dylan. Laoise is from Cork like myself, and Dylan here is American, but he's living here a few years now. They really are taking the country by storm, so we're lucky to get to see them at all. They'll be hitting the States next month so there'll be no stopping them after that.' Conor smiled.

'Yerra go way outa that, you auld charmer. Watch this one, ladies, he's a bit of an operator. We're only playing a few Irish bars and folk clubs, but to hear him go on you'd swear t'was to Carnegie Hall we were headed!" Laoise grinned, giving Conor a friendly shove.

'How long are you going for?' Ken asked with a grin, clearly charmed by this exotic young Irish woman.

The young man spoke up and though he had a slight American accent, there were definite overtones of an Irish brogue. Lucia wondered if it was acquired, to blend in with his exotic girlfriend. She took to him instantly, seeing the vulnerability in him.

'It's just a little tour, some Irish clubs, one or two festivals…' He reddened as all eyes were on him.

'I think people will love what you guys do over there,' Irene said. 'That instrument sure looks complicated though. I was trying to see what you were doing but there is just so much going on.'

His face lit up at the mention of the pipes. 'It's an amazing instrument, I'm so lucky to get to play it. I never even heard of it until I came to Ireland four years ago with my mom on a tour. That's how I met Conor, and Laoise too.' Again he blushed and Lucia just wanted to hug him. Laoise was deep in conversation with Conor so he was happy just to talk to them. She could see him relax in a smaller conversation.

'Well, you guys are incredible,' Declan said. 'I can't believe how talented you two are. How long have you been playing?'

'Thanks. I've been learning for about four years now, so in piping terms I'm a raw beginner. Laoise's dad is teaching me; he's great to go see if you want to hear really good piping. I practice a lot but the progress can be slow sometimes.' Declan smiled at the sweet American boy who was clearly in love with the Irish livewire who had just tuned into their conversation.

'Don't mind him!' She grinned. 'He's a prodigy. I wouldn't be with him otherwise, would I, Conor?'

'I don't know how he puts up with you, that's the truth. Bossing him around all the time, but he seems to like it. You have a way with the boys, Laoise,' Conor quipped back. It was clear they were very fond of each other. 'Sure my small lads are mad about you too. They have us driven cracked asking when you two are babysitting again.

Ana says the harp is the only thing to put the boys to sleep. She said for you to text her before you go, by the way.' As he spoke his phone rang and his face lit up. 'Speak of the lady herself, excuse me, folks.' He answered his phone and walked away to talk to his wife in peace.

'Thank you so much for "Danny Boy", it was my dad's song, and Declan's dad too, and you did such a wonderful version. I...I explained it to Conor the other day. He would always sing it and now... Well, it moves me like no other song can...' Irene couldn't go on.

'No problem, I'm glad you liked it. Conor told us it was one of your favourites. It's mine too, I really like it even though it's not a song you hear much, more of an Irish-American song I suppose, but it's so sad, and the melody is lovely. I hope it didn't make you too lonely.'

'Not lonely, exactly, it just reminded me of my dad. It was beautiful.' Irene smiled.

'So are you guys enjoying the trip?' Dylan asked. 'Conor's great, isn't he?'

'It's a lovely vacation, and he really is. Is there anything he doesn't know?' Ken joked.

'My mom is always teasing him, saying she reckons he makes most of it up, but then she's got kinda a bad view of men. She likes Conor a lot though,' Dylan replied.

Lucia was intrigued. 'Where is your mom now? Back in the States?'

'No, she never went back either. We came on a tour, and well, she thought she might find a new husband on it, by then she'd had four, but it didn't work out that way. She helped an old lady get this guy she liked to think she was hot or something, and she realized she was good at that kinda thing so she has a business now, doing stuff like that, here.'

'Conor mentioned something about her before. It's an intriguing idea for a business.' Declan grinned.

'Oh yeah, and she's so busy. Women who are afraid their husbands are cheating, or who have just lost interest or whatever, they go to Corlene and she teaches them the arts of seduction and how to dress and how to get their man back. She's amazing,' Laoise explained. 'People come from everywhere, the UK, America, everywhere. And she sorts them out.'

'That's a useful service, I guess.' Ken grinned, taking a drink from his pint of Guinness and winking at Irene.

She punched him playfully on the shoulder. 'I hope I never need her services,' she joked, mock threatening.

'You never will,' he whispered into her ear while giving her a quick squeeze.

'Hey, mister, we better get back before Jamsie has a coronary.' Laoise nudged Dylan as the bar manager gestured impatiently for them to return to the stage. 'People are leaving and he hates that.'

Laoise and Dylan went back onstage to rapturous applause. Irene confided in Lucia that she didn't drink much at home but she'd gotten a taste for Bailey's coffee since Conor recommended one after dinner the first night. They were absolutely delicious and she was on her third of the night. Ken was a committed fan of Guinness for years but vowed to Declan that he'd never touch a drop again in America after tasting what it should be like in Ireland.

'How are you enjoying the trip?' Lucia asked Irene as Ken and Declan were deep in conversation.

'Oh it's wonderful. It's such a gorgeous country, don't you think? And so tranquil. We lived in Brooklyn most of our lives so it's all sirens and traffic and noise. It's hard to imagine anything like that exists here, isn't it?' Irene sighed. 'Though I read in the paper this morning there are gangs in Dublin, battling it out for supremacy, all to do with drugs... It's everywhere.'

It obviously pained her to think of this lovely little island ravaged by crime and drugs. 'Though I guess this part is different from the cities, and no matter how bad Irish criminals can be, I think they could be nothing like Paulie Sacco and the rest of them. Have you been following that? His trial is starting next week; it's all over the news back home. I was watching something on YouTube earlier about him....'

Lucia paled at the mention of her father's name, and she saw

Declan had overheard it too. Ken was still talking, but Declan wasn't listening, she could tell.

Recovering just enough, she muttered something about going to the ladies room.

She stood in the stall, trying to regulate her breathing. Did Irene and Ken know something? Why would they just mention her father? Of all the crooks in America, they know about the case of Sacco? Did they try to befriend her and Declan on purpose? What if her father had sent them?

Forcing herself not to panic, she walked out and examined her reflection in the bathroom mirror. She looked fine; her face didn't betray the trepidation she felt inside. She had to talk to Declan.

She bumped into Conor in the hallway as she exited the ladies room.

'Hi, Lucia, are you having a good night?' he asked. 'I'm glad to see you both out, it's not good to be cooped up inside all day.'

'Oh yes, thanks, Conor, they are amazing,' she said, nodding in the direction of the stage. Suddenly a thought came to her. 'I wonder if you would do me a favour though. I have a bit of a headache, and I think I need to lie down.' She smiled weakly, still shaken from the shock of hearing her father's name mentioned. 'Could you ask Declan to meet me outside with my jacket? I don't really want to go back inside there again.'

'Of course I will, no problem. Will I get you a cab? It's a ten-minute walk back to the hotel but it's raining outside. I'd drive you but I walked here myself.' Lucia was touched that Conor was concerned, and she didn't like lying to him. Telling lies was her default position it seemed these days. She felt weary of the entire thing. 'Y'know, Conor, a walk in the lovely Irish mist might be just what I need.' She smiled. 'But thank you, it was kind of you to think of me.'

'No problem, our mutual friend is around anyway, I spoke to him earlier. There's been no developments in the States, nobody's gone anywhere, so you're safe. I'll just go get Declan and you can stand in the porch outside, in out of the rain but away from the noise.'

Declan appeared beside her in a matter of moments, worried she was in pain.

'I'm ok, I just…the mention of my dad just rattled me…'

They walked along the street, soft mist falling from the dusky sky. He couldn't see where the agent was, but he was sure one of them was around. Conor had explained that in Ireland, it hardly ever got really dark in the summer. In June there could be twenty hours of daylight.

Declan was trying to calm her down. He stopped once they were away from the busy street and turned her to face him, gripping both her upper arms gently and looking into her face.

'Lucia, listen to me, there is no conspiracy here, sweetheart. The Sacco case is all over the news. He appeared for a preliminary hearing yesterday, I saw it online but I didn't want to bring it up in case…well, I dunno, in case you freaked out or something, but honestly, anyone, especially East Coast people, would know about it, it's huge. Ken and Irene are from Brooklyn, of course they're going to know about Paulie Sacco. The biggest mob trial in years they're saying. So it's just a coincidence, ok?'

'You don't know that for sure—' Lucia started.

'Lucia, do you trust me?' he asked urgently.

'Declan, it's not about that…'

"Do you or don't you?' he insisted.

'I do,' she conceded with a sigh.

'Well, then trust me now. It was a coincidence, nothing more. So sure, I can't be a hundred percent certain, but you can't be one hundred percent sure you won't get hit by a car and killed tomorrow either, right? You can't live your life as if it might happen though. This is the same. Paulie Sacco is a huge mob boss and the FBI are gonna nail him, and put him away for years hopefully, with my help if I can, and then all of this will be over. We just need to sit tight, and do nothing until they tell us.' Lucia looked at him, and she prayed he was right.

They walked hand in hand back to the hotel.

CHAPTER 12

*N*ext morning Declan woke to Lucia's sighs of frustration as she knelt over their suitcase, looking for something to wear. They had grabbed the first things they saw when they'd left. Declan had bought some things in the airport, and a few more things the day they were in Limerick, but she'd worn everything she brought.

'I'm going to have to go shopping, I've nothing to wear.'

'Sure, let's go get breakfast and we can go get some things then. We're free to wander around the town this morning anyway. Ken and Irene are taking one of those horse and buggies to a castle by the lake. He's organized for them to have a picnic and everything.'

'He's such a sweet old guy. And to think he's going to lose Irene, soon by the sounds of it. It's so sad.' Lucia shook her head.

'He doesn't see it that way though. He's amazing, they both are. They just think they've had a good long life, and it's drawing to an end. He says he won't stick around without her, and I think he means it. I don't know, maybe he's right.'

Lucia looked at him in surprise.

'You really think that? But suicide is a sin, isn't that what you've preached all your life? That only God can decide when our time is up?'

Declan shrugged. In so many ways Lucia was a much better Catholic than he was. 'So much of what I preached makes very little sense to me now, Lucia, honestly, and I know the church's position on it, but why should Ken stay here without Irene if he doesn't want to? Their kids are grown up and gone, his life would be so empty, and he just sits here and what? Waits to die? Is that what a God that loves us would want for him?'

Lucia considered what he said. So much of their relationship, especially early on, was spent hammering out aspects of faith, of dogma and doctrine, that this was familiar territory for them.

'I see your point, but the Lord puts us here and it's up to Him when we leave. If we start taking everything into our own hands and removing God's hand from our very lives, then what have we got? An empty, Godless society. That can't be good surely?'

Declan smiled at her purity even if he didn't agree with her. 'Well, leaving matters of existential importance to one side, shouldn't we go downstairs, get some breakfast, and hit the stores to find you some clothes?'

'Sure, underwear first, then existentialism.' She grinned and took his hand as they walked to the elevator.

The breakfast room was busy and the smells of cooked breakfast were making Lucia feel a little nauseous again, but she was determined to eat something. Elke had warned her of the possibility of needing hospitalization to be fed intravenously if she or the baby weren't getting enough nutrition. Lucia knew she wasn't saying it to scare her, but she was pointing out how vital good food was for the baby's development and so she vowed to do her best. The thoughts of being in hospital, in Ireland, filled her with dread. She would hate to be away from Declan, so she took a yoghurt and a pastry from the buffet and asked Declan to make her some ginger tea, which she'd read was good for nausea.

Elke and Zoe were sitting at a table for four and gestured that they should join them.

'Good morning.' Elke exuded serenity. 'How are you today?' The slight trace of a German accent was still audible despite many years in the United States.

'Oh a little better,' Lucia said, glancing down at her tray and trying to swallow the urge to retch. 'I'm going to eat this anyway.'

'Good. Start with the tea, it's easier to digest liquid than solid, and try one of these.' She reached into her bag and produced a bag of what looked like hard candy.

'What are they?' Declan asked

'Pastilles, made from essential oils of sour raspberry, green apple, lemon, and tangerine. They are very sour but they help.'

Lucia popped one in her mouth and immediately winced.

Zoe chuckled. 'Gross, right? I take them the following morning sometimes if I've had a little too much to drink. They do work, you'll feel much better, but yeah, they're vile.'

Lucia smiled though it was a struggle to finish the piece of candy.

'So what are you guys up to today?' Zoe asked. 'I'm going shopping but Mom hates crass commercialism, so she's going to commune with nature or something.' She nudged her mother playfully.

Elke rolled her eyes in mock frustration. 'You have so many clothes already, why do you need more?'

'I've got to get something for Gabriella. Though I don't know what. Everything looks good on her though, she's gorgeous.'

The look on Elke's face said it all: clearly she wasn't a fan of this Gabriella.

'I'm sure once its criminally expensive she'll like it.' Elke smiled to take the sharpness out of her comment.

Declan sensed a conflict and jumped in to divert it.

'We're going shopping too, well, Lucia is, I'm going to hold the bags. Shopping isn't my thing either, Elke, so I'm with you there.'

'Hey, if you don't want to go, why don't Lucia and I hit the stores and you guys go look at some cows or whatever and we could meet up for lunch?'

Elke seemed open to the idea but Declan didn't want to leave Lucia.

'Well...I don't know, Lucia's not that well...' He tried to extricate them gently. Lucia interjected before he could get any further, 'Y'know what? A bit of girl time might be nice... I'll be fine,' she said gently, her hand on his arm, touched by his concern. 'You hate shopping, you said it yourself, so why don't I go off with Zoe and get what I need, and I'll meet you later? This national park looks amazingly gorgeous but I'm not really in a hiking state of mind right now. You guys should go, enjoy it.'

'You're sure?' Declan asked, the question loaded with all the information neither Zoe nor Elke knew.

'Absolutely. We'll just stay around this little town, and if I get tired or sick, then Zoe will have to deal with it and not you. You're off throwing up detail for today!' She chuckled, feeling much better.

'Great.' Zoe grinned. 'Mom, give her a few more of those disgusting things to suck, just in case. I'm no nurse, I'd make a terrible caregiver, so let's try to avoid any puking.'

'She's not lying, you have been warned,' Elke added with a grin, glad of Declan's company on her walk.

'Well, if you're sure. I brought my camera on this trip so I might take it and see if I can get some nice shots. That old abbey looked amazing last night with the sun setting behind it when we were walking to the pub.' He'd only thrown his camera in the bag as he was leaving, as a prop to make him look like more of a tourist; he'd never intended to actually use it, but now that they were here and he had the chance, he might as well.

'Cool. Hey, Lucia, we might get something cute for the baby.'

'Do that.' Declan squeezed Lucia's hand and held her gaze for a moment. This was really happening, exhilaration outweighing trepidation.

Just as they were gathering their things to leave, Conor appeared at the table.

'Good morning, folks, how are you all today?' Conor asked. 'How are you feeling, Lucia?'

'Oh much better, thanks, the walk home in the mist last night was so refreshing. It gets so hot at home this time of year, the coolness here is wonderful.'

'I'm not sure my countrymen and women would agree with you, Lucia. All we do is moan about the weather here. They say t'would be a perfect little country if we could only put a roof on it!'

They all laughed. There was something about the Irishman that brought a smile to everyone's face.

'I feel desperate looking at you. Us men have a lot to be thankful for, haven't we, Declan? Ana was in a bad way with the twins too. It was awful watching her, and it wasn't just the mornings either; for the first few months it seemed to be all-day sickness. She reminded me though after she met you and I told her how miserable you were, that she went to some woman, I'd forgotten. She gave her something herbal, don't ask me the name of it now, but I'll text her and find out. Don't worry, it's nothing harmful, Ana wouldn't even take a Panadol when she was pregnant for fear it would affect the babies, but she used to take this stuff each morning before getting out of bed. It smelled absolutely disgusting, I will say that, but it really worked. My mother, God rest her, would say it's the sign of a fine healthy baby though so there's that at least, though it's not much consolation to you at the moment, you poor girl.'

'Thanks, Conor. Don't go to any trouble though.' Lucia smiled.

'It's no bother at all. I'll give her a call there in a minute. She'll be dropping the boys to playschool so she can catch her breath for an hour or two. I'll get back to you.'

Declan and Elke took off for the forest, and Lucia and Zoe strolled into town. It was a lovely sunny morning, and the atmosphere in the town was one of calm relaxation. Most people were on holidays, it seemed, and the stores catered mainly to them. They passed a coffee shop and the aroma that Zoe sniffed appreciatively made Lucia almost retch.

'I used to love coffee, absolutely love it. My dad made the best espresso...' She stopped herself. How could she have mentioned him? Whenever she smelled really good coffee, it reminded her of the mornings she and her father would share. He let her drink coffee when she was ten years old, and her mother seemed to have no objection; she never cared what Lucia did. Other kids weren't allowed, she knew that, but her father sanctioned it so it must be ok. She loved those mornings, before anyone came to pick him up, or before the staff arrived, and they would sit on the bench by the pool and he would put his arm around her and they would drink coffee together and be happy.

'Is he dead?' Zoe asked gently, assuming grief to be the reason the conversation stopped so abruptly.

Lucia thought for a moment. 'Yes, yes, he's dead.'

'I'm sorry, you must miss him. Especially now that you're going to have a baby.'

Lucia smiled at the kindness in the other girl.

'Sometimes, yes I do. Sometimes I miss him very much.'

'Maybe, if the baby is a boy, you could name him after your dad?' Zoe suggested.

'Maybe.' Lucia wanted to change the subject and luckily she spotted a baby-size t-shirt covered in shamrocks on a stand outside a gift shop that said 'The Leprechauns made me do it.'

'Isn't that adorable?' She picked it up.

'Cute.' Zoe smiled, glad Lucia seemed cheered up. 'You should get it.'

They shopped all morning, and they even found a really nice maternity shop where Lucia got some jeans and a few tops and Zoe went into an incredibly chic store and bought a silver mini dress for Gabriella. Lucia bought Declan a shirt and a gorgeously soft knitted sweater in blue and green wool, which she could imagine would make his colouring even more striking. It felt great to buy things for him, like he was really her man. She paid for everything with cash; she'd withdrawn five thousand dollars from her account before leaving the states. She couldn't use a card because her father would spot it, so cash was the only safe thing. He always dealt in cash too, carrying several hundred dollars in his wallet and secreting great wads of money throughout the house. As a child, she sometimes found money in drawers, in the back of the dog's kennel, all sorts of places. One time, the housekeeper called a maintenance guy because the tumble dryer was making a weird noise only to discover the extractor hose was full of money.

'I don't know about you but I'm starving!' Zoe announced when both their arms were laden down with shopping bags.

They had arranged to meet Declan and Elke in a café so they made their way there. The friendly waitress directed them to a booth where they were waiting.

'Wow, you sure did hit the stores!' Declan smiled, relieved to see her looking so well.

'I got some really great things, and some maternity stuff too. And I got you a present.' She smiled as she pulled out the sweater.

'That's gorgeous,' gasped Elke, touching the soft wool. 'And the colour is so vivid.'

'Thank you, I love it.' Declan kissed her.

He and Elke had had a great time as well; they'd even spotted some deer on the lake shore. The photos looked wonderful, all moss-covered ruins, verdant green woods, and glistening blue lakes. This place really was as close to paradise on earth as Lucia could ever imagine.

They ate lunch; Lucia managed a scone and some peppermint tea and afterwards a crushing exhaustion came over her.

'I think I'll go back and take a nap.'

Elke looked at her. 'Yes, good idea. You look tired but it was good for you to get out and take some fresh air and exercise.'

'Let's take a cab back to the hotel. We'll see you guys later. Thanks for your company today, Elke, I really enjoyed it.' Declan kissed Elke briefly on the cheek, something he would never have done as a priest, as he gathered Lucia's many bags.

Despite the craziness of the entire situation, he was enjoying the sensation of being a non-clergy member of society. He was constantly amazed in retrospect at how much of a barrier people put between themselves and him as a priest. Because it was all he ever knew as an adult, people's willingness to share and open up with him just as another person, not a priest, was a revelation. He and Elke had talked a lot about pregnancy and what he should expect over the coming months, but they had also talked politics, her divorce, her relationship with Zoe, and her dislike of her daughter's girlfriend Gabriella. People confided in him before, of course, but it was different now, more balanced. She expected him to reciprocate and he did in as much as he could without revealing everything that was going on. When he was a priest, and people told him their stories, they didn't expect to hear his in return. This new level of human interaction was welcome, if a little strange.

CHAPTER 13

*A*s they hailed a cab, Declan spotted George and another man, presumably another FBI agent, sitting at a sidewalk café across the small street. There was a constant stream of traffic, horse-drawn carriages and bikes, but they managed to hold each other's gaze for a second. Lucia didn't notice them, but Declan felt relieved that they were there. Back in the room, they were just settling in, Lucia showing Declan all her purchases, when there was a knock on the door. They both started and stood without moving for a moment.

'It's George,' they heard through the door and they exhaled.

Declan opened the door and the agent walked into the bedroom. 'I need to tell you something, there's been a development. '

Declan assumed they'd got some feedback from the authorities about the priest- penitent privilege or the efforts to have the case heard in another state but the look on George's face suggested that he wasn't coming to update them on the progress of the developing case.

'What? Is it something bad?' Lucia was scared.

'Sacco arranged to have Fr Orstello kidnapped and interrogated.'

The news made Declan's blood run cold. Poor Fr Orstello; he was elderly, ill, and depressed at the state of his beloved church, and now this. All because of him. The guilt was crushing.

Taking a deep breath, George began telling them what had happened.

Apparently the old priest had been putting out the trash. He lived alone on the ground floor of the building where Declan and the parish office occupied the second floor, insisting he needed no live-in help. The ladies of the parish were wonderful, and Declan was there if he got into difficulty, but he was a stubborn old guy and liked to do things for himself. As he slowly and painfully pulled the trash bin out to the kerbside for collection the following morning, a car pulled up beside him. Before he knew what was happening he'd found himself shoved into the backseat. A canvas bag was put over his head and no one in the car said a word.

'But I thought you were watching the Saccos. How did they get to him without you intervening?' Declan was distraught.

'We weren't watching Fr Orstello, we had no reason to, and Sacco sent some local hoodlums to pick him up, kids out of juvie, nobody who would spark our interest in this case.'

'What happened?' Declan was pale and Lucia reached out to hold his hand.

'Well, from what we can gather, he was brought to the dock area, one of Sacco's warehouses, but even the family aren't really talking about it. Our inside source says Sacco is fuming, but it would seem that either Father Orstello told him nothing or told him lies. Either way, his body was found last night floating in the harbour. He'd been shot in the head.'

Declan felt like he couldn't breathe. He fought back tears, squeezing Lucia's hand.

'This is all my fault. He wouldn't have been in this position if not for my actions. My selfishness has led to an innocent man's death. I...I can't...' He couldn't go on.

Lucia rubbed his back as the agent stood silently.

'I'm sorry for your loss, Declan, I really am.' Winooski sighed. 'But now can you see how much we need to put Sacco and everyone associated with him behind bars? I don't mean to use your friend's death to force your hand, but he died for nothing if Sacco gets to walk away from this.'

Declan looked up, the pain of what he'd been told naked on his face.

'Now, I'm sorry but we need to focus on what to do next. He took Fr Orstello last week because he didn't know where you were. That's no longer the case thanks to Facebook, and so now we know he's looking for you, and more importantly, he knows where you both are.'

George fixed Declan with a steely gaze.

'To add to this, it seems you were right about the confession law. Your testimony would most likely be viewed as inadmissible. There's no precedent for it; in some states it's been overruled but never in New York or New Jersey. Since all the sex abuse scandals though, the judiciary are giving less and less weight to it, but since this isn't that kind of case, our legal team doesn't think it's going to fly.'

'So Declan won't be able to testify? And Fr Orstello's murder goes unpunished? And we are left without protection because we are of no further use to you?' Lucia was fighting panic.

Before George could answer Declan spoke. 'There's more, not just Paulie, I know more.' He sat with his head in his hands. They waited; Declan then stood and thrust his hands deep in his pockets, clearly conflicted about what was coming next. He'd never mentioned this aspect to anyone, not even Lucia. If he told them everything it might save them; then again, it could put them in even greater danger.

'There are others involved...' He spoke quietly; there was no going back now. George spoke slowly as if to a child. 'We know that, Declan. Paulie Sacco's empire includes cousins and brothers-in-law and others; we intend to get them all in one go, not just Sacco. It's the best way of making sure the family doesn't continue in his absence.'

Declan shook his head. 'That's not what I mean. I know about deals done between Paulie and Fabio Dias to flood the East Coast with heroin.'

'Go on.' George was interested. Even if Declan couldn't testify in court, anything he could tell them would be helpful.

Declan glanced at Lucia and took a deep breath. 'Well, as you know, Dias is Costa Rican but he has direct links to Columbia and Mexico, and they, he and Paulie between them, are flooding the East Coast with narcotics. Dias is a much bigger operator than the Saccos, but Paulie has influence over some officials involved with the Union County Dockland, so Dias needs him to get the stuff in. Since 9/11 security is so much tighter, and Dias hates that he needs to rely on Sacco. They pretend to get along, but they hate each other. The wedding of Lucia and Antonio was supposed to be a very public statement to their suppliers and everyone along the chain who were nervous about how acrimonious the relationship was between the two men that everything was ok. Now, I would imagine, our disappearance would have confirmed everything that anyone associated with the deal was worried about. It's a multimillion-dollar industry and both Sacco and Dias do very well with it. If you think Paulie Sacco is dangerous, well…Fabio Dias…he has aspirations of being the Pablo Escobar of this generation.'

George was clearly very interested in this information. 'So you know for a fact they were working together?'

'Yes. I've met Dias twice. I was asked to mediate between two young guys, one from the Dias camp and the other a Sacco who had a grievance and threatened to do each other harm about six months ago. Nobody could get through to Ernesto, that's Paulie's nephew, and he was threatening to shoot one of the Dias gang. He was flirting with Ernesto's girlfriend or something stupid like that.'

Declan glanced at Lucia, who was sitting on the bed, stunned.

'Ernesto is dating Adrianna's sister Maria. Is that who they were fighting about?'

'I think so.' Declan nodded and went on. 'It all kicked off when the Dias guy was in Jersey for a delivery of a consignment of drugs. After the shipment arrived safely and was on its way to be distributed, they all went out, Dias guys and the Saccos, but only the young guys and their girlfriends, had a few drinks and probably some of the merchandise, I don't know, things were said. These gang kids, they are raised on violence and pride, a horrible combination. Saving face, not being seen to be disrespected, it's a huge thing with them. The irony is they actually have no respect for anyone or anything, but anyway. They were dragged apart that night but Ernesto wasn't letting it go. I was asked to intervene; Paulie needed to keep everything sweet with Dias but couldn't be seen by the family to back down from a slight, so this compromise was arranged, that I would negotiate. At the time I wanted to refuse, but they were threatening a gun battle, and knowing them, it could have happened anywhere. All I was thinking was, they could kill innocent people if it went ahead. I spoke in confidence to Bishop Rameros, and he said I should do it, try to work out a deal. I hated it, I hated being involved and I wished I wasn't, but I felt I was being guided by God to try to make the best of a horrific situation. Dias allowed it, once Paulie assured them I could be trusted. Paulie spoke openly to me about what was at stake if a stupid squabble between two hotheaded kids were to spill over. He and Dias had a very profitable thing going and they were both anxious for it to continue. Obviously that wasn't my motivation; Paulie knew I was appalled by the whole thing, but I thought if I could avert this feud then maybe I'd save some innocent person getting caught in the cross-fire. I went to his house in Philadelphia, Dias is Catholic as well, he even asked me to bless his boat once but I knew the boat was being used for drug trafficking so I refused. He didn't like that, but he accepted it. Said he admired a man of principle.' Declan grimaced bitterly.

'So you heard this while outside someplace?' George asked.

'Yes.'

'This is better. It means it doesn't come under the seal of the confessional and therefore stands a much better chance of being considered admissible. When you first mentioned the seal, I was a bit taken aback to be honest. It's not something I'd ever come across before. I mean, I'd heard of it, of course, but it never featured in any case I was involved with, but you are a hundred percent right. It's mostly useless testimony if it happens in a confession box or if the penitent is given absolution. In this case, we might be lucky. Because Sacco wasn't looking for absolution, nor did you give it, we might have a shot, but it's still a gamble. The defense could say that the accused confessed, as if to God himself, and with the sure knowledge of confidentiality, so it can't be used as evidence. But a social conversation, in a house, well, that might be different.'

'You said you met him twice?' George went on.

'Yeah, I met him on another occasion, in Sacco's house. I was there because the family were celebrating a baby's christening, Julio and Cristina's baby, remember, Lucia?'

Lucia nodded. She remembered it so well; she was in love with Declan by that stage but had not yet said anything. It was torture, being so close to him and yet unable to express how she felt.

'Paulie insisted I go back to his house for lunch after, and Dias was there. I'm not sure why exactly, they hate each other as I said, though they were friends in public. Maybe it was to show the family that everything was ok between them; some of the made guys were getting a bit rattled as I said. It was probably a PR exercise, he was good at that.'

He stopped talking and the room fell silent, each person lost in their own thoughts. Declan knew George was glad; this was a breakthrough. Lucia couldn't believe that Declan was in so deep. She knew he was on friendly terms with the family, performed the sacraments on various family members, but the news that he was in that deep with them horrified her. Suddenly she needed to get some air.

'I'm going outside, just to the garden, I just need to be on my own for a minute.'

Declan immediately went to her side. 'I'll come with you.'

'No, no thanks, I'll be ok, I just need some time alone.'

She left the bedroom, the strain of all of this feeling like it was crushing down on her.

Declan and George stood in silence, neither knowing what to say.

'Will what I told you change your legal people's minds, do you think?' Declan's mind was racing.

'Possibly. I don't know. It's certainly better than what we had before, but I don't know. They'll still say he saw you as a confidant and because you were a priest...'

'And if they don't think it will work? Where does that leave us?'

'Well, from an official standpoint you are just members of the public. I mean, you can go to the cops, say you're worried, but I won't lie to you, the level of protection you're getting now won't go on if we can't use you in court. It's wrong maybe, but it's how it is, resources, money, you know how it goes.' George was apologetic but at least he was being straight with them.

'Then he'll come for us, for both of us, I know he will. There's no way he'll just let Lucia carry our baby and give birth. Not when the child's existence is a symbol of how he was humiliated. That's how he'll see it.' Declan stood with his back to the room, looking out into the beautiful grounds of the hotel.

'I don't think he'd go that far, honestly, according to our intelligence.' He was trying to reason with Declan but Declan was adamant.

'It doesn't matter what the FBI know or think they know!' Declan snapped, the strain of it all evident. 'You don't get it, none of you do. He knows he's being watched. He doesn't act rashly, out of temper like a normal person, he waits, watches, and then exacts his revenge. That's what he's doing. In his eyes, she betrayed him, as did I. He won't ever forgive us and we'll have to pay. I know how he thinks, he *will* hurt her. I'm not just worried about the possibility of this happening, you have to understand, it's a certainty.'

'But, Declan, she's his only child, he adores her, you said it yourself.' George was trying to restore some calmness. 'Sure, he'll come after you but she—'

'No, George, that's not how he thinks. I know him better than anyone. She betrayed him, and nothing that happened before means anything. Please trust me on this.' Declan was getting frustrated, trying to make them see. He took a deep breath, steadying himself.

He went on, 'Talk to your people, see if what I know can be used. In the meantime, I need to get her away, someplace he will never find her. If they think my testimony will be accepted, then I'll tell them everything, they can tape me, video me, whatever, I'll sit in the witness

JEAN GRAINGER

box and tell them everything, and I don't know everything, George, but I know a lot. I know where many of the bodies are buried, literally, where the money is, who's in with him, which politicians are in his pocket, who he loves, who he hates.'

'Ok, leave it with me.' George left.

CHAPTER 14

*L*ucia sat on the bench, so many emotions clambering for attention in her mind. She needed to be alone with her thoughts. Declan was going to testify against her father, and his testimony would be the thing that would put him and all the men in her family behind bars for years. He'd never told her the full extent of her father's empire or how deeply he was involved, and while she knew it was to protect her, it still hurt. The idea that the FBI could decide his testimony was usable and take Declan away filled her with terror and dread, but he would presumably have to go back to the states to testify. She needed to think, and for the hundredth time since all this happened, she wished she could talk to her father. He'd always been a listening ear and a source of sound advice her whole life; the idea that she had to go it alone from now on without him, and that she and Declan would be the reason for that, left her in an emotional spin. She should hate him, and she did, but the part of her that loved him couldn't be turned off like a switch. He had tried to marry her off to Antonio to prove a point to his business associates, but she believed in her heart that if she'd said she didn't want Antonio, then he would have called it all off. Or would he? It was impossible to tell now.

The old Lucia would have been sure but now that she knew

what she knew, she couldn't be sure. She wished she could think more clearly. She knew it was impossible, but she longed to speak to him, just the two of them, alone. Would he really kill her as Declan thought he would? She just couldn't believe it, though all the evidence suggested he was much more the man Declan knew him to be than the fantasy she had created. But it wasn't a fantasy, she argued with herself, he was really her dad, he really loved her, they were really close. If only she could see him, she'd know for sure. She gazed up into the clear sky as dusk was enveloping the idyllic scene of mountains and lakes. A dog barked, children squealed with delight as they played with water pistols on the hotel lawn, life just going on. Never before in her entire life had she wanted to just get away, from everyone and everything, but she did now.

Declan walked over and sat beside her.

'I know you wanted to be alone, but I just wanted to check you were ok. George is checking in with the legal people again, with the new evidence, and he'll get back to us... I'll go back inside if you'd rather.'

'I know why you didn't tell me, I do, but to hear you say it, heroin. Somehow the other stuff, the girls and the racketeering, were not ok, of course not, but kind of what he inherited. He never inherited heroin. I can't believe it...and Antonio? Was he in on this too? This match to cement the two families? Is that why he was ok with never seeing me?' She was exhausted, the strain of the past week bubbling to the surface.

'I don't know, Lucia, about Antonio. He never came up, apart from Paulie saying how happy he was for you guys.'

'He sold me. That's the truth, isn't it? He sold me to a drug dealer's son to secure his disgusting business.'

'You don't know that. Antonio and you met, he fell in love with you...' Declan was trying to calm her down; all this stress was so bad for her and for the baby.

'Antonio was planted, and all I had to do was go along with it, and you know it as well as I do.' She looked into his eyes, there was something there, something he was holding back. 'Tell me, there's something else, I know it.'

Declan couldn't bear to hurt her further, but now was the time for honesty if they were to have any future.

'Well, it was the belief in the Sacco family that Antonio was gay. I only know this because someone in your family wanted to talk to me. He was concerned that his son was showing homosexual tendencies, and this man was worried because he'd noticed that he and Antonio were texting and calling each other, but Paulie walked in on the conversation. It was just after you guys started dating, and it stopped. But it was probably just talk, you know how it is.'

'He never touched me, or even kissed me properly. I always thought it was a respect thing, until we were married, and then when he was away so much... It all makes sense now. Did my father know about Antonio's sexuality?'

Declan paused. 'Well, he'd heard the rumours, and you know the kind of talk that goes on in that culture about homosexuality.'

'Oh God, I thought that behind all of this he loved me, I really believed he did. When I was a kid, he was such a great dad. I know it's hard to imagine but he really was. My mother was so cold and didn't care what happened to me, so when my dad pulled me onto his lap and cuddled me I felt like the happiest girl in the world. But it was all a lie, all of it. He put making money from selling drugs ahead of me, and then was happy to marry me off to a man who could never love me. That's how little he feels for me.'

Declan stood and put his arms around her as she sobbed for the man she thought her father was.

Eventually they returned to their room, Lucia feeling like she would simply collapse if she didn't lie down. Declan knew he had to tell her the whole truth, but up to now there had never been a right time. He tucked her in and sat on the edge of the bed.

'At least I don't feel so guilty about leaving Antonio at the altar, he's probably relieved,' she whispered. 'I wondered why you seemed to not feel guilty about Antonio. Of all the issues this situation raised, you never said, poor Antonio. I found that strange.'

'I believe Antonio has had at least one homosexual encounter so he knew he was gay and he was willing to marry you anyway, so no, I didn't feel sorry for him. He's a bright young man. If he has any sense, he'll get as far away from his father as he can and live the life he wants to live.'

'I hope so. I should be angry at him I suppose, but I'm not. We were both just pawns in this horrible game. I'm just glad I'm here with you and not on some five-star island with him, with us trying to think of something to say and both of us dreading the inevitable.'

'If I'm honest, I could never bear the thought of him and you together. That day at the christening party, I only went to see you, though I was barely able to admit it to myself at the time. This doesn't show me in a very good light, but looking back, I remember feeling relief when that information was given to me. Even then, I hated the thought of anyone else being close to you, even though I was a priest and had no claim whatsoever to your affections. I should have told you, I know that, but I was so confused myself, and it all seemed to be set up and you know how those men in your family talk. I'm sure they were convinced I was gay as well because I didn't have some woman on the side. They are so sexualized, even when they are little boys; it's all they know. Women are either saint-like mother figures that they expect to be replicated in their wives and daughters, or they are disposable vessels for their gratification.'

'Would you have gone ahead, let me marry him? Done the ceremony even?'

He knew from his years in the priesthood that nothing was more corrosive to a relationship than lies. If people were honest, then so many other bad things could be avoided.

'I'd love to think I wouldn't have, that I'd have said something to stop the wedding going ahead, but I can't be sure. That's the truth. I loved you then, and I love you infinitely more now, and the idea that anyone else would hold you or kiss you…well, it causes me actual physical pain, but I can't say for one hundred percent certain.'

'"I would never have done that" would be a better answer.' She smiled.

'But that wouldn't be the truth, and I promise you, Lucia, I will never lie to you.'

'Ok, and I know you won't.'

'We're moving on to Cork tomorrow. What do you think we should do? Stay with the tour or stay here or what?' he asked.

'I guess we wait until George gets back to us. What time is it?'

'Just after six. Why don't you get some sleep? I'll be right here.'

Declan sat and watched her sleep. She looked so young, so innocent. He didn't know how he was going to do it but he would have to protect her.

His phone vibrated, a text. His heart thumped though Conor and George were the only people with the new number.

'Hi, Declan, Conor gave me your number, you've been on my mind. Hope everything is ok. If you need to talk, you know where I am. Eddie Shanahan.'

Declan smiled. How kind of him to think of them and their predicament.

'Thanks, Eddie, it was great to meet you, thanks for the listening ear. I'd love a chat sometime. We're in Killarney now though. God Bless.'

Immediately the reply came.

'Semi-retirement means I've plenty of time. An hour and a half by car. When suits? Tomorrow evening? Could be there by 7.'

Declan's first instinct was to thank him but say he could never put him to that much trouble, but something stopped him. He remembered the warmth and straight-talking manner of the Irish priest, and suddenly meeting him again was a very comforting thought. So many things were whirling around in his head, it might be good to talk it out with someone with no vested interest. And Eddie didn't strike him as the kind of guy who made offers he didn't mean.

'If you're sure, that would be wonderful. Thanks, Declan.'

'I'm sure. See you then.'

No sooner had he read the text from Eddie when another popped on the screen.

George this time.

'No go – Legal says inadmissible due to nature of relationship. I'm sorry. Talk tomorrow. G.W.'

So that was it. The FBI didn't want him, or they couldn't use him; whatever the reason, the end result would be the same. The agents would be recalled, Sacco knew where they were, and without protection, it was only a matter of time. The buttery light of an Irish summer sunset illuminated the room as Lucia slept on and Declan considered what to do. Whatever else happened, sitting around and waiting for Sacco or one of his henchmen was not an option.

CHAPTER 15

As they pressed the button for the elevator the next morning, their hearts sank when the door opened. Tony and Valentina were standing inside.

'Hey, how you guys doing?' Tony boomed.

'Fine, thanks,' Declan answered without enthusiasm. The man was a buffoon, and because of him and his foolishness, Sacco now knew where they were. Also he hated the way he leered at Lucia, and the way he spoke to and about his wife was just horrible.

'What do ya think of those earrings, Lucia?' he asked, pointing at Valentina's ears. 'Real emeralds and white gold. The guy wanted too much but I got him down to half. Amateurs, these Irish, don't know nothing about business. I'm hagglin' since I was knee high to a grasshopper. Show them your bracelet, honey.' Valentina reluctantly held up her wrist. On it was a huge gold bracelet encrusted with diamonds. Lucia thought it was horribly gaudy but she smiled appreciatively. As Valentina raised her arm, Lucia noticed the skin around her elbow was bruised. Looking closer at the woman's face too, she was sure she could see bruising under the makeup. 'Got that at Tiffany's, you need to get Declan here to invest in some nice pieces for you, Lucia. You're a great-looking girl but you could do with a bit of ...I dunno, something...'

Valentina blushed crimson and Declan breathed deeply to control his temper. The man was insufferable, but they had enough problems.

The lift pinged and the doors opened into the hotel lobby.

Valentina turned and spoke to Lucia, the first time either of them had heard her speak more than a word or two the whole trip.

'I hope...you is feel better, you looking better...' Tony grabbed her arm and almost yanked her away. Lucia felt so sorry for her. Underneath all the makeup and the designer clothes, she seemed nice, and judging by her accent and halting English, she hadn't been in the US very long. If that idiot was hurting her, then they needed to do something.

Instinctively she ran after them. 'Declan and I were about to go and have breakfast, would you like to join us?' Her question was addressed to Valentina. Declan followed her, looking bewildered, mystified as to why on earth she was drawing the dreadful Tony on them. He answered for both of them.

'Sure.' Jerking a thumb in Valentina's direction, he insulted her, 'She don't got much to say so it'd be good to talk baseball for a while.' He addressed Declan, 'You see the score in the Red Sox game? Those Yankees don't know what they're facin', that Fernando Abad pitches like nothing I ever seen...'

Declan mumbled something in reply while making frantic eye gestures at Lucia.

They passed a few others from the tour on their way across the dining room, smiling and waving as Declan, Valentina, and Tony weaved behind Lucia. Ken and Irene were sitting alone, at a long table with plenty of space.

This was the exact opposite of what he had in mind this morning, but Lucia seemed determined. He'd had very little sleep the night before and he was exhausted, but Lucia had slept for fourteen hours straight so she seemed better. He hadn't said anything yet about the text from George. He wanted to tell her but to have a plan B when he did, something he was still working on. He was glad Eddie was coming tonight; even though they'd only met once, he felt a connection to him and thought he could hammer out some ideas with him about their next move.

Just as they settled in to the table, exchanging morning greetings with the others, Lucia announced, 'I'm going to need the ladies room actually. I should have thought of that before I sat down. Valentina, would you come with me?' She smiled sweetly in Tony's direction.

'Sure, she can go,' he replied, irritated at being interrupted mid-rant about the Red Sox.

'I wasn't asking you,' Lucia muttered under her breath. Irene seemed to pick up on something, and she certainly overheard Lucia's retort and realized something was not quite right and she announced, 'Let's all go. We'll leave the men to talk sports and order some more coffee!'

Once out in the lobby Irene beckoned the women to her room; Conor had gotten her and Ken one on the ground floor to make their stay a little easier.

Valentina looked like a rabbit in the headlights as she and Lucia followed Irene into the bedroom.

'Is this not bathroom?' She looked bewildered.

'No, dear, this is my room, you're quite safe here,' Irene said and beckoned the other woman to sit on the bed.

Lucia sat on the other side. 'Valentina? Is everything ok?'

'What? Ok. Yes. Is ok, I ok, I must go, Tony will...' she panicked.

'Please, Valentina, I know you're frightened, but how did you get those bruises? Did Tony hurt you? We can help you, I was a nurse for many years, and I worked with women who were being hurt, I can help.' Irene's voice was soothing.

Lucia smiled. She had never asked Irene what she did for a living, but now that she said it, everything made sense.

Valentina's eyes filled with tears. 'I...my English...not so good... I cannot understand...'

'It's ok. We'll get there together. Where are you from?' Irene was gentle and spoke very slowly.

'Sakhalin Island. Siberia.'

'Ok, and did you meet Tony there or in America?'

'In Sakhalin. He work, coming there, for oil work, he very rich and he em… He…' She winced, frustrated that she couldn't find the words.

'Hang on, I've an idea,' Lucia suddenly spoke. 'Conor's wife, she's Ukrainian but I think Conor mentioned that she was a teacher and spoke Russian as well. Maybe she can help us?'

'Can you contact him? Is he in the hotel?' Irene asked, glad to have found a way to communicate with Valentina, who was clearly in need of help.

'He's in Room 319 I think.'

Lucia picked up the phone and spoke briefly to Conor, asking him to come to Irene's room. Within moments there was a gentle knock.

'Is everything ok?' Concern etched on his face as Irene opened the door. Lucia and Valentina were still on the bed, Valentina showing her bruises.

'Yes, fine,' Irene murmured, 'but we have a situation here that maybe your wife could help with. Valentina here is Russian, and we think she is being abused by Tony. She's got bruises all over her and she's clearly terrified of him, but her English isn't really good enough for her to communicate, so we were wondering if your wife could speak to her and translate.'

Conor took in the sight on the bed. People thought his job was a doddle, driving around the country, eating in fancy restaurants, and telling a few yarns here and there, but nothing was further from the truth. Some tours were like that, but there was nearly always something. This time, though, took the biscuit. Nobody would believe it; as if there weren't enough to contend with in Declan and Lucia, now he had a battered wife who didn't speak English.

Conor walked over to her and knelt in front of her, taking her hands.

'Valentina, is Tony hurting you?' he spoke slowly and quietly.

'Yes.' She nodded, tears brimming in her big brown eyes.

'Does he have your passport?'

She looked confused so Irene took her own passport out of the drawer beside the bed and pointed at it, and then at Valentina.

'I not have...' Fear crossed her face again, probably terrified they were going to report her or something.

'Ok, I am going to help you. But first, I must get your passport. Do you understand?'

'He don't give...is... I don't know.' She was quivering now; Tony obviously terrified her.

Conor took out his mobile and pressed a button. He crossed the room, his back to the women. Ana answered immediately.

'Hi, pet, listen, we've a bit of a situation here. There's a woman on the tour, she's from Siberia and she's here with her husband, but it seems he's violent. Her English isn't good enough to explain properly, can you talk to her? Explain that if I'm to help her I need her passport.' He listened for a second then turned back to Valentina. 'Valentina, my wife speaks Russian, she will talk to you now ok?'

Valentina looked at the phone for a moment as if she didn't trust whatever was going to happen next, but seeing Conor's reassuring smile and the phone in his outstretched hand, she half smiled and took it.

Almost immediately the conversation flowed between the two women and the small group looked on, fascinated but bewildered.

'Why do you need her passport?' Lucia asked.

'Well, if Tony gets wind of the fact that we are trying to help her, then his first instinct is going to be to get her away from us. If he doesn't have her passport, then he can't leave the country with her.'

'Of course, sorry, I must have a bit of baby brain.' Lucia smiled.

'Look, ladies, I think all things considered, you better let me handle this from here on in. Neither of you are really in a position to involve yourselves in any more than you are already dealing with... Maybe if you head back to the restaurant...' Conor was trying to be diplomatic but before he could go on Irene interrupted him.

'Excuse me, Conor, but with respect, I'm actually the one with the most experience here, so I'll be helping Valentina, and nothing you can do or say will stop me, ok? Let's not argue; she needs a woman on her side, and while your help will be needed too, this is a joint operation.'

147

Conor's face cracked into a broad smile and he raised his hands in submission. 'Ok, ok, I know when I'm beaten.'

'Good.' Irene smiled.

Valentina handed him back the phone, and he walked over to the window again.

Anastasia was very upset by what she'd heard.

'Ok, oh my God, this is so terrible, he is such a bad man, Conor. You must help her.'

'Go on. I'm going to put you on speaker so that the two women on the tour who are helping her can hear it as well, ok?' Conor pressed a button and placed the phone on the small coffee table.

'Ok, so she telled to me, no told to me, that she was working in a bar in Sakhalin, she is not from there, from a smaller town somewhere else on the island, and she was serving them, this Tony and some other men who were doing some deals over there, the whole island is really an oilfield. Anyway, he told her that he needed a manager for a bar he own in America and she can go there and work for him. So she is happy with this new opportunity and she goes and he fixes everything for visa and everything, but when he get her to America he say she must not work in bar but instead be with him. She says she don't want, she want the job he promise, but he beat her and he force her… I don't know what is the word.'

'Rape?' Irene intervened.

'Yes, this, many times, and then he make her marry him in City Hall, and he say if she says anything like she don't want, he will make her sent back to Siberia or else she will go in prison because her papers are not correct. She is so scared from him. He is a very bad man.'

The three digested this information.

'I'll need to get the guards,' Conor spoke. 'They have a human trafficking section but when it's not in our jurisdiction I don't know…'

'Hi, Ana, can you ask Valentina if he raped her here in Ireland?' Irene asked as they all sat around the phone, Valentina wedged between Lucia and Irene.

'Of course.' Ana then said something in Russian and Valentina replied, 'Da.'

'There we go, the crime was committed here therefore he can be arrested by the Irish police.' Irene was so matter-of-fact, Lucia guessed she must have been hardened by all she saw.

Conor picked his phone up and took it off loudspeaker. 'Ok. Ana, I'll call you later, love. I'll just need to deal with this now. I'll give the phone back to Valentina; can you just explain to her that we are going to call the police and that they will take care of her and take Tony into custody? And that they have people who speak Russian so that she'll be ok,' Conor said.

'Ok, be careful, he sounds horrible. This must be the craziest tour you ever had.'

'It's certainly up there. Anyway, I'll talk to you later, pet, love you.'

Conor handed the phone to Valentina, who by now looked a state with black makeup smeared all over her face from crying.

Again they conversed, and as she hung up the phone, she seemed calmer.

Suddenly there came a pounding on the door of the bedroom. Irene acted fast and shoved them all into the bathroom.

'Who is it?' she asked through the door.

'Tony. The dame at the desk said my wife was in here, I want her out here now.' His voice brooked no argument.

Conor called the police from the bathroom and explained how urgent the situation was. Valentina sat on the side of the bath shivering in fear at the sound of his voice.

'Oh I'm sorry, Tony.' Irene sounded so calm. 'They were here, Lucia got sick so we brought her in here, but then she said she needed some herbal thing from her room, so Valentina went with her to get it; she was a little unsteady on her feet. They'll be down any minute, I'd imagine. I'd let you in but I'm just taking a shower; poor Lucia threw up on me. Actually, could you tell Ken why I'm taking so long?'

'What room is she?' he barked, totally ignoring her request.

'What room is who, dear?' Irene asked innocently.

'Lucia for Crissakes! What room is Lucia in? Do I got to go back to that dumb broad at the desk?'

'Let me see...I think she said 106, or was it 406? Oh no, hold on, that was the other hotel, I think she said 260, yes, I'm almost sure. Valentina was so kind, she's such a nice person.'

Irene prattled on for another minute before checking in the room's spyglass that he was gone. Just to be safe, she went over and closed the heavy drapes on the window before opening the bathroom door.

'He's looking for her. Have you called the police?'

'Yes, there's a patrol car around the town anyway, they'll be here any minute.'

His phone rang. 'Yes, that's me. Conor O'Shea, yes, I'll see you there in a minute. Tony Davis. Thanks.' He hung up and addressed the three women. 'Ok, now you three stay in here, and keep the door locked until you hear me outside. I'll go out and talk to the guards.'

Conor slipped out of the room and turned left towards the lobby when he was spun around and felt a fist crash into his face.

'Where is she?' Tony screamed as he tried to land another punch. 'Don't give me no crap about that Lucia and her pukin'. Where is Valentina?'

Conor was leaner and fitter than Tony and blocked his next punch easily, while simultaneously landing a devastating blow to Tony's abdomen that left him winded and doubled over. Hotel staff came running, followed closely by Ken and Declan. Other tour members followed behind out of curiosity. The hotel manager, a burly man in his fifties, dragged Tony to his feet, twisting his arm up behind his back.

'Are you ok, Conor?'

Conor winced and then grinned at the other man, whom he'd known for over twenty years.

'Grand, Mossy, grand altogether. Glad to see you though.'

'Yerra you were doing fine on your own, Conor.' He tightened his grip on Tony, who screamed in pain.

'Let go of me, you stupid bogman, get your Paddy hands off me, I'll sue your ass, you won't be left with a pot to...'

The guards separated the group and took in the scene, and the younger of the two was about to handcuff both Conor and Tony.

'Not him, just the other one,' the older policeman said quietly. 'You all right, Conor?'

'I'll be ok. Thanks for coming so quick, Jim.'

Tony was by now almost apoplectic with rage. 'Get your hands off me, you moron, I'll make sure you end up on food stamps, I know a lot of people, important people, not from this stupid little green hole either. Get your hands off me, you'll pay for this, I want to see my wife...Valentina! Get out here now! You know what I can do, Valentina!'

The younger guard took custody of Tony and the other one cautioned him,

'Tony Davis, I'm arresting you on suspicion of assault causing actual bodily harm. You do not have to say anything but anything you do say may be taken down and used as evidence.'

Tony was unceremoniously dragged to the waiting police car.

Irene's door opened and she, Lucia, and Valentina appeared.

'Oh my God, Conor, are you ok?' Irene saw the blood streaming from Conor's nose onto his shirt.

'I'll live.' He winced. 'My boxing days are long gone though.'

The hotel doctor was called and Conor was cleared as being fine apart from the punch on the nose. A representative from the Russian Embassy was on the way from Dublin, and in the meantime a social worker and a female police officer took Valentina to the local hospital. The huge influx of workers into Ireland from the former Soviet states in the last decade meant that there would definitely be a Russian speaker in the hospital, but Conor gave them Anastasia's number just in case Valentina needed someone to talk to. She was nervous and reluctant to go alone, but Irene explained as best she could and promised Valentina they'd make contact later. Conor knew the older woman wanted to accompany her but he'd had a word with Ken, suggesting that the hospital with all its germs and bugs might not be the place for Irene's already weak immune system, and he agreed wholeheartedly. After a good deal of persuasion she finally consented to let Valentina go.

Elke and Zoe hustled everyone from the tour back to the restaurant to finish their breakfast, giving Conor a chance to get cleaned up. Before he went back to his room, she gave him a small glass jar with tiny white balls inside and a tube of cream.

'Arnica.' She smiled. 'Super strength, I give it to mothers after birth to reduce bruising. It will help, though you'll probably look a bit battered for a few days. Swallow two of the tablets, don't bite them or touch them with your fingers, and apply a little cream to the nose and your hand.'

'Thanks, Elke. Ana just said this must be the maddest tour I've ever had, and while the one I was on when she and I got together was fairly unbelievable, this one takes some beating.'

'Don't worry, I'm sure people would understand if you wanted to cancel today's trip. We could just stay around here today instead.'

'Not at all, I'll be grand. If you could just let people know we'll go at ten instead of nine thirty, that'll give me time to get cleaned up and grab a bit of breakfast before we go.'

'Sure, and take that arnica as soon as possible, it really is amazing stuff.'

'Will do.'

CHAPTER 16

'Tour going ahead as normal, folks, the Dingle Peninsula today, though how we'll make it as dramatic as this morning's events, I'm not too sure.'

A ripple of laughter came from the group as they saw with their own eyes no real harm had been done to Conor. A shower, a clean shirt, and some of Elke's homeopathy worked wonders, and they were glad to be on the road again.

As he'd showered, he'd wondered what to say regarding the business with Tony and Valentina. He'd decided the truth was the only way. They would have had bits of the story already anyway, not that those directly involved would have been gossiping, but Tony's exit from the hotel had been fairly loud and revealing.

'So, just to fill you in. Tony and Valentina have left the tour, separately I hasten to add. He has been arrested pending an investigation into assault charges, and she is in the care of the health services, so please rest assured that they are both getting the treatment they deserve.'

He looked in the rearview mirror and noted the odd wry smile. Tony was a pain and he had been rude to everyone at one time or another, so there was not going to be any tears shed over him.

Valentina, on the other hand, while she rarely spoke to anyone, seemed to be very much in their thoughts. Several members of the tour asked about her as they boarded, after they'd clarified that Conor himself was ok.

Declan was deeply lost in his thoughts. Lucia seemed in much better spirits today. The good night's sleep seemed to have done her some good, and she had even managed a slice of toast and some tea after all the business with Tony and Valentina died down.

She was chatting across the aisle with a couple from California who were celebrating their fiftieth wedding anniversary. Her pregnancy was common knowledge by now so everyone was extra kind to them both.

He watched as they drove through lovely little towns, the houses all painted bright colours. Conor explained it was to brighten the long winter days. People seemed to be in less of a hurry here; on the sidewalks people had time to stop and talk, and people shopped in their local stores. They passed a school, a small building with a football field beside it and bike racks outside. He wondered if kids cycled to school here. It wasn't something you saw too often in the States anymore; maybe it still happened in rural communities, but in New Jersey a kid would last ten seconds with the manic traffic. Conor said the city centres of Dublin and Cork were just the same, but out here in County Kerry these little towns looked like a great place to live, to rear a family.

That was all he wanted, and he knew Lucia felt the same. She had had the trappings of extreme wealth all her life and it held no attraction for her. The more he saw of this country, the more he could visualize them living there together happily. Raising their child, children maybe, them attending a local school, walking down a street where people knew who they were, where they belonged, and their parents were just Declan and Lucia Sullivan from New York, who just decided to live in Ireland. He wondered if he could get citizenship based on his grandparents.

He daydreamed for a while, but every time this perfect peaceful family life seemed like a solution, the gripping terror threatened to engulf him once more.

He'd been sure at four am he'd come up with the only answer but now, in the cold light of day, his confidence dissipated. The FBI were still around, but that was short-term. He knew that when they got back tonight, George Winooski would be saying that there was no way the Department of Justice was going to sanction the cost of keeping two agents in Ireland, watching over them, when his testimony was inadmissible. They were going to be on their own, and Sacco would catch up with them eventually, of that there was no doubt in Declan's mind. He'd considered leaving Ireland, going to some other country, but without a visa it would be madness. Also they only spoke English and they wanted to blend in, not stick out like sore thumbs. The one country where an American might actually fit was, ironically, Ireland. There were so many US citizens with Irish blood that a steady stream of traffic moved both ways between the two countries.

The FBI investigation would go ahead, but Declan knew that without his testimony they were not confident of victory. Sacco had wriggled off the hook so many times, and it looked like he was going to again. Even if they did manage to secure a conviction, it would be on a nominal charge, with a short sentence imposed, and most of the family still free to carry out Paulie's orders. George had admitted as much. Nobody would talk, no matter what the inducement; the family were just too intimidating.

They visited a long white beach with pristine aquamarine water and watched the surfers as they caught the huge waves, and the bracing Irish breeze felt good on his face. Lucia stayed in the bus; she'd fallen asleep again. He was glad that today of all days she wasn't her usual eagle-eyed self, sensitive to even the slightest change in his mood. He needed to think.

His fellow passengers were blown away by the scenery: the ring forts where Celtic people lived three thousand years ago, the tiny beehive huts perched precariously on the cliffs, homes to the solitary early Christian monks who lived on eggs and devoted their lives to

God. He wondered what they'd make of him and his predicament. They, like him, were men of God, but he feared that was where the similarity ended.

They ate a lunch of smoked salmon and pickled cucumber, creamy root vegetable soup, and the most melt-in-the-mouth dessert called, unappetizingly, 'bread and butter pudding.' Declan remembered his granny making it and loving it, so he encouraged his fellow passengers to give it a try. They were glad they did as they bit into the deliciously crunchy sugar-toasted dessert, layered with custard, raisins, cinnamon, and slices of white bread.

'Have you tried this brown bread ice cream?' Lucia asked, eyes wide in surprise.

'Apparently they use the stale bread and make breadcrumbs, then coat it in a kind of crunchy caramel and then they whip the mixture into vanilla ice cream. It should be gross but it's actually divine.'

He grinned as she ate another spoonful. It was so good to see her eating.

They were sitting alone as the café was tiny. Now would be a good time to tell her George's news, but he couldn't bear to see the distress cross her face again. Despite all the drama, she was better than he'd seen her since they'd arrived, and he didn't want to shatter her fragile and temporary happiness. It would wait.

Conor told them stories of Viking raiders in the seventh century, plundering the gold-rich monasteries, of mythology, where the warriors of the Fianna got into frequent scrapes with magical beings of all kinds. He even sang them songs.

He told them the stories of those who left during the 1850s for a new and terrifying life in the United States, often with only the clothes they stood up in and a dream, sometimes not even speaking English. He was so knowledgeable about not just the Irish in Ireland, but he was able to detail the Irish connections of Gene Kelly, Henry Ford, Alfred Hitchcock, Mel Gibson, and Tom Clancy. He explained how Michael Flatley, the creator of the famous Riverdance, learned Irish dancing as a little boy in Chicago. How the famous Captain O'Neill, chief of police in the same city, feared by those involved in organized crime back in the twenties, was also a wonderful Uileann piper, just the same instrument that young Dylan had been playing the other night in the pub. This Chief Francis O'Neill, as he was known, dedicated his life to his dual passions, stopping mobsters and collecting and writing down the tunes of the old country. As Conor told his tales, some funny, some tragic, all interesting, the group were enthralled.

The scenery was once again breathtaking as the sun twinkled on the azure Atlantic and shipwrecks, islands, and sheep dotted the coastline.

They stopped for an Irish coffee on the way home, where Conor insisted on treating the group, to make up for the delay in leaving, he said. They all objected but he was determined. The pub was the home place of Tom Crean, an explorer who accompanied Scott on three expeditions to Antarctica. His was the one where Amundsen pipped them to it, the man of the house explained as they sipped the mouth-watering combination of coffee, Irish whiskey, sugar, and whipped cream. With pride in his voice he told them how Crean won the Albert Medal for his thirty-six-mile solo trek across the Ross Ice Shelf to save the life of his friend and fellow explorer Edward Evans on the expedition that took the life of Scott himself.

Everyone had a wonderful day and thanked Conor warmly as they got off the bus.

Lucia went into the hotel quickly; another side effect of pregnancy was the need for a bathroom more or less constantly.

Conor drew Declan aside as he bade the rest of the group a good evening.

'You're very welcome, I'm glad you enjoyed it. Don't forget, bags out at eight, we're leaving for Cork at nine on the dot, barring any more incidents!' He waved them all off and he and Declan sat back in the bus.

'George said my testimony won't be admissible.' Declan was glad to get it off his chest.

'Yeah, I met him this morning, he filled me in. I doubt they'll hang around now that they don't need you.' Conor was worried. Without the FBI agents they were very vulnerable.

'I know. He hasn't said it yet but I know it's coming, I mean, why would they? I'm nobody really in this case they're building; neither is Lucia. Our involvement is personal, not criminal.'

'So now what?' Conor was normally the one jollying everyone along, assuring everyone that everything was going to be ok, but he was so tired and his hand and his face were hurting. He longed for this tour to be over, to get home to Ana and the boys and forget any of this happened. The man who died in the pool was in the morgue in the Embassy in Dublin, awaiting repatriation, Tony was in custody, Valentina was in the hospital. Ken had confided to him that Irene was fading and that they might fly home early, and the situation with Declan and Lucia was so messy and complicated and dangerous, he tried not to think about it. He had said nothing to Ana; she would have a fit if she thought he was in danger like that. He felt sorry for them, it was a terrible situation but he was a husband and a father and his family needed him. He sighed deeply.

'I'm meeting Father Eddie Shanahan later. He texted and offered to come down. It's so kind of him, and I really feel I connected with him. I've an idea about what I could do to fix this, but I don't know if it would even work, it's crazy. And I'm not going to tell you because you've done enough for us. You're dealing with so much as it is, but know this, Conor, you have mine and Lucia's eternal gratitude. This will be solved, or at least you won't have to deal with it, very shortly. I promise you that.'

Maybe he should have said it was fine, or that it was all going to be ok, or that he'd keep going despite the danger they were in, but he just didn't.

'Ok, Declan, be careful anyway, and I hope you can solve this. You need to stay safe, for yourself but also for Lucia and the baby, just as I have to for Ana and the boys.'

'I will, Conor. Thanks again for everything. How you stay so cheerful and upbeat with all of this going on, I've no idea, but you do look tired.'

'I am. It's been a long tour so far, I won't lie to you, but I suppose

I've been doing it for so long, it's kind of second nature to me, you know? Though I would give anything to sleep in my own bed tonight. But since that can't happen, I'm going to just get a sandwich sent up to the room and try to get an early night. I'll be fine again tomorrow.'

Declan glanced out the large front window of the coach in the direction of the entrance to the hotel car park.

'Well, you might not get to sleep in your own bed, but it looks like your home just came to you.'

Conor's face lit up at the sight of the silver SUV with Ana behind the wheel. She pulled in beside the bus.

He got out and waited for her to open the door. The smile he gave her when she did was one of pure love.

'You came.'

She smiled. 'Of course, you needed me. The boys are with Dylan and Laoise, they're having a, I forget the word, a sweepover?'

Conor did not seem like a man for overdoing the public displays of affection, but as Declan walked into the hotel, he watched as Conor wrapped his big arms around his tiny wife, lifting her off the ground, and kissed her as if they were the only two people in the world.

Eddie was in the bar waiting for him, doing the *Irish Times* cross-word. He was dressed in his clerical garb, something rarely seen these days. Priests were so afraid of the reaction they might get they wore civilian clothes most of the time, but Eddie wasn't most priests. His white hair was still sticking up all over the place, but his blue eyes twinkled in his weather-beaten face. As Declan sat down opposite him, he tapped the paper with his pen and took off his glasses.

'ABCEFG, One can affirm. Three letters.' He smiled questioningly.

'Er, no idea, I'm not a crossword guy I'm afraid.' Declan had booked Lucia a maternity treatment in the hotel spa so he had time to talk to Eddie in peace. He felt awful lying, or at least not telling her the whole truth, but he needed to get it all clear in his own head first. It was going to be hard enough to convince her to agree without the plan sounding half-baked. He'd hammer it out with Eddie, and hopefully address all the objections Lucia would no doubt raise when he told her what he was going to do.

'Nod. No D, you see?' He filled in the three little boxes.

Declan looked blankly at him.

'No D, look, ABC...EFG, and to affirm is to nod. Ok, fair enough, your head isn't in the game, as they say.' The old priest smiled. 'How are you?'

'I'm ok. Considering. Look, thanks so much for coming all the way down here, I really appreciate it. I know you said it was only an hour and a half, but when we did that same trip in the bus, it sure took longer than that.'

'Ah Conor has to take the scenic route; there's a main road too. Anyway, don't worry about it. You were on my mind, and sometimes it helps to talk to someone not directly connected.'

'It does. Conor has been so kind, he's really great, but this trip has really taken it out of him. Not just our stuff but others as well. It was nice earlier though, we were talking in the bus when his wife turned up out of the blue; she got sitters for the kids so they'll get to spend some time together. He needs that.'

'Ana is the best thing that ever happened to him. If ever there was a confirmed bachelor, it was Conor O'Shea. Many's the lady gave it her best shot but never a bite, as they say, but Ana melted him and he's a different man. He was always a grand fella, decent, y'know? But he kept himself to himself, but now he's such a devoted husband and father, 'tis great to see.' He looked squarely at Declan. 'But we're not here to talk about Conor, are we?'

'No, I guess not.' Declan steeled himself for the first pair of ears to hear his plan. Eddie sat in complete silence as Declan outlined the developments since they'd last spoken and the idea he had, mulling it over and over in his mind for the last twenty-four hours. When Declan finally finished speaking, Eddie said nothing for a moment, cleaning his glasses on his sweater.

'And you're sure this is the only way? It seems reckless and dangerous. I have to say that.'

"If there's another way, I can't see it.'

'And what will your man from the FBI make of this? They'll have to be in on it if you do it. And I can't see him agreeing.'

'I know. But I'll have to try to convince him.'

They spent the next half hour going over the plan, and despite Eddie's strong reservation, from both a practical and a moral perspective, he offered all the objections Declan hoped he would. It prepared him for the meeting with George Winooski.

At nine thirty, three pots of coffee and an enormous plate of sandwiches later, Declan felt ready.

As Eddie put on his coat he stood. 'Don't come out with me, I'm grand. I can't say I wish you luck, I can't condone your plan, but the longer I'm on this earth the more I realize that nothing is ever black and white. So I'll say that I'll pray that you get to live a happy life with Lucia and your son or daughter, and that this terrible situation gets resolved as best as it can be. I'll put it in God's hands now. He's directed you all your life, Declan, and you answered His call when He wanted you. Call on Him now in your hour of need; He won't be found wanting. God bless you.'

The two men shook hands warmly, and something told Declan that he and Fr Eddie Shanahan would be lifelong friends.

He sat for a long time after Eddie left, alone in the hotel bar, mulling it all over.

He was surprised at how clear he felt. He was absolutely sure he was doing the right thing. The chat with Eddie really helped him to see a clear path through this situation from a spiritual and personal perspective. His conscience was clear. God had sent him to the Sacco family, and God had sent Lucia to him as well. He had not the slightest doubt that what he and Lucia felt for each other was real, and he desperately wanted to build his life with her. He also knew with equal certainty that while Sacco had breath in his body, he would never allow it. In prison or not, his tentacles stretched far; a lot of people owed him favours. All it would take was a phone call. It wouldn't matter where he and Lucia went, he would find them.

The FBI had a file two feet thick on Sacco and his family, but they didn't know him. Not really, not the way Declan did. He thought back to his time as the family priest; he was privy to more than anyone else because Sacco had trusted him.

Increasingly he had been used over the years at sit-downs between the Saccos and other families as the voice of reason. He often talked it over with Bishop Rameros, who always asked the same question.

'If you weren't there, would the situation be worse or better?' The answer was always that the outcomes without his intervention would undoubtedly mean more pain, heartbreak, and grief. Not just for those involved, but for innocent people caught up in the whole horrible thing. It had never sat easily with him, but he truly believed that this was where God had wanted him to be, deep in the murk, and He wanted him to be a light for good, even if sometimes it was only the faintest glimmer. He thought back to so many instances, where he would counsel against a whack on a kid for acting outside the family and Paulie might agree and commute it to a kneecapping. Or Declan would urge him to show leniency towards the family of someone he believed to have betrayed him, asking him to focus on the perpetrator only, not his wife and kids. Sometimes, he was so revolted by what he had to do, he needed to offload it. Bishop Rameros was a man he trusted, and he told him the gory details in what he knew to be the strictest confidence. The bishop just let him talk and then they came, together, to the same conclusion, that the presence of Fr Declan Sullivan in the lives of the Saccos was to the betterment of society rather than to its detriment. It was his calling, and in so many ways it was a very hard cross to bear, but he did it and tried as much as possible to direct Paulie on the right path. Amazingly, Paulie Sacco really believed in God, and he also believed that by doing as Declan suggested some of the time, he was following God's law and securing his place in heaven. It was ridiculous, and absurd, but it was what Paulie believed.

Over and over, Declan had deliberated on the morality of what he was doing. He found it preposterous that Paulie believed that God was on his side, or at least that God forgave him his multitude of sins so long as he repented, and Declan's continued presence in Paulie's life gave truth to that belief. He wished he could go back to a simpler time, when he was in the seminary, when things seemed so clear.

Who was he to judge Paulie Sacco for his sins when he himself was justifying the breaking of his vows with a girl much younger than himself, a girl who trusted him in his capacity as her confessor, and he was convincing himself that God had somehow directed him to her? The more he thought about it, the more ludicrous it all seemed.

In the seminary, he had read a biography of a priest in France who had sheltered Jews during the war. The priest was betrayed and ended up in a concentration camp. He discussed in the book how he survived by not thinking about what would now be called 'the big picture.' Instead he focused on the minute, tiny victories, and he encouraged those around him to do the same. He found that to be very useful advice in his dealings with the Saccos.

Paulie Sacco was a product of his world, nothing more or less. It didn't excuse him or his behaviour, but some of the stories he told Declan, of witnessing extreme violence as a young boy, being forced to be tough by his macho, brutal father, being denied love as a punishment by his mentally unhinged mother, all of it went to create the monster that Paulie had become, and sometimes Declan felt sorry for him. On the very rare occasions when Paulie opened up about his childhood, the stories would break your heart. Love used as a weapon, in a family already in possession of a huge arsenal. To gain his family's love he had to be vicious; the more vicious he was, the more respect he earned, the more approval was given.

The Mafia talk all the time about family, love and loyalty, but it's not real. It couldn't be if he could treat Lucia as he did. He didn't love Lucia in the way that Declan's father loved him, or the way Declan himself felt about his child yet unborn. He wasn't capable of it. Declan

163

knew that the rage Paulie felt was directed at Paulie himself as much as them. He'd trusted Declan and felt his version of love for Lucia and those were emotions very foreign to him. He neither trusted nor loved anyone else as far as Declan knew, and from his perspective, the only ones he did had betrayed him spectacularly and publicly. It was no wonder he was murderous.

He probably should regret his feelings for Lucia—he knew how much trouble it had caused for so many people—but he couldn't. He had tried so hard to resist his feelings for so long, refusing even to acknowledge them to himself. The day she came to see him, when she said she was thinking of becoming a nun, his overwhelming reaction had been one of panic. She couldn't become a nun, because then she could never be his. This information had hit him like a thunderbolt; he wanted her in his life, not just as a friend. He knew it with exactly the same certainty he'd heard his calling to the priesthood years earlier. His mother had asked him at the time if he was sure of his vocation. And he could always answer definitively that he was. Now, he wasn't sure. He loved the priesthood, and believed he had been given a job to do by God, but he also knew that he wanted, needed her. He had to choose and for him there was no contest. Lucia was his life.

On the way back to the hotel room, George fell into step beside him.

'We need to talk.'

'Sure, come up. Lucia should be back now.'

They walked in silence to the bedroom door, and George respectfully waited outside while Declan went to check that Lucia was dressed.

She was sitting on the bed, reading a magazine about pregnancy and birth Elke had bought her.

'Oh you're back. I was starting to worry. I had such a lovely massage...'

'George is outside, he needs to talk to us.'

'Oh, is something wrong?'

'No, I don't think so. Let's see...' He opened the door and George walked in, his huge frame almost filling the room.

'Hi, Lucia, Declan, how are you two doing?' They caught each other's eyes; his demeanor had changed, he was friendlier than he had been. Declan knew what was coming next.

'Well, as I said in the text, our legal people tell me that because of the relationship between you and Paulie Sacco there is no point to putting you on the stand. The defense would cite priest-penitent privilege, as you correctly pointed out, so...em...'

'We're of no further interest to you,' Declan finished quietly for him.

Lucia looked from one man to the other.

'But does this mean you're leaving? That we have no protection now?'

'Well, you'll have the protection of the Irish police for the time you are here, and once you get back if you feel in anyway unsafe, you can go to your local police department and...'

'But I don't understand... One minute you're telling us we are in real danger right now, even all the way over here and then in the next —' Lucia was getting upset and Declan interrupted.

'Lucia, our issue with your father, or more to the point his with us, is a personal one, not criminal. The FBI can't be involved. George just came here to see if I would testify, no other reason, and now that my testimony is no good, he can't stay here babysitting... You understand that, don't you?'

'But he...'

'Wait though, both of you, I've been thinking and I'm sure there's another way around this. Can I ask you both just to keep an open mind, don't shoot me down before I get to explain. Will you do that for me?'

Both Lucia and George nodded in agreement.

'Ok.' Lucia looked more scared than he'd ever seen her. He was more convinced than ever that he would have to get them to agree; they couldn't live like this.

They both sat in silence like they promised as he outlined his plan,

George looking at him like he was insane. When he finished speaking, before Lucia had a chance to say anything, George spoke.

'Absolutely no way, none. Even if I put it to my boss, and I wouldn't, not in a million years, they'd never sanction it. No.'

'But it makes sense. Think about it; it takes out the element of chance, the possibility that Sacco or any of the consigliore wriggle out of it, or their lawyers find some little point of law that wasn't done properly. You know as well as I do that Sacco isn't above getting at a judge. Even if he doesn't, you said yourself his lawyers are the best money can buy. He is slippery and he's wriggled out of it before. This way, there's no way out. Guarantees an outcome, and saves the taxpayers a lot of tax dollars.'

George couldn't believe what he was hearing; it was just insane. 'No. Just no. I can't agree to it, Declan, it's too... I don't know... It's just crazy, and anyway it's not my call to make. I want to help you, I do, but this... This is suicide.'

Declan Sullivan looked at George and got the measure of the man. One of the things the priesthood teaches you was how to read between the lines. George was a cop to his marrow; he believed in the good fight, that people deserved to be protected from scum like Sacco and Dias, but that there was only one way to do it, and that was through the legal system.

Declan would have to convince him that in this case the ends justified the means. He was in this thing deeper than anyone could imagine and that was his leverage. He'd been over it and over it; this was the only surefire way of ending everything for good. He probably should feel more guilt, have more qualms, but he didn't. This was right, maybe not legal, but it was right.

CHAPTER 17

*J*ust as George was about to continue to shoot the idea out of the water, his phone rang. He went outside to answer it, but before Lucia and Declan had time to talk he was back in the room.

'Is everything ok?' Declan noted George's face was like thunder.

'Not really, no. Sacco was arrested this morning, and immediately his team clicked into action; they knew it was coming. It seems they have unearthed something, some bit of paperwork that wasn't done properly. It's a small thing but we can't afford any slip-ups. They're looking to have him released on a technicality and stuff like this... well, it just can't happen. We've thrown everything we've got at this. If we don't secure a conviction this time, then we won't get to go again. It's now or never so any little mistake can cost us.' George rubbed his unshaven chin. He looked tired and strained.

'If there's even a tiny way out, he'll find it. He gets his way, George, always. Why do you think that none of the other East Coast families ever tangle with him? They squabble among themselves, over turf, deals, insults, real and imagined, everything, all the time, but never with Sacco. The only one who isn't afraid of him is Dias. He doesn't give a damn who Sacco is, and the Mafia don't mean anything to him. In his eyes, all that racketeering, girls, dope, protection, that's all child's play. He is a drug dealer, plain and simple. Cocaine and heroin, to high-end markets and in huge volumes. He has his own internet network that you guys are a million miles behind in terms of technology. All their phones operate on satellites that law enforcement can't block or decode; in fact, you can't even see it. He has the best accountants, tech guys, lawyers, permanently on the payroll at huge expense, but Fabio Dias can be forensically examined and you won't find so much as a parking ticket. He's untouchable and he knows it. The only impediment to him dominating the drugs market in the whole of the Americas, north and south, is Paulie Sacco. He refused to allow Dias's merchandise to flood New York, New Jersey, Boston. He has enough control of the ports to get whatever he wants in, enough high-ranking people are in his pocket.

'Dias is exporting to Europe and Asia, everywhere, but he couldn't get at the lucrative East Coast market, and it drove him crazy. He didn't need the money, but he's not used to being challenged, and Paulie isn't used to being overruled. Sacco arranged for anyone working for Dias to come to a nasty end, and Paulie then made it clear that he wasn't going to stand for it. The other families are no shrinking violets, as you know, they've seen off plenty of challenges themselves over the years from Irish, Chinese, and Russians, but Dias is a whole other ball game and nobody else would take him on. The other dons are just watching and waiting to see what's going to happen. Sacco and Dias have sat down, and it's fairly cordial, both men are genial and friendly on the surface, but neither was willing to give an inch. Dias said he wanted that market and access to the ports on the eastern seaboard, and Paulie laughed and refused point blank. The whole thing is at an impasse. If this were two mob families, they'd work out a split, some kind of deal where nobody loses face, but Dias won't do that. He wants it all. Dias had more money and probably more firepower, he's a more modern criminal, but Sacco is the figurehead of East Coast organized crime. He can't lose face, so even if he wanted to back down from Dias, he couldn't. He'd lose all respect with the other families. They'd move in and take him down. This case you people are building is a distraction from the big issue in his life right now, this game of chess with Dias.'

Declan knew by George's face he was surprised at the level of knowledge he had.

'And he's told you all of this?' George asked.

Declan glanced at Lucia, who was sitting in shocked silence on the bed. She was processing what he was saying. There were things about her father he hoped she'd never need to hear, but that time had passed. If he was to get them to agree he'd have to be explicit.

'Yes. As I said, he trusts me. I had many crises of conscience, feeling that I was somehow implicated by just knowing what was going on, but I tried, as much as he'd listen to me, to urge him in the direction of good and away from evil. I'm only marginally successful at best, but I've squared it in my own head that at least I can divert some bad things from happening. He thinks in some warped way that he's a good man: he takes advice from a priest and sometimes he can be prevailed upon to show mercy. In his book, that absolves him of the many sins he commits.' Declan stopped. George looked incredulous. 'I'm not defending him, I'm just trying to explain.'

George nodded. 'I know you're not. I'm just trying to process this.'

'So that's why my idea is the best shot we have. If we don't get rid of Paulie Sacco for once and for all, and I mean kill him, or at least orchestrate that someone else does, then my family won't ever be safe. Not only that, I don't expect you to sanction this just to ensure mine and Lucia's safety. There's a much bigger issue here. If something isn't done, this feud will escalate and you are going to be looking at a gang war, the ferocity of which will put the 1920s in the shade. If Dias moves against Paulie, tries to force his hand, then the other families will get behind the Saccos. Not out of loyalty, but because they would see themselves as next. These people are ruthless, they won't care who gets caught in the crossfire. By intervening now, we are sparing the country that.'

'And why are you only telling us this now?' George asked.

'Well, I did tell you that he and Dias were working together, but I thought I'd leave the gory details for the stand. To be honest, I didn't want to expose Lucia to it. She knows a lot, but some of it...well...I wanted to spare her. I know this must sound totally contrary to everything a priest stands for. The fifth commandment says thou shalt not kill, and I'll have to answer for this when my time comes, but I honestly believe in my heart that Paulie Sacco is an evil man, incapable of love or empathy or compassion. He's cold inside; there's no good side to him. My own reasons are selfish, I admit it, and I'm not going to suggest that I'd be offering this as a solution if I wasn't in the position I am. He will stop at nothing to exact his revenge on us, on me.

'But in terms of the world generally, there is no redemption for him. If the FBI could prove all the crimes he has committed in his lifetime, an impossible task by the way, then he'd get the death penalty. This way, the end result is the same. No person on earth will ever benefit from having Paulie Sacco in the world. The case you have won't stick, I know it won't, and deep down you know it too. My evidence has been deemed inadmissible, and even if it had been allowed, once his lawyers bring up that I got his daughter pregnant, then they'll go after me and make me out to be so scared of Sacco and the family that I'd do or say anything to save my own skin. Nobody else will testify, even if they are saying now that they will; they won't in the end. He'll scare them so badly they won't risk their family's lives.'

He looked once again at Lucia. He'd hoped he'd never have to tell her this story, but it was life or death.

'Remember the last case against him? In the eighties? You had an African-American guy called Orson Cambridge ready to testify, a drug counselor working in a shelter in Brooklyn. Remember him? Well, he pulled out at the last minute because Sacco kidnapped his three-year-old twins and threatened to cut their fingers off if he even so much as whispered to the police. He held those kids for four weeks while the case went on. Cambridge and his wife nearly went insane with worry, and they never spoke to the police. Paulie told them in graphic detail what abuses he would put the children through before killing them if they did. The FBI even charged Orson with wasting police time and it went to court and everything, but Cambridge never said a word. Sacco mailed bits of their hair to his wife, along with a sharp knife. Another day he sent a vial of blood to their house; they didn't know if it was the twins' and they couldn't get it tested without people asking questions. Another time he sent them kid porn pictures, not of their kids but of others. They were nearly out of their minds. When he told me what he'd done in confession, the day the trial was over and he got off, I remember how loud my heart was beating in my chest. I asked him if he'd harmed the children, and he laughed and said he hadn't but that he still might, to teach people like Cambridge a lesson for daring to rat on Paulie Sacco. I thought as quickly as I could, and said the only way I could give him absolution was if he returned the children to their parents. He believed I had the power to forgive sins, no matter how bad, and I used that power that day. I asked him to tell me where the children were and I said I would get them myself and bring them home and if he allowed that, then I would give him absolution. He never really bought into the part of the sacrament that requires the penitent to be truly sorry for what they've done. For him it was simply a matter of committing the sin, going to confession, and wiping the slate clean again until the next time. An infantile attitude really.'

Lucia spoke for the first time, her face pale. 'So what did you do?'

'I went to the address he gave me. They were there, filthy and undernourished, being watched by a guy off his head on crack, but they didn't appear to have any injuries. I took them and brought them to a doctor I knew, one who patched up gunshot wounds and so on, and didn't feel the need to reveal it to the authorities.'

Declan noticed George's look of distaste; it was because of people like this doctor that gun crime went under the radar so often.

'No, Doctor Caputo isn't what you think. He and I often talked about it. He had the same qualms as I had but the alternative was to let these kids bleed out, and often that's all they were, kids. His father

171

was a made guy, back in the day. He's dead now, but if it wasn't for his mother working her butt off, sending him to school and keeping him away from the family, he'd have probably gone the same way. Don't judge him; he's one of the good guys.'

'Go on.' Lucia's voice was barely audible; George sat stony-faced.

'Well, I called Orson Cambridge and told him I was going to get his kids and take them to the doctor. He knew he couldn't take them to the ER without answering loads of questions and how Sacco would feel about that, so I assured him they seemed ok and asked him to meet me at the doctor's office. They were being held in the Bronx but the doctor's office was in midtown, off Sixth Avenue, so I got there before the Cambridges, who lived in Brooklyn. The doctor checked them over, and apart from rashes on their skin from sitting in their own excrement and being seriously underweight, they were ok. I asked him if he thought they'd been sexually abused, and he was fairly sure they hadn't. The poor babies were so traumatized, they weren't even crying. I will take to my grave the moment of reunion when Orson and Delores came in. She howled and screamed and just fell apart. The kids were so thin and miserable-looking, but they were alive. I explained to Orson how I managed to get Sacco to give them back, and we talked about what to do next. I gave him the best advice I could, to go home and gather their things, sell his house, and move states away from Sacco forever, start again, get some therapy for him and his wife, and possibly for the children as well. Sacco won again, but there was no changing him, and that family staying there and living in terror was a horrible prospect. So they did as I suggested: they left and never came back. And that's just one story, George. I could tell you fifty more, but I just want you to really know that I know exactly what you're dealing with.'

'You don't have much faith in the authorities, do you, Declan?' George remarked wryly.

'Not where Sacco is concerned, no, I don't. He laughs at you guys, they all do, because they win so often.' Declan shrugged.

'Ok, so your plan? I'm still against it but explain it to me again anyway.' Declan was sure he heard a slight shift in tone.

'Ok. Before anything about the wedding of Lucia and Antonio, Fabio Dias was getting fed up with Sacco killing everyone he sends east. Not because he cares about his operatives, you understand, but because it's an insult and it disrupts trade. As far as Dias is concerned, he's tried everything. He and Paulie used to be ok; Dias brought the stuff in, Paulie made sure that it happened but then Dias wanted to distribute the drugs on the East Coast and Paulie refused. After that Dias was hamstrung; with Paulie out of the picture he had no way of getting the stuff in. He went in there all heavy-handed, no luck. He tried threatening Sacco himself; that nearly ended in a gun battle in a deli near Battery Park. Dias was losing money and face, so last month Dias *asked permission* to have a shipment come through the Port Authority. Sacco has the chief purser there on his payroll. Sacco charged him sixty percent, an outrageous cut, and Dias was angry but paid it because he had no choice. The yacht was at sea and needed to dock. Word was getting out internationally that Dias was being whipped by Sacco and he was losing power. At least by doing a deal, he could dress it up overseas like he had gotten what he wanted. Reputation is everything in this game.' Declan tried to gauge their reactions but failed. George was listening intently but Lucia was unreadable.

'Sacco was happy with the arrangement. He made sure the right people heard the terms of the deal, showing once again how formidable Paulie was. It was great for his ego and his reputation; apparently he was in Carmine's, that's the restaurant they always go to, with the consigliore, laughing about how he could get Dias to do all the work, and take all the risk, and Sacco can skim off the top. The wedding between Lucia and Antonio was the only thing holding the relationship together from a public perspective. Paulie was so into the details of it, and he seemed so happy at the match, that those who were dissenting were convinced that everything was still ok between him and Dias. The reality was, nothing could be further from the truth.'

'And he just told you all this?' George interrupted.

'No, but because Paulie trusts me, the others do too. One of his made guys is struggling. His mother has cancer and she doesn't want to go into hospital. There's a lovely nursing home run by the parish, and he dropped by to see if I could pull some strings to get her in. It came up in conversation.'

'Go on.' George was transfixed.

'So,' Declan said slowly, 'Dias also trusts me, after that intervention with the two young guys. My idea is to go and tell him that the next big shipment, due on the sixteenth, is a setup. He knows about the FBI investigation; it's common knowledge. In fact he's hoping you guys will actually pull it off. It would solve his problem. My plan is to go to him, tell him that Sacco plans to tell the FBI everything he knows about the drug shipments, implicating Dias of course, in return for a lighter sentence. I'll be honest about my motivation: I'm trying to save my own skin. He may or may not know we are here, it doesn't matter. I'll tell him that Sacco told me all of this before the wedding, when he had no idea there was anything going on between me and Lucia. If it works, and he believes me, Dias won't allow Sacco to give evidence against him; he knows too much. And Dias hates him anyway so he won't have any qualms about killing Paulie. He wipes out his arch enemy, he gains control of the East Coast drug market, and he looks to the criminal world as the one who wins in the end. For Dias it's win-win.'

'And you think he'd believe you? And why wouldn't he kill you there and then for humiliating his son by being left at the altar?' George asked.

Declan was beginning to feel a spark of hope. If George was asking questions about the details, maybe he was considering it. Declan thought about going on a solo run, telling no one, but Dias was being watched. If the FBI didn't know what was going on, he'd be picked up right away. Not to mention the fact that he'd need their help to get to Dias. George was right—to go back to the states at this stage was suicide, so he'd need protection to get to Philadelphia. After that, he'd be on his own.

'I can't guarantee he won't, but it's worth a try. Because I'll confess about Lucia, he'll know exactly what Sacco would do to me if he finds me. He wants Sacco out of the picture anyway, then it suits both of us. Who knows, maybe Antonio is ok about the wedding being off? From what I know of Fabio Dias, he's not the kind of man to make decisions with his heart anyway. I'm hoping he'll see it as an opportunity to rid himself of his enemy and rival for once and for all. I'll supply the information and he does the deed. What stopped him up to this was the fear that he'd stir up the whole hornet's nest and the other families would get involved, but if they think it was because Sacco was turning state's evidence, they'll have no sympathy for him. They hate rats, so even though Dias is outside of their thing, they'll let it go. Secretly most of them would be delighted if Sacco was killed, though there'll be a huge outpouring of public grief.'

Lucia hadn't moved a muscle since he started speaking. He wished he knew what she was thinking.

George sat back in the chair exhaled slowly.

'So that's the plan. You just stroll into Fabio Dias's office and say "sorry about the Antonio mix-up, Sacco wants to kill me for getting his daughter pregnant and you've never trusted him, here's another reason not to, he's going to rat you out to the cops as part of a plea bargain so why don't you take him out and solve both our problems?"'

George was trying to sound incredulous but Declan knew he was mulling it over. It was probably the last chance to get Sacco; the court case was looking more and more unsafe.

'More or less,' Declan responded.

'And if he doesn't believe you?' George asked.

'Then he'll kill me, and we're no worse off than we are now. You have my written testimony, signed and witnessed. Arguably that would carry more weight in court if I were dead, and the court case goes ahead and you hope for the right outcome. But this way, if Dias believes me, and I think he will, then he'll stop Sacco himself.'

George thought for a moment. 'And why involve us at this stage?'

Declan smiled. 'Come on, George, you know why. Without the FBI's help, I'd be dead before I got out of JFK.'

'I'll have to run it by some people.' He stood up. 'They'll most likely say no but I'll do my best.'

175

'You are in favour of it then?' Declan asked.

'No, I'm not, but I happen to agree with you. We're not going to get him this time by legitimate means either. There are too many things that could go wrong, and I can't have Lucia's and the baby's blood on my hands because I didn't try everything.'

CHAPTER 18

*T*hey sat quietly without turning on the light. The room was darkening but despite it being close to eleven pm it wasn't black outside.

He moved towards the bed but when she didn't move he sat on a chair beside it.

'Talk to me.' His words hung in the air.

'Those babies... The Cambridge family... I can't get it out of my head.'

'I know. I'm sorry you had to hear it and they're ok now...'

'But what about the ones you couldn't save? The ones you didn't even know about?' Her eyes were huge, like saucers. She looked haunted.

'I don't know, Lucia, but it's why he has to be stopped someway. The legitimate way would be best, of course, but that just isn't going to happen. It has to be my way.'

She gazed into his eyes. 'But you might die.'

'I might. But you and the baby will live in peace, because he'll kill Paulie. Even if he kills me too, he'll finish your father. As I said the only thing stopping him up to now was the fear of the other families, but if they think that Paulie was a rat, then nobody will defend him.'

'I'm afraid.' Her voice was a whisper.

'So am I, but this is the only way. Will you let me go? Stay here, with Conor and Elke and the others? There's still six days left in the tour. I could go and be back before the tour is over and at least I'd know you were ok.'

She moved over on the bed and he lay beside her, her head on his chest.

'I won't do it without your say-so.'

She lay there in silence for a while. She'd thought of little else. He was her dad, and if Declan did as he was proposing, her father would almost certainly be killed. Despite everything, a part of her still loved him, or at least loved what she'd thought he was. But then she thought of poor old Fr Orstello, and the Cambridge kids, and God alone knew how many others, and she knew someone had to stop him. He would never repent; there was no hope of him even feeling regret for his actions. The FBI couldn't secure a conviction, and even if they could, he'd get out sometime. Not to mention how he could still influence the outside world from inside prison. Declan's solution, however horrific and terrifying, was the only way.

'I can't see any other way. I wish I could, but there just isn't. I'm sick at the thought of it, mainly for how much danger you'll be in but also, if I'm honest, for the fact that I'm sanctioning the murder of my father. I know you understand, he's a monster, and he has to be stopped, but...'

Declan stroked her hair. 'He's your dad, I know.'

The rest of the night dragged as Declan waited for George's answer. He considered, if they refused, just enacting his plan on his own, without the intervention of the FBI, but now that they knew what he was up to, they'd stop him. He'd have to have their help. They tried to read, to nap, to watch TV, but couldn't settle to anything. The minutes ticked slowly by.

Eventually, just after three am, George returned.

'Ok, we'll do it. You fly tomorrow from Shannon at nine am. We'll get you disguised as best we can when you land. A female agent will accompany you from the airport to Philly. Sacco won't be expecting you to travel with a woman. You'll wear a wiretap and we have a team backing you up. We'll—'

'No,' Declan interrupted. 'I said he trusted me but every single person gets patted down and checked before meeting Dias. I can't wear anything, nor can I have anyone around me. They are incredibly vigilant, they see everything. I have to go alone and unarmed.'

'But—' George began.

'He's right,' Lucia interrupted. 'He knows what they're like. Better than most. If he's to do it, it has to be his way.'

'But it's madness to go in there alone,' George argued. 'But then, this whole plan is ludicrous, so maybe you're right. Sacco is watching JFK, Newark, and La Guardia. He's pulled in every connection he has for the manhunt for the last forty-eight hours since the Facebook thing. He knows now that you aren't being shielded by the church.' He paused and looked at both Lucia and Declan.

'You do know what you're doing?' he asked. 'If this backfires, you'll be on your own, you understand that, don't you?'

Declan nodded. He knew only too well, but it was their only hope. Either way, he thought, he was probably a dead man, but if eliminating Sacco could save Lucia and their baby, then he'd do it. He was surprised at how calm he felt.

'And you're sure you can do this? How will Dias get at Sacco if he does go along with your plan?'

'I'll tell him to go to Carmine's next Thursday night, that's three days' time. Sacco is out on bail so they'll be celebrating. Even if they are worried they won't let the world see that, they'll party harder than usual to show everyone they are invincible. All the made guys, along with their wives, eat there together religiously every Thursday night. Have done for years. They'll all be there, his brothers Joey and Sal, probably Marco, he's married to Paulie's sister Rita, and Giovanni, who was married to Paulie's other sister Maria before she died of breast cancer. He has two nephews as well, Tito and PJ, Paul Junior, who may or may not be invited. That's the inner sanctum, the made guys. They would each have others working for them, and tipping up to them, giving them a cut of whatever they were running, but they wouldn't have anything to do with the Dias thing. That's inner circle only.'

'You really think this is going to work?' George was still skeptical.

'I can't be sure, obviously, but I think so. Sacco has it out that he's looking for me, and Dias will know what that means so I'm going to be open with him. The story all makes sense. Stick as close to the truth as I can.'

'And he won't think it strange that a devout priest would be basically asking one gangster to wipe out another one? To be honest, I'm not convinced. I accept that you know more than we do, but I'm just not sure he's going to buy it. Dias is as slippery as an eel, and he seems to be untouchable. He's not dumb, that's for sure. I think you're crazy.' He shook his head.

'I can't give a cast-iron guarantee, but I think it's worth a shot. I think I can convince him. He's jumpy about Sacco anyway, he hates that he needs him, and personally he can't stand the man. I really think the whole wedding, even if Sacco didn't set it up, would have been very embarrassing for Dias. He'd want to send a message to the world that nobody disrespects him, not even Paulie Sacco. He would believe that Sacco would sell him out; he knows through the media that there is a lot of evidence against Sacco. We know it won't stick, but Dias doesn't know that. Sacco turning state's evidence and dropping Dias in it is not remotely beyond the bounds of possibility. He doesn't trust him an inch. Dias is only looking for a reason to whack Paulie, who isn't popular with the other families either. They hate how he dictates to them so nobody will shed real tears for him, plenty of crocodile ones no doubt, but nothing real,' Declan finished. He knew he'd convinced the other man.

'You'd better pack. We'll leave at six and its almost four now. I'll leave you to it and see you in the lobby in two hours, ok?'

'Ok. Thanks.'

George nodded and left.

Declan threw a few things in a bag, he didn't care what; he just wanted to go and get it over with.

'Will you explain to Conor? I'd ask him to take care of you myself, but I don't want to disturb him.' He spoke over his shoulder as he threw in his passport and wallet. 'And just lay low, don't go anywhere on your own, stick with Elke and Zoe or Irene and Ken, and I'll be back right after I speak to Dias. Whatever you do, don't leave. I need you to swear to me, Lucia, that you'll stay here with Conor till either I get back or you hear from George.'

'Ok…I'll stay.' She stood behind him and he could hear the fear and pain in her voice.

He turned and put his hands on her shoulders. 'I love you, and I love our baby. I'm going to do everything I can to secure our future, to make sure we live in peace for the rest of our lives, and if I can't, then I'll die trying. This is the only way, you see that, right?'

She nodded, unable to speak.

'And I know he's your dad, and we've talked before about how there was a side to him…'

'Stop. I thought there was. I was wrong. What he did to those babies, he's…evil. So wicked, there is no redemption, no mitigation. My only reservation is you, not him.'

She kissed him and held him for a moment, and he placed his hand on her slightly swollen abdomen.

'It's going to be ok, Lucia. I think it is.'

'I'll be praying,' she said, 'every second you're gone.'

They sat and talked, about their future, about the baby, where they would live, what they would do. In that comfortable hotel room in Ireland, it seemed like a real possibility. They both wished they could just stay there together forever, forget the outside world existed at all, but all too soon it was time to meet George.

She clung to him, terrified it was the last time, and he did his best to reassure her.

'I'm coming back, ok? I'm going to do this, and get right back on a plane the second I can. Don't worry if you don't hear anything. Remember bad news travels much quicker than good, so if you don't hear anything, then that's good. I'll keep my phone off in case Dias or Paulie is tracking me.' He kissed her and held her tightly and then he was gone.

CHAPTER 19

*D*eclan glanced over at his travelling companion. She'd picked him up at Atlantic City Airport. The FBI must have thought it was the one Sacco'd be less likely to be watching. She wasn't like any cop he'd ever seen. Tattoos and piercings everywhere, loads of dreadlock-style plaits tied back from her face with a tie-dyed hair band. She wore Doc Marten boots and jeans that were more rips than fabric and a Sex Pistols t-shirt. The team from the FBI did a good job on him as well; once he'd cleared customs he had been taken to a secure area and transformed. He now had a fair-haired ponytail, some dirty jeans, and a frayed checked shirt. With his stubble he looked totally different. The instruction was to drive to Philly and then to change into his normal clothes, at a motel on the outskirts. Not priest's garb obviously but just a pair of normal jeans and a sweater. Remove the wig and have a shave. He had to convince Dias he was telling the truth, so looking as close to his old self as possible was paramount to the success of the plan.

He played the conversation over and over. How to even get into Dias's house was going to be tricky. The FBI had given him a prepaid cell phone, and he had Dias's number, or at least one of his guys, Cristiano, from the time they'd arranged the sit-down. If he picked up, and if he agreed to either let him talk to Dias or at least pass on a message, and if he agreed to meet, then he was at least going to have a shot. There were a lot of ifs between now and then though, he acknowledged grimly. The woman agent didn't say much, just looked out the window, but she seemed ok. He drove; it was only an hour trip.

They arrived at the motel around lunchtime. The agent, who didn't introduce herself as anything more than Jen, had booked it online and gotten a code sent to her phone so no contact was needed with anyone. Declan thought they were being unnecessarily cautious but he supposed they knew about this sort of thing. He would have preferred a room to himself, but if anyone checked, they didn't want to arouse suspicion.

They took turns in the bathroom. She insisted he go first, and once he'd showered, shaved, and changed his clothes, he felt like himself again. He gazed at his reflection, noticing himself for the first time in a long time. His physical appearance had been something he gave very little thought to until he'd started to have feelings for Lucia. He wondered if he looked the full twelve years her senior or not. His hair was still quite dark, though graying at the temples, and he was in good physical shape. He knew he looked more like his mother than his dad, with his green eyes and pale skin. Lucia thought he was handsome; she told him often enough. He just hoped he was enough for her, not that it would matter if this whole thing backfired. He allowed himself a moment's daydream of them together in a little house, with their baby. He'd have a job, teaching maybe. That was the thing, a resume that showed all work experience as being a priest probably wouldn't get him very far. A degree in theology might land a job at a Catholic school for someone else, but hardly for an ex-priest who had gotten a parishioner pregnant. Still, that was another hurdle, and nothing could progress until he enacted this plan. Could it work, he wondered. He had to sound very confident for the FBI, but inside he wasn't anything close to convinced.

Jen was lying on one of the beds watching TV news and eating pretzels from the mini-bar when he emerged from the bathroom. The anchor was interviewing someone from the NRA about the state response to gun law, and he was citing the organized crime problems of East Coast cities, which made it unsafe for ordinary citizens not to carry a weapon.

'Are you telling me that in the world we now live in, you wouldn't feel safer sending your son or daughter on a night out in New York or New Jersey or Philadelphia with a pistol? Of course you would. Too often innocent people get caught in the crossfire between the ever-increasing numbers of gangs. The Mafia shooting at the Russian gangs, the Puerto Ricans shooting at the Mexicans, the Chinese shooting everyone... I'm telling you, we live in a dangerous world and we need to be prepared—' Jen flicked the channel.

'It's all yours, I'll be a while.' She smiled. 'There's a pizza place at the junction if you're hungry, they deliver; there's a number on the nightstand.'

'Sure. Will you share one?' he asked.

'Yeah, but nothing with mushrooms,' she added.

Declan ordered pizza and thankfully they also delivered beer so he got a six-pack as well. When he hung up, he decided now was as good a time as any to call Cristiano.

Taking a deep breath, trying to steady the butterflies in his stomach, he scrolled until he found the number.

It rang and rang and he was just about to hang up when someone answered.

'Yeah?'

'Is this Cristiano?' Declan asked.

'Who's this?' the voice asked. Declan was fairly sure it was him.

'It's Fr Declan Sullivan. I need to talk to Fabio.'

There was silence on the other end but Declan knew they were tracing the call.

'Where you at, Father?' Cristiano asked.

'I'm on my way to Philadelphia. I'll be there in a few hours.' Declan tried to keep his voice steady.

'You delivering a message from someone? Is that it? 'Cause you can just tell me and I'll make sure that whoever needs to hear it does hear it.'

'No. I'm coming on my own, and on my own behalf. Can I see Fabio, or at least speak to him on the phone, Cristiano? It's really important.'

More silence. Then a click.

'Fr Sullivan.' The smooth faintly accented voice of Fabio Dias came on the line. 'You are the last person I expected to hear from.'

'Hello, Fabio, thanks for taking my call. I need to see you. Urgently. I can't go into it on the phone, but I'm sure you've heard that I am no longer connected to a mutual acquaintance of ours. There's something you should know. On the word of the Lord I am acting on my own behalf only.'

He could imagine Dias smiling behind his huge mahogany desk in his oval-shaped office. He had the flag of Costa Rica behind him and the whole room looked presidential. Declan remembered how silly it looked but nobody dared question Dias's taste in décor.

'You don't have my almost daughter-in-law with you then? It must be quite tricky being you right now. Sure, we can talk. Come this evening, around ten. We'll talk then.' The line clicked once more and went dead.

Declan's heart was pounding and he jumped when there was a knock on the door, but it was just the pizza and beer. He tipped the guy and turned back into the room to be greeted by a very different Jen.

The dreadlocks, tattoos, and piercings were all gone, and her short blonde hair was slicked back from her face. She wore cream chinos and a blue button-down shirt. Smiling at his reaction, she explained, 'I used to work in movie makeup, horrors mostly, and then I was head-hunted by the FBI. I can turn anyone into anything, it's a skill I know.' She winked and took the beers from him, cracking one open.

'But it looked so real...' Declan was mesmerized.

'That's the idea, but it's all fake. But I think we're safe enough now. So, did you call him?' she asked as she bit into a slice of pizza.

Declan smiled. This transformation took some getting used to.

185

'Yes. I'm meeting him tonight at ten.'

'How'd he sound?' she asked

'Like himself. Smug, as if he was laughing at me. He mentioned Lucia.'

'Did you think he wouldn't?'

'No. I guess not.'

'Did you get any sense of how things were between him and Sacco?'

'No. He's a very clever operator. You never know what he's thinking, and anyway the conversation lasted only a few seconds. He just said it must be tricky being me and asked if his almost daughter-in-law was with me.'

'There's a chance Sacco had second-guessed you and has already contacted Dias to get in touch with him if you were to make contact. You might be meeting more than Dias tonight,' she added ominously.

'I had thought of that. I don't think so, but then who knows?'

'Well, we're watching Sacco twenty-four/seven. If he starts making for Philly, we'll know.'

They watched TV for a while, some mindless comedy, and Jen took a nap fully clothed on one of the twin beds. He knew he should do the same, he'd need to be up again in a couple of hours, but what she'd said was going round and round in his brain, driving him crazy. In the end, he was eighty percent sure she was wrong. He'd want to catch Declan himself. Paulie would never humble himself like that in front of Dias of all people. He sat on the bed, leaning back against some pillows, and took from his wallet a photo of Lucia. He'd taken it with his phone one day when they were walking in the woods on one of the stops with Conor and had it printed at a pharmacy in Killarney. The light was dappled on her face and she was laughing. His heart ached with love for her, and for the child she carried. The hours ticked slowly by until Jen's alarm beeped on her phone.

'So, Father, had we better get going?' she asked, instantly awake.

'I guess we should. How should we do this?'

'I'll drop you in one of the suburbs and you can catch the bus into the city, then depending on time, either walk or take a cab from the station to Dias's place on Delancey Street. You have my cell; call me when it's safe and I'll arrange pickup. Take a bus or train out to a suburb again, but be careful, some areas of Philly aren't the safest for a skinny white guy.' She smiled.

'Ok.' Declan exhaled slowly.

'You'll be fine. I just hope she's worth it.' She gave him a smile.

'She really is,' he replied.

CHAPTER 20

*J*en had dropped him at Allegheny Avenue at 8.30pm, with instructions to take the bus to Eighth and Christian Streets. From there he could walk to Dias's place. As she pulled the rental car into the traffic, leaving him on the kerb, Declan fought down feelings of panic. This was it; he was on his own now. Jen warned him that there was a good chance either Dias or someone working for Sacco was looking out for him so he needed to be vigilant, though when he asked her what he should do in the event of one of them tried to kill him, she had no answers. As he waited he decided to drop his bag in a locker in the station. Emerging, he noticed a small church across the road. He was too early anyhow, it was only about a twenty-minute bus ride to the city centre. He ran over. If he ever needed the intervention of the Lord, it was now.

The church was a Catholic one, not that it mattered to him, and thankfully it was deserted.

He slid into a pew two thirds back from the altar and knelt. Declan rarely prayed in a formal sense when he was alone. His life was more like one long stream of consciousness, an ongoing conversation with Jesus. The real presence of the Lord in his life meant he never felt alone; God was always with him. He knew other people didn't understand what he did, why he dealt with gangsters and drug dealers, but God did, and that was what mattered.

'Dear Jesus,' he began. For the first time in his life he had no idea what to say. Surely it was wrong to invoke God's blessing on a mission to have one criminal wipe out another, all because of a lie told by a priest? This was so ridiculous, it was like the plot of a bad gangster movie. How on earth had it become the real story of his life? Declan's head ached. He was lost, lost to himself and possibly lost to God.

Kneeling there, he waited for some inspiration to come to him, some sign that what he was about to do was justified, something more than inciting violence and hatred, but God, if he was listening, was maintaining radio silence. He waited, trying to still his thoughts, to pray the prayers of his childhood, the ones that never failed to ease his troubled mind over the years. The silence went on and on. Nothing. He tried to focus on Lucia and Eddie praying for him back in Ireland, and while the thoughts of them brought him a small degree of comfort, he felt nothing of their spiritual strength.

He took in the interior of the church, but in an instant it seemed meaningless to him. For the first time in his entire life, Declan wondered about the existence of God. Perhaps there was nothing. Maybe this was all a construct of a species that couldn't cope with the concept of an existence independent of any higher power. There was no real evidence, he had to admit, and there was so much evil in the world. He'd tried to explain faith to people so many times; it wasn't something you could develop, or invent. You either believed or you didn't, and it was a far deeper emotion than anything our conscious mind could grapple with. He felt empty and alone, and the feeling made him feel almost physically sick. Even in the worst days, after the sudden death of his parents, he never felt totally on his own because God lived within him, He was always there. Now He was gone.

The conflicts that others grappled with bubbled to the surface. The questions parishioners and nonbelievers alike had asked him down through the years: Where was God when priests were abusing little children? Where was God when innocent people were having their lives destroyed by war? Where was God when a crack baby was born screaming for a fix? For the first time there was no answer. He fixed his gaze on the sculpture of the crucified Christ behind the altar, the blood running from the crown of thorns, the piercing in his side from the spear of a Roman soldier, the holes in his hands and feet. The grotesque nature of Catholicism struck him, the fact that parents would not allow their children to watch violent movies, and yet each week took their kids to mass to be subjected to these gruesome images. He hated the feelings this unfamiliar crisis of faith invoked.

He felt himself longing for the absolute certainty of his life up to this point, but the doubts kept coming, wave after destructive wave, disintegrating everything he thought he knew. Maybe he never had a vocation, maybe it was just because he was reared in the faith, had been a studious and thoughtful child who enjoyed the solitude and peace of the church. He was never abused by the clergy, he served as an altar boy from the age of seven, the priests of the parish were regular visitors to their home, he was educated by Jesuits who were inspirational and kind. The more he thought about it, he was just conditioned to the priesthood, primed and trained from birth not to question but to have an all-encompassing, undiluted faith in both the Lord and the Catholic Church. He wasn't an undereducated man, he understood the abuses the Catholic Church engaged in over the centuries: the sale of indulgences, nepotism, absenteeism, the ruthless extermination of anyone who disagreed with them. He remembered the ripple of laughter when his history teacher, Fr Antonio, declared that Martin Luther had a good point when he nailed his ninety-five theses to the door of Wittenberg Cathedral in 1517. The church was corrupt and needed to take a long, hard look at itself. Then and now, he said, the church and the Vatican needed to constantly be self-aware and critical, never complacent in its certainty of its own virtue.

Trying to come to terms with all the anomalies he faced daily—the vast wealth of the Roman Catholic Church compared to the extreme poverty of many of its flock, the manner in which the abuse scandals were covered up, the dogmatic approach to divorce, homosexuality, abortion—were all things he struggled with. When he talked it over with Bishop Rameros, as he did regularly, he came to the same conclusion every time: that the church was made up of individuals, flawed human beings, and like all human beings, it was neither completely good or completely evil. He just held a deep conviction that there was more good than bad, that the church provided such solace to people; the fact that he could say with certainty to a bereaved widow that she would see her husband again in the next life brought comfort. The social outlet the church provided for those who needed a friend, the good that was done for the poorest of the poor. It was an imperfect organization, of that there was no doubt, but he really believed that people's lives were better when they were a part of it. Even the Saccos. They were ruthless and utterly without qualms when it came to the most heinous of crimes, but they believed, and his interventions had saved lives.

The church of late certainly did not display any traces of virtue. The abuse scandals, one after the other, all over the world, shook him to the core. And then, to watch the church, his beloved church, who collectively preached every Sunday the messages of love, repentance, forgiveness, do the exact opposite, tore at his conscience. He watched in horror and disbelief as they continued to obfuscate, deflect, and lie.

A final icy wave of realization crashed over him. He couldn't do it anymore. He was overwhelmed with a sensation he couldn't adequately describe, a mixture of pain, sadness, and a tinge of relief. He looked around the cool dark church, the icons of the Stations of the Cross adorning the walls, the beautiful pipes of the pipe organ reaching high up into the nave, the ordered pews facing the altar. He admired the lovely flower arrangements decorating the altar. The sanctuary flame glowed red, indicating the sacred host was in the tabernacle. Everything looked and smelled so comforting, so familiar, he could just walk up there this moment and say mass. He would know where everything was, it would be just like home. He took a deep breath, the aroma of incense, beeswax, and flowers intermingled in his nostrils. He knew in that moment, with complete clarity, that there was nothing else, no God, no saints, no heaven. The dead were gone, rotting in the ground, this life was all there was. It was over.

He left the church feeling empty. How could he have entered it a short time ago, full of hope and in need of comfort, and emerge an atheist? The transition was so sudden but yet it felt as though the scales had fallen from his eyes, he saw the world as it truly was, and it was a strange feeling. He dismissed it; he had other problems to worry about. He decided to take a cab to the corner of the Dias property; the gangs of youths hanging around on street corners made him uneasy.

The last time Declan was at the Dias house in the affluent neighbourhood of Bella Vista, he'd been driven there by PJ, Paulie's nephew, and so had no idea how complicated or not it was to gain access to the residence. They were expected, so they just drove in through the huge electric gates. He remembered being appalled at the wealth on display, all gained through the misery of others, far more ostentatious even than the Saccos. Fabio Dias liked nice things. His clothes, his watch, his shoes all screamed money, and his house was exactly the same. Dias saw himself as an art collector and claimed to be quite knowledgeable on the subject. Paintings that Declan imagined were genuine adorned the walls. The large marble table in the entrance hall, Dias had explained, came out of one of the Medici properties in Florence. It had been in private ownership since the Renaissance and he was its current guardian. During his last visit, the way he had shown Declan around, explaining in intricate detail the provenance of the seemingly endless collection of art, sculpture, and furniture with no pang of guilt at the vastness of his wealth, fascinated and repulsed Declan.

Like Sacco, he believed fundamentally his own press, that he was an entrepreneur, a custodian of the art of the past, a benevolent employer, a good man. There were hospitals and schools in his native Costa Rica dedicated to his generosity, but nowhere in the whole conversation did he, or anyone around him, admit that all this money came from peddling drugs, the same drugs that destroy individuals and families all over the world.

The last time he was there, Dias had spoken to him about the situation beside the aquamarine kidney-shaped pool with a verdant green waterfall at one end. The white marble of the poolside area made his eyes wince, and he'd never felt so uncomfortable in all his life. Sprinklers ensured the green lawns remained so, despite the city-wide watering restrictions in place to conserve the city's water supply. Like everything else, Dias assumed the law did not apply to him.

He would take to his grave the image that had greeted him as they toured the grounds and discussed how best to proceed. Rounding a corner into the Italian Garden, Declan had almost jumped to see a fully grown tiger in a large cage, pacing menacingly.

Dias had laughed. 'Don't worry, Father, he has been already fed. This is Diablo. He takes some handling but I like him.'

Declan had been stunned. He'd thought of admonishing Dias for having a wild animal locked in a cage, especially a man-eating one, but he'd realized the futility of such a gesture, and anyway he'd needed to keep on his right side to resolve the stupid argument. When he looked back, that conversation seemed so difficult then. It was nothing compared to what he was about to do.

CHAPTER 21

*T*he small silver panel in the long white wall was the only way of communicating with the Dias compound. The gate beside it left not one inch of light through; it was a fortress within a city. Declan pressed the only button on the panel.

He was just getting ready to announce himself when the gate opened enough for one person to enter. He walked through and immediately the gate closed automatically behind him with a gentle click. Two huge Doberman Pinscher dogs bounded towards him but were immediately brought to heel by a sharp whistle from an enormous man wearing a cream suit with a black open-necked shirt.

'Welcome, Father,' he said. Declan wondered if he'd met him before, but he was sure he hadn't. He would have remembered him, he was over six feet and easily weighted three hundred pounds. He was of Latino origin, with dark hair and eyes. On his fingers he wore a variety of rings, which on another man might look effeminate, but this man exuded power, both physical and psychological.

'Thank you,' Declan replied. His heart was pounding in his chest. There was no going back now; he was in the beast's lair. He pictured Lucia in Ireland, trying to act normally, praying that this nightmare would soon be over, and he steeled himself. He had to do this, and

Dias would have to buy his story. He wished he was in his priest's garb. Like Sacco, Dias too had been raised a Catholic and somewhere underneath all the avarice, crime, and decadence, it meant something to him. In his own way he was quite devout. Declan had noticed lots of religious artwork the last time he was there, and Dias had explained how he'd donated a Caravaggio to his local parish.

The man led him first to a Perspex cubicle, like those he'd seen at very high-tech airports, and the man gestured that Declan should walk inside and place his feet on the shoe-shaped symbols on the ground.

'Please raise your arms.'

Declan did as he was asked and screens flashed in front and behind him. Declan was in no doubt that this security check was far more advanced than those used at airports. He was right to go in with nothing.

He had no phone, was completely out of contact with anyone. There was no point to the FBI watching the compound; it was such a citadel it was impenetrable. George had explained that warrants had been issued on a number of occasions, and law enforcement authorities got in but never found anything incriminating. Dias would smirk as they searched, confident there was nothing to be found. It wasn't illegal to be vastly wealthy, every painting on display; every antique could be proved to have been acquired by legitimate means. The tiger was news to George; obviously it was removed when the surprise searches took place, which led George to question how much of a surprise the operations really were to Dias. Though George hated to admit it, there must be someone in authority tipping Dias off. The Dias empire included hotels, casinos, yacht charter companies, mining corporations, oil exploration ventures, so many legitimate businesses, with squeaky clean books, that there were almost endless streams of revenue. His really lucrative narcotics business was easily subsumed into the others. Declan had often heard Sacco exclaim how he wished he had Dias's accountant, the man was clearly a genius, but no one could poach him away from the Costa Rican's employ. What's more, nobody would dare try.

'I will take you now to Fabio,' the man growled. 'Please follow me.'

This time he wasn't led to the pool area but into the house and up the huge marble stairs. Declan walked silently behind him, on thick cream carpet down corridors decorated by art and sculptures. The house was totally silent and Declan wondered if Dias lived here alone. Antonio's mother was never mentioned. Lucia said Antonio had explained that he never knew her and that she wasn't in his life. She knew all too well the pain of an absent mother so she didn't pry any further.

He hoped he looked miserable enough to add credibility to his story. A man on the run from Sacco, in fear of his life—he hoped he looked hunted; he certainly felt it. After what seemed like an incredibly long walk in a domestic house, the man opened large double doors with a theatrical sweep. If the situation weren't so grave, Declan knew he would have smiled at the ridiculousness of the gesture, as if he was being presented to royalty.

He entered a room that overlooked the entire property. Not the oval office of his previous visit this was more like a viewing area, with vistas over the grounds, and past Dias's property onto Cianfranni Park. The room was entirely devoid of furniture, the floor covered in deep pile scarlet carpet. The white walls were bare apart from a gigantic painting of a tiger, probably a portrait of the one he kept as a pet. A huge semi-circle of glass made up one wall, the aquamarine pool complex glittering below, the perfectly manicured lawns with abundant flowering plants stretched to the end of the complex. Because the property bordered a public park, the view gave the illusion that Dias owned acres and acres of land in the middle of Philadelphia. Declan had no concept of how much a property like this was worth but he guessed multiples of millions.

'Fabio will be with you shortly,' the security guy said and backed out of the room. Dias insisted everyone call him Fabio, not Mr. Dias or Sir. In some stupid way he felt it made him one of the team. He was fond of saying that nobody worked for him, they worked with him. The irony of the fact that anyone who displeased him ended up dead seemed lost on him.

Declan was nervous, and he felt nauseous. He put his hands in his pockets so the shaking wouldn't be visible. He was positive he was being watched, by security and probably by Dias himself. Should he sit, pace, stand? He decided to walk to the glass and stand with his back to the room, gazing out at the gardens. He kept his hands in his pockets but squared his shoulders and steadied himself with a few deep breaths. After several minutes the soft click behind him indicated the doors opening. He turned to face Dias.

He looked exactly as Declan remembered. Dressed in dark jeans and a pale pink shirt, perfectly shaved and without a dark hair astray on his head. He wasn't a tall man and he had a slight but athletic build. He was magnetic though, Declan had noticed that before as well; he had charisma and when he spoke to people they seemed to light up. He exuded energy, and if he didn't know better, Declan would have described him as genial and friendly.

'Father Declan, here you are. You led us to believe you were in Ireland of all places.' His voice was cultured, that of a well-educated man. He almost purred. So he had spoken to Paulie. Declan wondered if Jen was right: was Paulie going to appear through the double doors any minute? He needed to hold his nerve.

'Thank you for seeing me.' Declan looked him in the eye. The game had begun.

'No problem. Can I get you a drink? Something to eat? You look like you should eat, you've lost some weight since I saw you last.' A simple observation, but the words hung heavily.

'No...thank you, but I'm fine. I don't have much of an appetite these days to be honest.' The urge to be flippant was absent; he needed to be sincere.

'Very well, perhaps later, after we have talked. Now, Father, I know this isn't a social call, so what can I do for you?' His eyes never left Declan's face.

He'd rehearsed this in his head so many times, should he build up to it? Launch straight in? He wasn't sure. In the end he decided straight talking was best.

197

'I'm on Paulie Sacco's hit list because I fell in love with his daughter Lucia and now she's pregnant.'

'Yes, the Lucia Sacco who was to marry my son Antonio.' Dias voice was neutral; it was impossible to tell what he was thinking.

'Yes. And both she and I are sorry for the upset we've caused. Especially to Antonio. Lucia wished she could have spoken to him, to explain...'

'Yes, that would have been the courteous thing to do, but then she's a Sacco. I was never in favour of the match, Father, did you know that? No? Well, I wasn't but Antonio seemed to like her and she's easy enough on the eyes I suppose...'

Declan resisted the urge to react.

'How is Antonio?'

'He's fine. Relieved, I think. He's in the Galapagos now, went with a friend of his, to get away from it all. He feels he's had a lucky escape; she wasn't worthy of him.'

Declan was sure Dias's words were aimed to get a reaction from him, but he stayed calm.

'I'm glad he's ok. As I said, it was never anyone's intention to hurt him.'

Dias nodded. 'So, Father, why are you here?'

'I need your help. And given the situation with Antonio I know I have no right to ask, but I have nowhere else to turn. Lucia and I love each other and Sacco won't or can't forgive it. He sees it as a betrayal of my position of trust within the family and he wants me dead.' Declan knew the only way Dias would go for the plan was if he thought him totally honest, so he was going to stick as closely to the truth as possible.

'Oh dear. That's not good news for you, Father. He's a vindictive man, our Paulie, you're right. He won't forgive that, ever. But why come to me? This is an issue between the two of you surely?'

'Yes it is, but it does implicate you. I'm coming with some information. And I want to be straight with you about my motivation. I'm telling you this, not to save you, but to save my family.'

'Go on, Father, I'm intrigued.' Fabio smiled.

In the movies the rat would extract a promise of protection in return for information, but this wasn't the movies and anyway Dias wouldn't honour any promise he would make if it wasn't in his interest, so there was only one way to do it: Give him the information and hope that he did what Declan wanted him to do.

'As you know, I'm sure, the FBI are building a case against Sacco and the family.'

'But you can't testify, seal of the confessional and all of that?' Dias was interested now.

'Indeed, but I was also privy to other conversations, outside of the confessional...'

'I must hasten to warn you, Father, if you have come here to threaten me, that you will reveal conversations you and I may have had...' All traces of friendliness gone, his voice was steely.

This was not at all how he wanted it to go. Declan forced down a feeling of panic.

'Absolutely not. That isn't my intention at all. If you'll allow me to finish, I'll explain.'

Declan swallowed and hoped there wasn't an audible gulp; he had to remain calm.

'Ok, go on.' Dias was on his guard.

'Sacco recently discovered that I wasn't in a monastery somewhere being protected by the church, but that I was in Ireland with Lucia and that I had been approached by the FBI and asked to testify against Paulie. Probably realizing that with my testimony he would face conviction, the case is very strong, he approached the FBI and offered a deal in return for a lighter sentence. Nobody, not even anyone in the family, knows this. He's going to sell out the rest of them and save his own skin.'

'I'm still failing to see what this has to do with me.' Dias was sounding bored now, all traces of hospitality gone.

'Well, it has, in that the FBI will only agree to the deal if he gives them information on you as well. They've told him that they can convict all the consigliore and several minor family members as well without him, so they don't need him for that, but they do need his testimony to go after you.' Declan fought the urge to keep talking, allowing this information to hang in the air.

Dias paused and then burst out laughing. Declan's heart sank. Dias wasn't buying it, he wasn't going to get out of here alive.

'That little worm. Does he seriously think I'm going to allow myself to be arrested based on his say-so? He can't touch me. If that's what he thinks, he's more stupid than I thought he was, and to be honest, I always thought he was a moron.'

Declan had one last piece of false information up his sleeve.

'He has video, complete with audio, of you and him in the ware-house in Newark when you came to check the conditions. I've seen it. He was going to use it if you didn't agree to compromise on the Ernesto thing that time. That's how I know, he told me not to give in too much to you, that he had something he could use against you.'

Declan felt slight relief as he saw the shadow cross Dias's face. He was taking this seriously now. He paused. 'Does the FBI know you're here?'

Declan paused. This was the trickiest part, to convince Dias that he was trusted by the FBI but that he was unworthy of that trust while still coming across as honest.

'No. I wanted them to be involved in this, I thought it was the best thing to do, but they refused. I suppose they can't be involved in something that is essentially criminal, even if it's what needs to be done. The FBI are not of the frame of mind that the ends justify the means.'

Dias smirked. 'That shows how much you know about the FBI, Father, but no matter, go on.'

Not knowing how to respond, Declan chose to ignore that remark. 'So in fact, up until yesterday I was in Ireland. Fabio, I can't believe that I'm in this position, but I am desperate, not for my life, but for my family. I thought I could testify, tell the police what I know and Paulie would go to prison for life, but that's not looking likely now. I was naïve I suppose. With the plea bargain he'll get ten, maybe fifteen years, out in seven, and in the meantime, the rest of them are still on the outside doing his bidding. You know Paulie, he won't rest, either from outside or inside jail, until he has punished me. Already he has murdered Fr Orstello, the other priest in the parish. I'm scared and I don't think the FBI or the courts can protect Lucia and me.'

Dias thought for a long moment, gazing disconcertingly at Declan. The lack of furniture, or anything to distract from the bare formality of the space, made the exchange almost unbearably tense.

Eventually he spoke, 'Father, I can't decide if you are naive, stupid, or very very clever. If you think the FBI just let you leave when you're one of their chief witnesses, then you are deluded. They have either followed you without your knowledge or you are lying to me and they are in on this. Either way, it's irrelevant; they know you are here. But that does not matter; they are outside this place twenty-four/seven as the kids say anyway. They think if they wait around long enough, then I will do something stupid. Of course I won't, so it's a waste of time. A waste of taxpayers' money. The donut place down the street would close down if I moved house, they are their best customers.'

Declan remained silent. If he laughed or smiled, it would come across as ingratiating himself. He kept his face as neutral as he could. Dias was thinking; gushing or pleading or trying to convince him at this stage would be totally counterproductive. He had to come to the inevitable conclusion himself.

'Are you lying to me, Father?' Dias's eyes bored into Declan's. Now was the moment of truth. Whatever happened next would decide the outcome.

'I'm not. Paulie Sacco is going to sacrifice you to save his own skin.' Declan hoped his voice came out steady and it did. He held the other man's gaze.

'Very well, if you say so. So what do you propose I do?' Dias asked eventually.

'That's up to you. He will testify if he isn't stopped though, that is a certainty. If he doesn't implicate you, then the plea bargain is worthless. If he does it and takes you down with him, he'll get out while he still has something left to live for. And the first thing he'll do is come after me if he hasn't had someone do it already.'

Dias nodded his head thoughtfully, and smiled.

'You want me to kill him, is that what you want, Father?' He was enjoying this. Declan couldn't really believe what he was about to say nor the conviction with which he was about to say it. A man who had preached the gospel all his life, who tried to abide by the commandments, to do unto others and all of that, was about to break the fifth commandment, not in anger or in a moment of passion, but with malice of forethought as they said in court.

'Yes. That's exactly what I want.' The words hung in the air between them, both trying to process, both knowing that it was a game of chess. There were no sounds coming from outside; the room was entirely soundproofed, probably bug proof as well. Declan was aware of the beads of perspiration gathering between his shoulder blades and in the small of his back. He hoped his face wasn't betraying him in a similar way; he had no way of knowing, there was no mirror in the room.

'So, I do this, what you ask of me, this huge favour, despite the fact that you stole my son's fiancée, and I save myself from being implicated in a long-winded and messy court case, and you and your family are no longer at risk of the wrath of a mobster scorned. That's it in a nutshell, isn't it? So all that remains is for me to decide if a, I believe you, b, I trust you, and c, if I want to do it.' He drummed his fingers together in front of his mouth in an almost prayer gesture.

'You're a dark horse, Fr Sullivan. Rarely do people surprise me, but you have. Yes, you certainly have. Well, thank you for dropping by, and I wish you luck. Roberto will see you out.' To Declan's dismay, Dias then simply left the room. What was he going to do? Was he going to do anything? It was impossible to say. Nothing he had said or done gave Declan the slightest indication of what would happen next. He fought the urge to follow him to ask his intentions, realizing the futility of such a move. Dias would do, or not do, as he pleased.

CHAPTER 22

*R*oberto reappeared and Declan retraced his steps and within moments found himself back outside on the grounds of the Dias compound, none the wiser.

Suddenly Roberto lost all his polite detachment and dragged Declan near the perimeter wall, smashing his huge fist into Declan's jaw. Stunned, he fell to his knees, the pain in his face excruciating. As he tried to get up, Roberto delivered two more punches to his abdomen. Declan felt a rib crack.

Blood streamed from his mouth as he struggled to get himself upright. Even if he'd not been caught unaware, there was no way he could fight back against this man mountain.

Just as Declan prepared himself for another blow, he felt himself being lifted by his collar and Roberto spoke directly to him.

'Now, Father Sullivan, I just want you to understand that we do not tolerate anyone speaking out of turn or placing Fabio in any awkward situations, so listen carefully. This never happened, you don't know us and we don't know you. You keep that in mind when you go to live your fairytale life with your little girl and your bambino, everyone will be ok. But if you don't, if you speak to anyone, anyone at all, well, then there will be consequences. You understand?'

Declan looked up into his eyes, dead of all emotion, and nodded. 'I understand.'

'Good, now off you go.'

Declan turned and hobbled in the direction of the electronic gate. Glancing one last time at the mansion, he thought he saw Dias standing at a window but he couldn't be sure.

He stood on the street outside, trying not to vomit with the pain. No cab would pick him up covered in blood, and he didn't dare go to the ER, so he walked as inconspicuously as he could back to the bus station to collect his bag.

Jen had warned him that he needed to get out of circulation as quickly as possible after the meeting, but Declan knew Dias would have someone follow him.

Nobody took any notice of him, and eventually he locked himself into a stall in the men's room of the station and gingerly touched his face. He felt around inside his mouth with his tongue; all his teeth seemed to be in place. The blood was coming from his cut lip, which he could feel was very swollen now. He lifted his shirt to see the beginnings of bruising around his rib cage, and he was sure one if not more ribs were broken. He went out to the sink and tried the best he could to clean himself up. Thankfully, he had some spare clothes in the bag, and with great difficulty he managed to put back on his blond wig.

He texted Jen.

'Getting back by myself. Am ok. Thanks.' He couldn't risk being seen with her; he was safer alone.

He turned his phone off as soon as the text was sent; she'd been given the job of bringing him back in one piece so she wouldn't be happy. He knew George would want him back to debrief him on how it all went, but he just had had enough. He just wanted to get back to Lucia; there was nothing more he could do now. He took the bus to the train station and got a train ticket back to New York. He bought a bagel from a stall on the way to the platform, hungry for the first time in days, but he couldn't eat; his jaw was too sore. Sitting in a single seat at the back of the carriage, he thought about his next move. The reality was, there was no next move. Dias would either act on the information or he wouldn't.

He changed at Penn Station for JFK, having bought a Yankees Beanie hat and scarf that he pulled down over his face as much as he could, and wrapping a scarf around his jaw to hide the swelling. The train journey was uneventful but despite his exhaustion, he was too jumpy to sleep. He eventually arrived at the airport train station. He checked his watch; it was almost five am. He walked up to the Aer Lingus desk.

'Yes, sir, how can I help?' asked the ground staff lady without a smile. She looked like she hated her job. Her coworker looked worse as she tried to check in an entire Chinese student group where nobody spoke English.

'I'd like a flight to Ireland please,' Declan said.

'Have you reserved online?' she asked.

'Er, no, I just walked in here...' he began.

'Well, this line is for online reservations, sir, I need a reservation number to process your flight.' Already she was looking at the next guest in the line.

'But do you have a seat this morning on the flight to Shannon?' Declan asked, trying to remain polite.

'Yes, sir, but without a reservation number—'

'But I can't give you a reservation number because I don't have a reservation, so can I just make a reservation now, here, with you? Please?' He could feel the frustration and tiredness combining, but he didn't want to be rude to this woman; she was just trying to do her job, he supposed.

Something changed in her. Maybe it was the sincerity of the please, or the state of his face, but whatever it was it worked.

'Ok, sir, I'm not supposed to do this, I hope you understand, but you look tired and...well...I sure hope the other guy looks worse.' He thought she gave a hint of a smile.

'Thank you.' He tried to smile but his face ached.

'Name?' she asked, a little bit more kindly.

'Father Declan Sullivan,' he responded automatically.

'Ok, can I see your passport please, Father?' she asked, curious now.

He handed it over, and watched her do a double take as the photo was of a dark-haired priest wearing his collar, and while there were similarities between him and the specimen in front of her, it was a leap to make.

He should have removed the wig, but in his pain and confusion he just forgot.

She processed his information, seeming perplexed once more when he insisted on paying cash for the flight. She looked incredulous when he said he didn't have a credit card.

'Does the church not give you a credit card, Father?' she asked kindly, as if she thought he was a little bit mentally impaired.

'No, ma'am, vow of poverty.' He felt like such a fraud.

Eventually, after she had flouted at least five rules of checking in, he was handed his boarding card.

He quickly went to the men's room again before boarding and removed the wig, and tried to flatten his hair down. He looked dreadful, and he didn't want to arouse any more suspicion. He sat beside a man reading news off an iPad in the hope that he would discover something about the case, but the man was only interested in the football scores. It was too early for the papers; only yesterday's were available. He'd just have to wait.

CHAPTER 23

*a*s Declan slept over the Atlantic, Lucia sat in a hotel room. She'd transferred to Cork with the rest of the group the day Declan left, making up some excuse about still feeling sick, and since they were there for three nights she couldn't face the daily tours.

She'd explained to Conor that Declan had gone back to the states to try to sort things out but left the explanation at that. She assured him that either way it would no longer be his problem in the next few days. He was kind and supportive and didn't ask too many questions.

The group had gone to Kinsale and Cobh on Cork harbor, as well as everyone getting to kiss the famous Blarney Stone that day, and by all accounts everyone had a wonderful day.

Elke knocked on her way back to the room and tried to get her to go have dinner with her and the others, but Lucia couldn't bring herself to leave the room. She ordered room service because she'd promised Declan she would try to eat, but she could think of nothing but what was happening to him. She watched American news on the hotel TV day and night, but so far there was no mention of anything. The incessant talk was getting on her nerves so she kept the sound down so it took a moment for her to catch a glimpse of a scene she recognized. Quickly she grabbed the remote, turning up the volume.

'...New Jersey area. Notorious East Coast crime boss Paulie Sacco was fatally injured in a shootout earlier today. An armed unit of the FBI Organised Crime division were alerted and called to a restaurant in Hoboken, New Jersey, associated with Sacco and his family in the wake of several eyewitness accounts of a gun battle. A number of other men, including several members of Sacco's immediate family, are reported dead. It is believed the shootout occurred when members of what is presumed at this stage to be a rival gang entered the premises and opened fire indiscriminately. Sacco's death culminates one of the FBI's most protracted and complex investigations in living memory. Our reporter Joe Lavino is at the scene. What can you tell us about the events of today's shootout, Joe?'

Lucia stood gazing rigidly at the television screen. She didn't dare look away in case it was a mistake. The camera moved from the studio to a reporter outside Carmine's, the site of so many birthday parties, christenings, and even weddings. Her Uncle Sal's fiftieth was there only last year and she remembered as a child how Old Carmine would spoil her when she came in to dinner with her daddy and she felt like the most important customer in the whole place. Young Carmine, his son, was really sweet too, a bit too fond of the bottle and the horses sometimes, and her father had helped him out financially once or twice, but he'd do anything for Paulie Sacco, or for his daughter if she'd ever asked. Police cars and sirens seemed to dominate the scene.

'Well, Helen, extraordinary scenes here, so far the FBI has been able to confirm the death of Paulie Sacco, his two brothers, Joey and Salvatore, his brothers-in-law Giovanni di Angelo and Marco Putti, as well as other minor players in the Sacco family. It seems this was a male-only dinner party, and it is understood that this restaurant, Carmine's, is a regular location for members of this organized crime gang. The owner of the restaurant was shot and died shortly after. Early indications suggest that it was a drug deal gone wrong, though who is behind the attack is too difficult to say at this stage. It seems from unconfirmed sources here that there was to be a mass arrest by the Organised Crime division of several members of the Sacco gang, who were to be indicted on a variety of charges from murder to rack-eteering.'

'So are we to understand that the FBI were on the brink of arresting the Sacco gang when someone else appeared on the scene and started shooting?'

'Yes, it would seem so, Helen. The FBI are, as I say, not forth-coming with the details at this point, but I understand an FBI agent was injured in the exchange, though not critically. The battle was almost entirely between the Saccos and the other group, but as I've said we have no information yet as to who that might have been.'

The studio anchorwoman's voice was heard again. 'And why now, Joe? It seems like Sacco has been under surveillance for years. Had there been a breakthrough in the case?'

'Nothing has been confirmed or denied by the FBI as of yet, but there seems to be a generally held belief among those whom I have spoken to that a witness very close to the Sacco family had agreed to testify and that his or her testimony would have secured a successful conviction. Obviously we will have to wait for the full details of this case to emerge in due course, but this is certainly a significant day in the fight against organised crime on the East Coast. For CNN News, this is Joe Lavino, Newark, New Jersey.'

The camera cut back to the studio. 'And in sports news today...'

Lucia stumbled back to the bed. She was afraid her legs wouldn't hold her up, such was the shock.

Was that it? Was it over?

Grief overwhelmed her. Her dad was dead. She'd never see him again. Apart from Declan, he was the only other person who had ever loved her, and now he was gone forever. She didn't even have the reassurance that she would see him again in heaven, because he couldn't be going there after the life he'd lived. Her faith taught her that in order to receive God's grace and entry into heaven, a soul had to have repented of their sins. Perhaps he had; maybe he had a moment before he died to say he was sorry and truly mean it. She prayed that he did.

When there were no more tears, she just lay on the bed for a few moments, her hands on her swelling abdomen, and prayed Declan was safe.

CHAPTER 24

*E*ventually, with trembling fingers, Lucia called George. She assumed he was back in the states and she wasn't sure what time it was there, but she didn't care.

She spoke with a steady voice, despite the gut-churning anxiety she felt. 'This is Lucia Sacco speaking, George. I've seen the news, I know what's happened. Is Declan all right?'

A slight pause.

'My condolences on the death of your father and uncles, Lucia.' He sounded sincere.

'Thank you,' she replied. Was he offering his condolences on Declan as well but couldn't say it? 'And Declan?'

'Well, I assume he is fine. I've not heard anything to the contrary at any rate, but I don't actually know where he is.' He sounded apologetic.

Lucia tried to keep the tremor of panic out of her voice but failed. 'What do you mean? You were supposed to be looking after him!'

'Lucia, as we explained, he was acting independently. That said, I understand you're worried, but honestly he's probably fine. He left our agent yesterday and he—'

'Why? Why did he leave?' Lucia was crying now.

'To carry out his plan. He contacted our agent by text after the meeting and said he would take care of himself. The phone we provided him with is no longer operational. We have tried, but he can't be reached, and his personal phone is switched off.'

'But I thought you were tracking him, keeping guard from a distance?' Lucia tried to steady her voice; she didn't want to be dismissed as a hysterical female and not taken seriously.

'Lucia, Declan is not under arrest, he is not a suspect, and frankly we have had a lot going on in the last twenty-four hours here with this case. I understand you're worried but I honestly think he is fine. Every significant member of the Sacco family has been under twenty-four-hour surveillance for the last few weeks so we are fairly confident that none of them has been in contact with Declan, and now none of them can, so please, try not to worry. He'll be in touch soon I'm sure.'

Fairly confident. That would have to do, there was nothing more the agent could say to allay her fears. 'Ok, thanks, George. Please contact me immediately if you do hear anything though, ok?'

'Of course, but I have to go now, Lucia. Take care.'

'Good-bye.' She pressed the end call button.

She'd just have to wait, try to be brave. They were dead, all of them. She didn't need to hear from the news who died because it was the Thursday night dinner, always the same. Sometimes they brought wives but often not, just the guys. Carmine would close for regular customers and he'd cook for the Saccos, the finest Italian food. Chianti flowed, and the conversation was always punctuated by bursts of laughter. Her uncles, Sal and Joey, her cousins, all gone. She'd never see them again. Carmine, always so full of fun, gone too. She remembered how he always made her the most magnificent birthday cake every single year when her dad took her there for her birthday. And most of all, her father. Dead.

She went to her bag and found her old sim card. George had given her a new one last week once the texts started coming from home. She should have destroyed it, he had told her to do that, but something had stopped her. She fiddled with the tiny drawer on the side of the phone, took out the new sim, and replaced her old one. It took a minute or two to reboot and then she put in her old pin. The phone began buzzing immediately: thirty-seven new messages, voicemails, whatsapp messages. She opened her inbox, scrolling through messages from Antonio, from Adrianna, from her Uncle Sal even, all asking the same thing.

'Where are u?'

'We're worried, call us.'

'We need to talk.'

Eventually there was a message from Dad. He didn't text, said he hated that technology but that wasn't true; he just didn't trust writing anything down. The vast majority of his conversations were in person and in private. She looked at the date: it was the day of the wedding. Last Saturday.

'Principessa, I don't understand. If you didn't want to marry Antonio, why didn't you say? I thought we were close, please call me. I love you, nothing is so bad we can't fix it. Daddy xx'

She remembered the video clip of the fury on his face as he left the church. That message was warm and kind. Which was the truth? She'd never know now.

She continued scrolling. More of the same, nothing new. One or two from cousins she rarely spoke to, but she heard the command of her father in them all. He was trying to get her to contact someone, anyone. There was no recrimination, no mention of Declan apart from that first message from Adrianna.

She got to the end and then there was another message, from a number she didn't recognize. Sent yesterday.

'Lucia, it's not safe for you here. Stay away. They are trying to trap you into coming back. They know everything about you and Declan and they know you are in Ireland but not where exactly. Don't speak to any of them, your father is controlling everyone. Emmanualla.'

Lucia read the message several times. Her mother had never said that many words to her since she was a child. Was it part of the trap? Why would she warn her if it was though, unless they thought she'd call her mother back, trust her? She looked for a message from

Declan, which she knew wasn't there. He knew she had a new sim card so if he was going to contact her at all it would be on that.

She swapped the sims again and turned up the sound on the TV.

'...now that Sacco and the consigliore are no longer a feature of the organized crime on the East Coast, someone else will undoubtedly seek to occupy the space once filled by them,' the expert was saying. Lucia was transfixed.

'It has emerged since the shootout that there was some sort of history between Sacco and several other families, that they were either associates or friends or bitter enemies, nobody knows for sure. But what do you predict will happen now, Dr Leytonstone?'

'Well, an incident such as this is unprecedented, even within the notoriously quarrelsome East Coast mob families, but yes, you're right. Within crime circles it was widely believed that Sacco and his family was trying to dominate the East Coast, and in particular, the New York narcotics market. As you point out, they are dead, so the entire thing is in a state of flux. We'll just have to wait and see...'

The flight touched down in Shannon, and Declan walked blearily to the passport control area. He was surrounded by a combination of excited Americans on vacation in Ireland and Irish coming home. He caught a glimpse of himself in the glass of the arrivals doors. He looked awful, unshaven, hollow-eyed. He just wanted to get to Lucia, ensure she was ok, and then sleep.

His phone beeped with messages the moment he turned it on. Lucia used to laugh at him with his old-style phone. It had no internet or fancy apps but it made and received calls and texts, and that was all he needed.

Lucia. 'Declan, please call me. I'm so worried.'

Eddie. 'Call when you get back, I'll pick you up.'

Instantly he pressed call.

'Declan?'

'Yes, it's me, thanks, Eddie.'

'Where are you?'

'Just landed in Shannon but you don't have to, I can rent a car—'

'I'm on the way. Be outside in twenty minutes.'

Declan felt relieved. One problem less. He texted Lucia. He had no idea what was happening, who was watching him, or interpreting his communications. He sighed. He was probably paranoid but this sudden projection into the world the Saccos and the FBI inhabited made him so jumpy. He didn't want to be too specific in his text but he wanted to reassure her.

'Am ok. Back here. See you soon. Phone off. xxx'

He walked through arrivals with ease. Irish airports made him smile. You could get from your seat on the plane to your car in fifteen minutes.

Eddie was at the welcoming area. .

'You ok?'

'Yeah. Exhausted, but ok.'

'Well, it worked I suppose.' Eddie said nothing about Declan's face.

'What do you mean?'

'Don't you know? I suppose you must have been flying, here.' He handed Declan a smartphone and he opened the internet search engine and typed Paulie Sacco.

The entire story opened up in front of him and he read in silence and with mounting horror the events that unfolded as he flew across the Atlantic. He felt sick. There was no triumph, or even relief, just disgust at what he had initiated. On and on he read, each word torture. They were all dead, and he had been the one to initiate it.

'Come on, let's get out of here.' Eddie led him away from the main arrivals area. 'I was planning on driving you to Cork but my car is out of action. A parishioner works here so he gave me a lift up. I was thinking we can rent one and I'll drive and then I can return it. Ok?'

Declan was too traumatized to respond with more than, 'Sure, ok.'

Eddie went to the car rental desk and within minutes they were crossing the parking lot to a nondescript silver car.

Eddie seemed to understand that Declan just couldn't speak.

As Eddie eased out into the early morning traffic Declan was lost in his thoughts.

This was his doing. Dias did as Declan wanted and confronted Paulie and something went wrong, or went right or... He didn't know anymore. Paulie dead. The others, by the sounds of it, were all dead as well and he had their blood on his hands. He thought of the cross hanging over the altar in his church back in Jersey. The symbol of Jesus's sacrifice for mankind. He closed his eyes. He felt so lost and alone. He couldn't pray, he never could face God, if he even existed, again.

Across the cities of New York and New Jersey mothers, grand-mothers, children were inconsolable because their loved ones were dead. He realized with a gut-wrenching pain that one of those chil-dren was Lucia. Paulie was her father and now he was gone, and Declan was the reason why. What on earth was he thinking? The events of the last forty-eight hours were surreal. His epiphany in the church, the meeting with Dias, everything seemed like a horror film playing over and over in his head. *But this was what you wanted*, the mantra kept appearing in his thoughts, *you set this up*. How could he have thought this was a solution? He was supposed to be a priest of God, at least he used to be, and a man of honour, and here he was, behaving like a mobster himself.

His father always said, 'You lie down with dogs, you're gonna get fleas,' when talking about the crooked builders who bribed city hall for contracts, something he refused to do. He said he wanted to be able to sleep with a clear conscience, and he urged his son to do the same. To be upright and honest in all his dealings, even if it meant losing out sometimes, a clear conscience was worth the price. He should have never allowed himself to get so involved with the Saccos. Their poison was contagious and he'd caught the disease. He was in no position now to judge them, he was just like them.

His reverie of misery and self-loathing was interrupted by a buzzing sound. His phone on silent was vibrating in his bag. He thought he'd switched it off but obviously not. Lucia's name was flashing on and off on the screen. Lucia, his darling girl, it seemed like a lifetime ago since he'd seen her. She was carrying his child, they were safe now, safe to live their lives. He needed time before he could speak to her. If he answered now, he doubted he would even get any words out of his mouth.

When the phone stopped ringing, he texted. 'Can't talk now. Am ok. Hope you are too. I'll see you in a few hours. Everything is going to be ok.'

He pressed send and hoped that was true. Maybe she'd had second thoughts. She knew about what he planned to do but not that it had actually happened. Now that her father and all her family were dead, maybe she thought differently.

Eddie spoke for the first time, 'We'll be in Cork in about two hours I'd say.'

'I…thanks…I…I'm…' He couldn't get the words out.

'Are you all right, Declan?'

'Yes, well, no actually, I don't know to be honest…'

'Ok, start at the beginning, treat it as a confession so I am bound to secrecy, talk to me as if you were talking to God himself, and leave out nothing.'

Declan didn't know where to start, but somehow the entire story tumbled out. He found himself unable to stop talking; the words poured from his lips in a torrent of fear, frustration, horror, and self-loathing. He told him everything, about the conversation with Dias, the realization he'd had in the church, the entire miserable tale.

'It's over now, it's done,' Eddie spoke quietly. 'Do you want to be absolved of your sins?'

Declan put his head in his hands, resting his elbows on his knees. 'I'm not sure if absolution is even a thing, to be honest, Eddie, and even if it was, then I am definitely not deserving of it. I don't think I believe any of it anymore. I have done a terrible thing, I've orchestrated countless deaths, I've let my parents down, I've let the church down, people, some really good decent people, trusted me and I betrayed their trust so I'm not worthy of their forgiveness either.'

Eddie kept his eyes on the road, then spoke.

'I don't have all the answers, Declan, I don't think anyone has. But I do know this: you didn't pull any trigger. I know you blame yourself and that this Dias character wouldn't have gone there and done what he did if you hadn't told him what you did, but at the end of the day they are all in this position by choice. It is the free will of each of those men to do what they do. They choose it, and not just once, but every day of their lives. You manipulated their hatred to turn them against each other, but they were in that position where they could be manipulated, by their own actions. They live lives of crime and bring untold misery into the lives of countless people by their actions; you don't. You've only ever tried to do good in the world, so no, you are not like them.'

He took a sip of coffee.

'As for your family, and your parents and all of that, well, I don't know you well but I think if you were a son of mine, I'd be proud of you. It was brave what you did. Anything could have happened but you did it to save Lucia and yourself and your child a life of fear and dread.'

Declan desperately wanted to believe what he was being told, but he couldn't.

'I wish I could say I should never have met her, then I'd still be working in my parish, doing what I should be doing, but I would be lying if I said that. I love her, but now, maybe it's different. What if she's changed her mind? He was her father and a part of her loves him still, despite everything. What if she can't forgive me for orchestrating his death? I wouldn't blame her. She could have anyone, you know. Not just a mob guy but anyone, she's beautiful and kind and generous and she wanted me. God knows why but she did and what have I given her? Nothing but pain and grief. I should have left her alone, maybe if I had, I'd still be a priest, still doing some good...'

Eddie sighed deeply.

'Ah now, would you listen to yourself? Wallowing. Pull yourself together, Declan, or you'll be neither use nor ornament to that girl. Lucia is with you because she loves you, and in a few short months you two are going to be a family so you need to focus on that. Forget about the *should* and *could* and think about what is. This has happened over and over, and the ones who fare best in my opinion are those who put their minds to the job at hand. Do you think you're the first man of the cloth to be turned? Of course you're not. 'Tis a ridiculous law in my opinion, but the lads over in Rome don't want our minds taken off the job I suppose. Or maybe they don't want to be paying out for our widows and children when we go, I don't know, but I do know that if they'd let us get married like men are supposed to there'd be far fewer problems. I mean, when a couple come in to me as their priest, asking for help, their marriage is in trouble, what in the name of God can I say? I haven't a clue and I don't know what it's like to have kids to rear, and bills to pay, and all the rest of it. Whereas if I'd a wife of my own, and I'd gone through the troubles that every marriage faces, then I might be of some use.'

'Did you ever consider it?' Declan was fascinated by the candour with which he spoke.

'So, did I ever feel tempted? Are you seriously asking me that?'

His blue eyes bored into Declan's for a second before returning his attention to the road ahead.

'Well, I…' Declan was afraid he'd insulted him.

'Of course I was, and anyone who says he wasn't is lying. What the church don't want to see is that while we are men of God surely, we are just men as well. With all the same needs and desires and all the rest of it as any other fella walking the road. I look at friends of mine, Conor O'Shea for example, he and I often go for a pint, though he's not a religious man at all, and I see the way his life has been transformed by Ana and the boys, and I wonder if I could have had something like that. I see other, older fellas, my age now, and they tell me about their grandchildren and their kids and all of that, and despite all the years of bills and fights and worry, they'd not change a thing. When they die, their families will cry for them, because they love them and they'll miss them. When I go, I'll get the full treatment, they'll be falling over each other up on the altar to concelebrate the mass, but will there be a single genuine tear of loss? Not at all. So, yes I did consider it, on more than one occasion. I loved someone once.'

His voice had dropped both in volume and in tone; it was as if he was being transported back in time.

'What was her name?' Declan asked.

'Maggie…she was a widow and we were very close, in a parish I was in before this one. I…I asked to be moved.'

219

'Did you not love her enough?' Declan was gentle.

'I did.' Eddie never took his eyes off the road. 'But I loved God more.'

Declan knew he didn't love God or anyone more than Lucia, and in that moment all the guilt he had felt dissipated.

CHAPTER 25

*A*s the car ate up the miles, they talked about everything. The baby, his romance with Lucia, his feelings at leaving the priesthood, the sex scandals in the church. They were completely at ease with each other, and the honesty was so refreshing after all the secrets and lies. He allowed himself to talk about him or her properly for the first time. Becoming a father was not something he'd ever considered; it had been something for others, and he would be there to support and minister and baptize and give communion to other people's children. The idea that one of them would be his own genuinely never crossed his mind. Non-clergy friends often asked him over the years how he coped with the whole celibacy thing.

Eddie grinned when he said, 'Conor always used to ask me the same thing. It's obviously something that most men couldn't bear the idea of.'

Declan explained that he could say with complete conviction that it didn't bother him, not in any real sense. In the same way as he viewed children, women were for others. His role was as confessor, as priest, as confidante sometimes, but never as a lover. He liked women, he had loved his mother, he even had friends who were women when he was a younger man, but before Lucia he wasn't ever close to any other women romantically. Once or twice over the years, opportunities might have presented themselves, but he was never tempted. A parishioner, a few years back, had tried to get a little amorous one evening. Declan suspected a philandering husband and too many cocktails were more the driving force than his charm and sex appeal, so he gently extricated himself and never referred to the incident again. She never brought it up either; she probably didn't remember it.

He realized as the car sped along the quiet Irish roads that God, for him, had become a fantasy where Lucia was real. A part of him hoped that his faith would return, once the shock of the Dias and Sacco episode dissipated, but so far it hadn't. He'd never thought faith was like that, like turning on a switch, or indeed turning it off for that matter. The irony of that realization wasn't lost on him; he would be a much better priest now, if he were to continue, because up to now, he didn't really understand people who said they would like to believe but they just didn't. He thought it was just a matter of submitting to the Lord's grace and His love would wash over you and sanctify you. But now he knew, it wasn't that simple. You can't make yourself believe something any more than you can make yourself feel something.

'Did you ever doubt it, Eddie? God, all of it?' Declan asked.

'I don't think so. No, I can't say I ever did. I often times wished it wasn't the case, that we could just go off and do whatever we liked, but I've always known God is there. I suppose, I'm not as convinced on some of the rules though, you know?'

'I do.' Declan nodded.

As he gazed out the window, Eddie put some classical music on the radio. He sensed Declan needed to be alone with his thoughts.

He loved Lucia, not as a priest but as a man. She was so beautiful to him, his physical longing for her was overwhelming sometimes, but the more he thought about it, he loved the idea of making a family with her, of pushing their baby in a stroller along the sidewalk to the park to feed the ducks and get ice cream. It was like that part of the world, the parents, the husbands and wives, were in an exclusive club, with membership rules that made his entry impossible. Now, though, he could qualify, and he found he desperately wanted to join.

If she forgave him for what he did, then he would have to find a way to support his family. It struck him as ridiculous that a thirty-five-year-old man had never considered that reality before. He worked for God, through the church, and they provided everything he needed. A house, his bills paid, a car, and a little pocket money each month, most of which stayed in the bank. The parishioners were so generous, cooking meals for him, and Sister Bernadine always knitted him warm sweaters for the winter. He wore clerical collar every day, though he only wore the black at parish functions. Mostly he wore jeans and a light-coloured shirt that allowed him to clip in his collar. Some of the older parishioners remarked upon it when he arrived first, but since he was very casual in his approach to everything they were used to it by now. They'd started calling him Fr Sullivan but he insisted on using his first name so generally he was just Declan or Father Declan. He went to the bar down the street to watch the Giants games, he got his groceries in the Chinese store two blocks away. He loved the feel of his neighborhood; it was multicultural and vibrant, and he felt at home there.

More and more of his brother priests had opted for lay-person clothes in the wake of the sex scandals that rocked the church, fearful of the public reaction. Eddie said it was the same over here, but not for him. He was a priest and he said he wasn't going to hide behind sweaters with logos of fellas playing golf. Declan had laughed at the image. He told Eddie the story of one elderly parish priest in Long Island who had been devastated when he started up a conversation with a child on the subway. The kid's parents were sitting either side of him and when he tried to engage the child, he replied in a loud voice, 'You are a stranger and a priest, I'm not supposed to talk to you and I'm not going anywhere with you and anything you do to me I'll tell my dad and the cops.' The script was obviously learned by heart and while apparently the parents had the good grace to look a little embarrassed, they also shared a conspiratorial glance of congratulation; they had protected their child.

The priest on the subway had to admit that the parents were probably right, but it sure made life hard for the vast majority who were not pedophiles, and who were disgusted and horrified to hear of the abuses. The old man never wore his priest's garb again outside of church after that.

It saddened Declan beyond words to see the way things had gone, but the reality was that these people were operating in the fifties, sixties, seventies, and eighties, probably even before that, when no checks and balances were in place. Nowadays everyone was aware of child protection, nobody could have any contact with kids without being fully vetted, and kids themselves were so much more aware. He and Eddie both wished the church response had been different, more honest, open. That they would give up the information the authorities so badly needed to secure convictions, to provide adequate support and counseling for the victims of these people, but they didn't. He used to love the church, knowing it was flawed but still an institution made up of good people. He still believed that, but there was a dark heart to the Catholic Church. Not among the rank-and-file faithful, nor the priests that served them, but deep in the centre of power. The church had proven to be chameleon-like over the centuries, appearing to change to suit the mores of the day but not really shifting, not fundamentally. That's why they survived and prospered through the centuries, he supposed; still, it made it hard to defend. Eddie said he felt the same way but that for him the church wasn't Rome and the Pope and all the pomp and ceremony. For him the church was the First Holy Communion class in the local primary school, who were singing songs and drawing pictures to decorate the church on their big day. It was the flower committee, the elderly people who attend mass every morning to pray, but also to see their neighbours; it might be the only human contact they get all day if they live alone. Declan could see his point, but he was angry at the powers that controlled all of those good people, and have the audacity to point out their wrongdoing when the sins of the church itself are gargantuan by comparison. He was glad at least that part of his life was over, trying to defend the indefensible.

He had a degree in theology and history; perhaps teaching might be open to him? Probably not in a Catholic school, a defrocked priest wouldn't be the image they're going for, but maybe in a public school. Lucia would probably like to finish her degree, so maybe they could have someone look after the baby while he worked and she studied.

He wondered if the baby was going to be a boy or a girl. Navigating the future as a child with Sacco blood in his or her veins was going to be complicated as well, unless they moved far away. There was so much to think about, so many possible permutations.

CHAPTER 26

*S*he was pleasantly surprised at how tiny the airport was. It reminded her of home. She showed her passport and smiled her thanks when the man standing beside her at the carousel dragged her huge suitcase off the belt.

'Thank you.' She smiled and watched him redden with pleasure as his wife struggled to pull her own case off, looking none too pleased.

She would need to rent a car. She rarely drove anywhere, the chauffeur brought her wherever she needed to go, and she wasn't used to driving on the left side of the road, but she would do this. She had to.

She approached a car rental desk.

'I want to rent a car please.' She smiled at the young man.

'Well that's what we do, have you a booking?' He grinned and winked.

'No, I didn't have time.'

'No bother, but it might be a bit dearer, y'know. You get the best deals on the auld internet.'

She found his accent hard to make out but she thought she understood him.

'The cost doesn't matter, but I need something not too big. I'm not used to driving on the left.'

'Right oh. So, can you drive a shift or does it have to be automatic?' he asked.

'I'm Italian,' she replied smoothly, 'of course I can drive a shift.'

'I'd say nothing gets past you, does it?' Again with the winking. She wondered if he was a little slow.

'Now, your passport and your credit card please.' He held out his hand and she handed them over.

'Now then, is it Mrs or Miss?' He glanced at her hand, bejeweled except for the ring finger.

'Miss,' she replied, growing weary. 'If you could do this as quickly as possible, I would be grateful.' She opened her wallet pointedly, showing several green bills.

'Right so, now, what kind of insurance do you want?'

'Just the regular kind will be fine,' she replied.

'Well, there's no such thing really as that. Like, with each policy there's an excess to be paid in the event of you damaging the car or someone else's car for that matter, so how much you pay now for the insurance will decide how much excess you have to pay.'

He explained, 'Like, driving here can be tricky enough if you're not used to it, d'ya know what I mean? Very small roads and fellas driving like lunatics and auld wans with no licenses, my granny for example, never did a driving test at all. There was so many people applied in the year she was supposed to do the test they just gave everyone a license. We make her ring us when she's going driving so we can all stay at home, she's a nutter so she is, and all her mates the same. Mental!' He cackled loudly at the prospect of elderly road hogs terrorizing Ireland's tiny roads.

He slid a laminated sheet across the counter. 'Take a look at that there, and sure, decide yourself. The cheapest one there has a five hundred Euro excess and only third party cover, the second one then has an excess of three fifty and has fully comp on your vehicle but only third party on the second vehicle except in the case where...'

The sheet was covered in legal jargon. Full of articles and part 4 and section a, in the event of, refer to section F1…she was exhausted even looking at it.

He pointed to the bottom of the sheet, the most expensive insurance. Maybe it was easier and she'd get away from this kid faster if she paid the highest premium.

'What do I get with that one?'

A broad grin spread across the young man's face that told her this was definitely a commission job.

'For that, madam, you can bring the car back in a plastic bag.'

As he clicked and processed the payment he was determined to chat. She desperately wanted to get away. The urgency that she felt since the night in Carmine's had not dissipated; she needed to get to Lucia.

'So where you headed, or are you just spinning around the place, see where you wind up?' her tormentor asked, the grin even wider.

'Cork.'

'Ah, great spot that, I was there last weekend with the auld doll and a few of the lads, mad craic it was. You should go to The Deep South pub, they have a savage cider there, some fella up the country making it out of apples and magic mushrooms or something, you'd be demented altogether on it, and cheap out too, they were doing a deal on pints of it, some kind of promotion, though that might be finished now,' he added with regret.

'Well, that would be a great pity but I'm sure I'll enjoy it anyway.' She smiled. The kid was harmless really and the idea that he thought a lady of her ilk would enjoy becoming 'demented' on some kind of homemade discounted hooch entertained her.

'Ah you will, and at least now if you give the car a few clatters on the way home some night, it won't matter a bit; you're covered!' This information seemed to bring him great joy as he clicked his fingers and gave her a thumbs-up.

'Great,' she responded, and since the kid seemed to expect it, she gave him a thumbs-up in return.

CHAPTER 27

The two-hour drive to Cork passed in a blur. He was sure that in other circumstances he'd be enthralled by the beautiful scenery, but all he could think about was seeing Lucia. He wondered for the millionth time how she was. He knew she was hurt and appalled at her father's life, and she was under no illusion any more as to what kind of man he was, but he was her father, and he'd never really shown her that side of him, the ruthless, psychopathic side. She'd heard it from Declan but never seen it with her own eyes.

Sure, he'd been enraged when she failed to show up at her wedding, but what traditional Italian father wouldn't be? He'd behaved exactly as many other fathers would, even in this day and age.

They stopped at a hotel on the way and used the restroom. He looked at himself in the mirror, thinking she'd be mad to want to have anything to do with him. He looked appalling, his face was going black and blue where Roberto had landed that killer punch, and his whole chest and abdomen ached. Eddie had given him some painkillers but they weren't touching it. He had lost so much weight and his hair was so much greyer than it had been a few months ago.

Eddie used the sat nav and found the hotel effortlessly. It seemed that every building in the town of Kinsale was dedicated in some way to serving the clearly thriving tourist industry. It wasn't surprising, the place was heartbreakingly beautiful. Patchwork green hills, ruined castles and forts jutting out of the headlands as below the boats in the blue harbour tinkled their riggings. It was lunchtime and several people were milling about the town, on bikes, walking, holding little kids by the hands. As he drove down the main street, he wondered if Lucia was in the hotel or out on a tour for the day. The itinerary said they were going to Cork City for a tour and to visit the University there. There were ogham stones in the corridors there, the ancient pre-Christian writing carved along the edges of tall rocks. He would have loved to have seen them himself; maybe he and Lucia could take the baby back there someday.

Part of him hoped she'd gone out with Conor for the day, but another part hoped she was in the hotel. The thought of waiting even longer would send him over the edge. The hotel was large and looked like an old manor house with a turning circle in front. Eddie followed the signs for the car park to the rear of the hotel.

He sat for a moment. Suddenly scared to face her.

Lucia was a devout person. Her faith was so much a part of who she was that it wasn't something that she could just remove, cut out, like he had. He needed to tell her before they discussed anything else. It could well be a deal-breaker for her. She'd loved him when he was a man of deep faith and conviction, and now that he wasn't, things might be different. He got out of the car and wished he could get showered and cleaned up before he saw her. He looked terrible and doubted he smelled much better, but he needed to see her.

'I'll leave you to it. Just be honest and you'll be grand. You have my number.' Eddie was gentle but firm; it was time to see her and tell her everything.

CHAPTER 28

*L*ucia lay on the bed staring at the ceiling. At least the baby-related nausea was gone. Whatever Conor's wife had given her really worked, even if it tasted vile. Her father was probably being buried in the next few days. She would be expected to go, to be there, beside her mother, a woman she barely knew, to grieve for a man they had complicated feelings for. She thought again about her mother's text, warning her. Should she contact her? She wished Declan was here; she needed him. She needed to talk through the events of the past two days with someone who understood. She tried to process what she felt; she'd done little else since the news sunk in. He was gone, dead, and so were her uncles, Sal and Joey. Sal had always made her laugh when she was little, throwing her up in the air and catching her in his big bear arms, and Joey liked to talk to her about books. He'd never admit to his brothers but he was actually a bookworm, loved reading thrillers and stories of political intrigue. Though they weren't her choice, she'd talked to him about his favourite writers and what made them great. He was quietly spoken and gentle in his manner; she couldn't imagine him doing the kinds of thing she knew he did. It was like they were all Jekyll and Hyde characters, her father most of all.

She knew that on some level she must grieve—he was her father, whatever else he was, and that must mean something, but it didn't. She only felt relief; it meant he couldn't hurt anyone anymore. He couldn't hurt Declan. She looked at her watch again. Four pm. Where was he?

The tour was due to end the day after tomorrow. She thought that maybe she should go home, be there for the funeral, say her good-byes, but then she knew her father's funeral would be a media circus. His daughter couldn't pass through JFK or La Guardia unnoticed, and now that the bump was beginning to show, well, that would be tabloid manna from heaven. She decided to suggest to Declan that they stay on in Ireland until after the funeral at least. No information about it had been released yet, and she'd had almost no contact with anyone in the family. She decided to put her old sim into her phone again. She didn't know why exactly, but she wanted to feel some way connected. The phone flashed with more messages. Some from college people who'd heard on the news about the shootout, and one or two from family, but then she scrolled down to another from her mother.

'Lucia, I really hope you're safe and well. Don't come back for the funeral, it won't help anyone. He's gone now, and that's the end of it. Take care of yourself. I hope you find happiness, *Dio ti benedica*. Mama.xxx'

Lucia cried when she read it—tears for the relationships she should have had with her parents but that she now never would. She considered replying, she even wrote a few words, but nothing seemed adequate so she left it unanswered. It was much too late now to try to salvage a relationship with her mother. In many ways her father was to blame for that as well, always running his wife down, or simply ignoring her throughout Lucia's life. Whenever a decision was to be made, a question to be asked, advice sought, it was to her father she went, never her mother. Her mother rejected her emotionally because she saw her as Paulie's daughter only. He certainly behaved as if he was the only parent she had. She wondered why he did that, to make himself more important than his wife in his only child's life she supposed. If she and Declan got to raise this child together, then they would be equal partners, both loving and being loved by the child equally. She would do everything differently: no private tutors, no decadence, just an ordinary happy childhood, with decent, law-abiding parents who loved each other. That was her fervent wish for the new life growing inside her, but nothing was certain.

Apart from those two messages to say he was ok and would be in touch soon, she'd not heard from him. She longed to know what was happening, but she knew he'd get there as soon as he could.

She sighed deeply. At least she felt safe here in this beautiful country with its merry people. She had never even considered Ireland; she'd seen movies and all of that, but it had never occurred to her to visit. Some latent racism against the Irish passed on by her father no doubt, he'd never had anything good to say about them, but she realized she loved it here, despite the terrible circumstances. She felt safe, here on the edge of the world. Most importantly, she wasn't anyone of interest. She wasn't Paulie Sacco's daughter. A thought occurred to her, that maybe they could stay here. Raise their child, get a job, a little house by the sea, and live simply.

The knock on the door startled her. It was probably Conor checking up on her. The group had gone sightseeing today, but she wanted to stay close to the hotel so Declan could find her should he need to.

She dragged herself from the bed and opened the door.

'Hello, Lucia.'

She couldn't speak, long seconds passed before she flung her arms around him and drew him into the room, closing the door behind him. She cried silent tears as she clung to him, he comforting her, rubbing her back, letting her cry. Eventually her tears subsided.

She looked at him as he winced when she hugged him. 'Oh my God, you're hurt, what happened? Did he hurt you?' Her fingers went to his swollen face, seeing it for the first time.

'I'm ok, a few cuts and bruises, but I'm fine. I'll explain everything.'

'Are you sure, he didn't shoot you…'

'No, nothing like that…honestly.'

'Ok, I can't believe you're here. It's over, Declan, it's all over, he's dead, and all the others, most anyway, are gone too, we're safe...' The words tumbled out of her, one crowding out the other.

'I know, my love, I know.' As she reached up to kiss him, he stepped back, out of her embrace. The hurt confusion on her face broke his heart.

'What's the matter?' she asked, dread filling her. She had talked herself into the fact that she would have to accept his decision to return to the priesthood, but now that he was here in front of her, she just couldn't bring herself to let him go.

'Lucia, we have to talk. There are things I want you to know and I need you to listen while I tell you, ok? Please, I just have to talk to you first...'

'Are you finishing with me, is that it? Are you going back to the priesthood? Just say it if you are, don't try to rationalize it, just say it and go.'

'Lucia! Stop, please, just sit down, and listen.' He led her to the bed and sat her down, choosing another chair opposite for himself. He needed to be physically removed from her to tell the story.

He began at the beginning and told her the whole thing, leaving nothing out, and she sat in silence, allowing him to speak uninterrupted. Even when he told her about the realization in the church in Philadelphia, the meeting with Dias, Roberto's threat, the conversation with Eddie, everything. He took full responsibility for the shootout. She knew of his plan but now that it had been executed; maybe she felt differently.

Eventually he stopped talking and the room was quiet. She looked at him, her face inscrutable.

She'd never looked lovelier to him, and he tried but failed to avert his eyes from the slight swell in her abdomen. Eventually she spoke.

'My father is dead because he was the boss of an organized crime family. He dealt in drugs and that's a dangerous business to be in. You're not responsible, Declan, not in my eyes.'

The moments ticked by.

'And what about the other thing, the fact that I don't believe in God anymore? Can you love a man who doesn't share your beliefs? I know how much your faith means to you, you can't just turn it off like a faucet.'

'Are you asking me to do that? To turn my back on my faith?' she asked, her eyes locked to his.

'No, of course not, but I don't believe, I really don't. I don't think there's anything out there. It's just us here on this earth, randomly, no great scheme.'

'But that's your belief, and you are entitled to believe whatever you want. I do believe in God and I won't change, but we are individuals. We don't have to hold the same opinions on everything. Do you love me? Us?' she asked.

'More than anything in the world.' She heard the exhaustion in his voice.

Lucia moved closer to him, standing right beside him now as he remained seated, drew his head onto her belly, and rubbed his hair soothingly.

'Just because you don't believe in God doesn't mean He doesn't believe in you. You might change your mind, and maybe you never will, but that has no bearing on how I feel about you. You're a good man, Declan Sullivan, a kind, honest, decent man, and I love you with all my heart, no matter what you think you've done or what you do or don't believe. I think you'll be a wonderful husband and father. If that's what you still want, then so do I.'

She led him to the bed and they lay there together, his arms wrapped around his family.

They fell into a relaxed sleep, their first in over a week, and so it took several rings before the hotel phone woke Declan. Blearily he lifted the receiver.

'I'm sorry, Mr Sullivan, but there's someone here to see you.' The young receptionist's voice gave no indication who it might be.

Declan's heart thumped in his chest. Who was it? Had Dias sent someone? But no, if Dias had ordered a hit, he'd hardly call the person down to reception. He tried to think straight. Lucia was fast asleep beside him.

'What is his name?' Declan asked.

'It's a lady, sir, one moment.' He could hear a murmured conversation and then she was back on the line.

'It's a Ms Emmanualla Favone?'

Declan took a moment to process it. Emmanualla? There was only one Emmanualla he knew and that was Lucia's mother. She'd told him about the texts she'd sent; was she actually downstairs? And if so what did she want?

'I'm on my way. Thanks,' he said and threw off the covers.

Lucia woke, sitting upright suddenly.

'What? What is it? Please, Declan.' She looked so young, her hair in waves around her head, her hand to her mouth in fear.

'Lucia, I think your mother is downstairs.'

'What? My mother? What?' She was totally perplexed.

'Well, reception just called to say Emmanualla Favone was downstairs looking to speak to us. Look, you stay here and I'll go down. If it's her then—'

'No. I'm coming too, wait for me.' Lucia bounded out of bed, throwing on the clothes she'd worn yesterday. Once they were both dressed they went downstairs. It was dinner time and several people were milling around the lobby, but Lucia saw her instantly. Her rich nut-brown hair was drawn up in an elegant chignon, diamonds glittering in her ears. She wore a cream Valentino suit and black crocodile high-heeled shoes. Despite her diminutive five-foot frame, she attracted considerable attention. Declan had only seen glimpses of her over the years, but now he could see where Lucia got her looks. The woman looked like Audrey Hepburn, and though she must be at least forty, she looked not much older than Lucia.

Declan hung back as Lucia approached her.

'Mama?' She was tentative.

'Ah Lucia, can we talk?'

'Of course, maybe come to our room?' She glanced back at Declan, whether to indicate to him he should come or stay down here, he was unsure.

'Of course, hello, Father Sullivan.' She extended her tiny hand and he took it.

'Mrs Sacco.' He nodded.

She smiled and her face seemed to radiate a warm glow. Lucia realized how rarely, if ever, she'd seen her mother smile.

'Perhaps we should begin again, how about with Declan and Emmanualla? I think we are both people who have some issues with our previous titles, no?'

Declan nodded. 'No problem. If you'd like to follow me?' He caught Lucia's eye, trying to figure out what she wanted him to do.

They walked in silence down the carpeted corridor. A million conflicting thoughts crowded Lucia's mind. Was her mother there to see her of her own volition? Or was she sent by someone? If so, who? Was she in danger? What did she want? And then the deeper questions, the ones she'd never allowed in. Why did her mother reject her? Was she so hard to love? What happened between her and Dad? Was it all her fault? Once they reached the door, Lucia turned to him. 'Could you give us a moment please, Declan? I... We...'

'Of course, I'll be downstairs. Just have reception call me.' He was worried; what if she was the one sent to harm them? But he instantly dismissed that thought. It was ridiculous; even if she was sent by someone, what could she do at this late stage?

The two women entered the room. The unmade bed, the remains of a room service meal, and a variety of their clothes were scattered around. Lucia made a vain effort to tidy up.

'Please, Lucia. Sit.' Her mother sat on the chair in the bay window of the hotel room and indicated with her hand that Lucia should sit opposite. Obediently she did as her mother expected.

'You must be wondering what on earth I'm doing here.' Emmanualla put her very expensive-looking handbag on the floor at her feet, and despite the steadiness of her voice, Lucia noticed her hands couldn't stay still. Unaware she was doing it, her mother twisted a ring round and round on her finger.

'Yes. Yes, I am. I know you sent me those texts and to be honest, I didn't know what to think.' Lucia tried to hide all the pain that threatened to destroy her resolve to keep it together. She thought of her baby, not even born yet, and the fierce love and need to protect him or

237

her that she felt, and looking now at her own mother, well, her failings seemed even more pronounced.

'I can't blame you. Not to trust me, why would you?' Her almost black eyes rested on her daughter's face, and the busy fingers stopped twisting the ring.

She sighed heavily, the weight of the world on her shoulders.

'I am going back to Italy, I belong there. And now, after everything that has happened, I cannot stay any longer in the United States. Now that your father is dead, I can go back without shaming my family. Before, no matter how much I wanted to, I couldn't do it.'

Her voice, low and gravelly, was American, with the vaguest hint of her Sicilian past.

'Did you always want to go back?' Lucia knew it was a loaded question. She wasn't enquiring as to what country her mother preferred; she was asking her why she wanted to leave her only child.

'Yes. I could lie to you, Lucia, tell you that I didn't dream of going home every minute of every day, but there have been enough lies. Now, it is the time for truth. I owe it to you; you deserve it.'

'Ok, go ahead, I'm listening.' Lucia was relieved to hear her voice steady, betraying none of the turmoil she felt.

'As you know, I am Sicilian and my brothers Marco and Pietro ran Palermo. They needed a contact, family really, in America to expand their empire, and so I was sold.'

Her words had the impact she expected as Lucia responded with incredulity, 'Sold?'

'Yes. Sold, for money. My father was dead. My mother begged them, said I was too young, that I didn't know this man, but Marco was adamant and Pietro backed him on everything, so I was sold to Paulie Sacco. The deal was, Sacco paid money and he got connected to all the Italian families. It gave him credentials not just in Europe but also with other families all across the United States. It was a formidable alliance, to join with the Favones. The Saccos were big then but not like they were up to recent times. It was the alliance with my family that made him strong, and he knew even then how invaluable that would be so he was happy to pay. I was just to cement

238

the alliance; I was nothing, just a pawn, and not even an important one.'

Lucia couldn't think of anything to say. How horrific that a young girl would be treated just as a commodity. She couldn't have imagined her father doing something like that, despite all she knew of him.

'So you had to go through with it?' Lucia tried to inject kindness into the words.

'Yes, the marriage, the move to New York, everything.' Emmanualla sounded tired.

'And then you had me?'

Her mother looked deeply into her eyes before speaking.

'Yes. He, your father, didn't even come to meet me at the airport, he sent Sal. I barely spoke to him until the wedding day. I was dressed and made ready by the wives of other Sacco men and then we got married. That night, I was so scared, and I felt so alone. I waited for him in the hotel bedroom, but he never came up. We returned to the house after the wedding, and it was back to as it was before. He worked all the time, I never saw him, we never spoke. Then one night, one of the women asked me about my monthly cycle, when my period was next due, and I told her. A few days after that, he came in. I had never been with a man before, but my mother had told me what to expect so I tried to be demure as she told me to be.

'He never spoke, not one word, and there was no kissing or anything like I'd seen in movies. He just told me to lie down on the bed and he did it. I just lay there, with him pushing and grunting, and then it was over. He got off me and walked out the door. Two weeks later my period was late and I was pregnant with you.'

Lucia was horrified. She felt sick, thinking of her father in that way, now especially. But a large part of her also felt so sad for that girl from Sicily, so far from everyone and everything she knew, irrevocably tied to a man who didn't love her.

'But you are beautiful. I've seen your wedding picture, you were stunning. Why didn't he want to?' Lucia could barely get the words out.

'I don't know. He never had a *gumar*, you know, a mistress? They all do, their wives know it, but your father never did. At first I thought it was because he might have been in love with someone else, but that's not it. He would never ever have admitted it, but he was homosexual.'

Lucia swallowed. The lump in her throat stayed there; she opened her mouth to speak but nothing came out.

'The pregnancy was fine and then one night you were born. He never came to see you, and he never came to my room again, not since that one night. The labour was hard and I feared I would die, but then the midwife put you in my arms and...' Emmanualla's voice cracked with emotion for the first time. 'And you were so perfect, so beautiful. I loved you instantly. All the loneliness, the misery, the confusion was not important. Just being your mother, that was all that mattered. He arrived and said only one thing. "You can't even do that right, I wanted a boy."

'But then, the midwife, she gave you to him and his face changed. He looked down at you and you opened your eyes and looked straight at him, and he fell in love, maybe for the only time ever in his whole life. He fell so in love with you, I hoped maybe it would be the start of us being a family, even then I wanted it to be ok, but no. He would come and take you away, down to his office, and for hours I wouldn't see you. He wouldn't allow me to feed you, gave you bottles instead, and it was him and you. No room for me. Then as you got older, you would cry when he left you with me again, or when he came into the room, you would instantly raise your arms to have him pick you up. He spent more time with you than I did and there was nothing I could do. I was trapped.'

Lucia knew instinctively that her mother was telling the truth no matter how much she wished it was all a lie. She wanted to do something, say something, but Emmanualla was determined to get her story told so Lucia just listened.

'I found him one night, in his den, watching a pornographic film with three men, when you were just a baby. You'd left your bunny down there and you wouldn't settle without it. Normally I never ventured into his areas of the house but you were inconsolable. I was shocked so I confronted him, asked him straight out if that was why he was such a bad husband. I told him I'd take you back to Palermo. We fought and screamed and I told him I hated him, that I wanted a proper man for my husband, a proper man to be my baby's father, and then he hit me. He beat me up really badly that night, and he said if I ever breathed a word of it to anyone I was a dead woman. That I'd get my wish to go back to Palermo all right, one piece at a time. And to hurt me further, he took you from me. I wasn't allowed to see you, to be anywhere near you. I would watch you play in the garden with the nanny and he would come out and roll on the lawn with you and throw you up in the air till you squealed with delight, but that was as close as I got. It broke my heart to have you so close but not to be allowed to love you. He poisoned you against me, I know he did. And when you came to me, when you were little, asking me to read to you, or speak Siculu to you, he would send a message, that if I wanted to survive I should keep my distance. He would have killed me except for the alliance with my family. He needed me alive, and at his side if necessary, but he hated me because I knew what he was. The more he loved you, the more you loved him back, the deeper it hurt me, and he knew it. That's why I couldn't be your mother.' Emmanualla sat back against the chair, and exhaled. The effort of telling Lucia the truth clearly had drained her. 'I'm so sorry,' she whispered as she finally allowed the tears to fall.

Lucia stood up and went to her mother. The older woman stood as well and they faced each other. All the rejection, the loss, the pain seemed to dissipate. Her mother was just another in the long line of victims of Paulie Sacco's life of hate.

'It's ok...it's not your fault.' Lucia embraced her mother for the first time she could remember, offering comfort and forgiveness. 'It's ok, we'll be ok.' Over and over she said the words as her mother cried in her arms.

All through the night they talked. Declan came back and they ordered some more room service. He was relieved to see that everything seemed to be all right. Emmanualla looked more disheveled than she had, but there was a lightness to her that he'd not seen before. They talked about the baby, and about the future, and while it was still very early days, and there was a lot to try to repair, he felt like there was a chance this baby would have a grandparent after all.

They talked a little about the night in Carmine's. And Declan noticed that Emmanualla was always anxious that Lucia understand how much her father loved her, even though she herself clearly despised the man. She told funny stories about Sal and Joey and the others, knowing how fond Lucia was of them. Lucia was a Sacco, that was the truth, and their blood ran in her veins. She was appalled at what her father and the family did, but she would never *not* be a Sacco. Emmanualla was putting her daughter's feelings ahead of her own, and that boded well for the future.

She assured them that it was a quick visit, but she stayed that night and took a taxi next morning to the airport to catch her next flight to Palermo. Emmanualla's mother was still alive, and even though they spoke on the phone regularly, they'd not seen each other in over twenty years. Emmanualla spoke of her sisters, Julianna and Chiara, as well as her brothers and Lucia's cousins in Palermo, people she'd never even heard of. As her mother left the next morning, Lucia knew they'd see each other soon.

CHAPTER 29

C onor was busy loading the suitcases onto the coach for the last transfer. The group had two nights in Dublin before flying back to the states, but Declan and Lucia had talked and he agreed with her suggestion that they stay on in Ireland for a few weeks, maybe head up to Galway and Mayo to find Declan's family roots. Emmanualla was staying in Italy indefinitely and had issued a genuine invitation to both of them to visit as soon as possible. Lucia was feeling so much better; the nausea was subsiding with each passing hour.

Valentina had been released from hospital and was doing ok so she decided to rejoin the tour. Everyone was thrilled to see her, and she looked so different when she arrived at the hotel with Conor while everyone was at breakfast.

He and Ana had kept in touch with her and they'd even gone to visit her in the hospital. She arrived back wearing jeans and a t-shirt, no jewellery and no makeup. She looked even younger than she had before. The bruises on her face and arms were fading to a purplish-yellow, but she looked so much more relaxed. Tony was in custody and the court deemed him a flight risk in his preliminary hearing so he was remanded in custody until his trial. Valentina had to stay in the country until the case came up as she was the chief witness, but Ana offered her a place to stay with them until then.

'That was really nice of you,' Lucia whispered to Conor as Valentina told of her plans in halting but better English.

'Not at all, it's the least we can do.' He winked and gave her one of his infectious grins.

As they walked out to the bus, he caught up with them again.

'So, how are you two?'

Declan put his arm around Lucia's shoulders.

'We're fine, though I look a bit the worse for wear I'm sure. A very, very long story for another day, but I think we're going to be ok. Conor, thank you so much for everything. I can't imagine what this would have been like without you, and Eddie and Ana and everyone. It's been so surreal but yet…I don't know, like I needed to see that there are good people in the world or something, you know?'

"I do. I'm glad it's all worked out for you. Maybe now you can enjoy the bit of the tour that's left without any drama.' He smiled as he helped Lucia up the step of the bus.

Ken and Irene were sitting happily in the front seat, and Elke and Zoe were farther back. Valentina was talking to a lady from Detroit whose father was Russian and who even spoke the language a little so they were having a language lesson.

Conor pulled out of the hotel car park and was his usual chatty, cheerful self. He explained about the European funding for the roads and how, despite what visitors might think, they were vastly improved on what they once were.

They visited an old monastery on the top of a hill, with majestic views towards the ocean, and they learned about the men of faith from long ago. How tough they were, and how they took on the marauding Vikings.

'The clergy have a reputation for toughness. They weren't afraid no matter how high the stakes.' Conor caught Declan's eye as he spoke, and both men smiled.

After a delicious lunch, which Lucia devoured happily, they went to a cultural centre where a band, including a mesmerizing harpist, played and then some of the cutest little girls and boys aged four to fifteen they'd ever seen arrived to show them some Irish dancing. The way the little ones' feet leaped and hopped to the music was amazing, and then they insisted on getting members of the audience up to dance with them. Declan was hopeless, nearly treading on the feet of a ten-year-old freckly Ginger Rogers, but Valentina it turned out really had a flair for it. The teenage lad she was dancing with was clearly smitten, and he did everything he could to impress her with his dancing. They watched in amazement as the young boys used brush handles as sorts of hurdles while they danced over them, easily throwing them from one hand to the other. Eventually winded and laughing heartily, they sat as the band played some waltzes. Declan danced with Lucia, something they'd never done before, and Valentina was asked up once again by her fourteen-year-old suitor. The whole group were dancing but it was Ken and Irene who stole the show. They moved together as if they were not two but one body. They weren't as agile as they once were, perhaps, but the way they danced together brought tears to the eyes of several members of the tour. They kept no secret of Irene's diagnosis and everything they did, they did mindfully. His eyes never left hers as they danced on and on, never putting a foot wrong.

Conor eventually, way behind schedule, managed to get everyone back on the bus.

The next stop was a magnificent castle, the home of the Butlers, Earls of Ormond, which was fully decorated and restored. Ken and Irene opted to stay on the bus; the dancing had worn them out so they were happy just to rest in the sunshine.

The guide told them stories of the many members of the Butler family who lived there, one in particular catching their attention. Elenor Butler ran away to Wales to live with Sarah Ponsonby, her lover, in the late 1700s. Their home in Llangollen became a retreat for writers and poets, and their bohemian lifestyle was quite the scandal at the time.

'I'm glad I live now and not then!' Zoe exclaimed as the guide retold the story of the chase after the midnight flit to get the lady of the house home. Every effort was made but it was in vain, apparently she was bound for the convent because of her refusal to marry.

They roamed the magnificent grounds and had coffee in the court-yard across the road, once the stables for the castle. As the sun shone in the small leaded windows of the café, Declan caught Lucia just gazing at him.

'What? Do I have cream on my face?' He was tucking into a mouthwatering scone piled high with butter, homemade jam, and thick whipped cream.

'No, I just realized that we're safe, and nothing can harm us. So often, our relationship has been fraught with problems. It's nice to only have cream on your nose to worry about. Do you think it is really over? I mean the Dias side of it?' she asked, sipping her tea.

'I do. Dias has no interest in me or you. He made sure Roberto got his point across, that if we stay out of his way, then he'll stay out of ours. It's over.'

He grinned and she thought he was never more handsome.

As they made their way back to the bus a little early because Declan had forgotten his camera and wanted to get one shot of the castle before they left, they spotted Conor on his phone by the door.

Declan could tell from his body language that something was wrong.

'Ok, yes, if you could. Yes, just in the coach parking area outside the castle, thanks.'

Conor's face was ashen.

'Conor, what's wrong?' Declan was worried.

Conor took a deep breath. 'It's Irene, she's dead. Ken is in there with her. They fell asleep after all the dancing and everything, and when he woke he couldn't wake her.'

Declan squeezed Conor's shoulder. 'I'll go in.' Conor nodded, relieved that someone who was more used to this could help out.

Ken was sitting on the front seat, holding her hand.

'I'm so sorry, Ken.' Declan spoke gently; the other man seemed lost in thought.

He nodded slowly. 'She knew it would be soon. She never

246

complains though, that was the hard part, worrying if she was in pain. She'd never say.' His voice choked with emotion.

'I don't think she was though. I've seen a lot of people at the end of their lives, and they can't hide the pain, it gets so bad, even with all the drugs. She danced with you this afternoon, we all watched you, and you never took your eyes off each other... Every person in that room was thinking the same thing. How lucky you two were to have known such love for so long.'

Ken nodded again.

'Ken, it's a long story, and I'll tell you another time if you're interested, but I was a priest. I know Irene was a believer, we talked about it. Would you like me to say a prayer, give Irene the last rites?'

Ken was shaken out of his grief for a moment. 'But you and Lucia?'

'As I said, a long story. I don't have to, only if you want me to...'

'Sure, she'd like that I think. She was raised Methodist, but she used to like going to hear the choir sometimes in the Catholic place down the street. I never was into it myself but I think she'd like it. She used to pray sometimes.'

For the second time in a week Declan found himself whispering the words of the last rites.

Irene looked so calm and peaceful.

'She looks like she slipped away easily, Ken,' Declan said as he finished.

'She did. I'll be following her shortly.'

Declan smiled and patted him on the shoulder as he held his wife's hand.

Outside the window Conor was on the phone again, sorting out an ambulance to take Irene's body to the morgue. Lucia was explaining to everyone else on the tour, who were keeping a respectful distance.

'Sure. It sounds like you've got a hell of a story of your own to tell anyway.' Ken's voice broke the silence.

'I do.' He saw the ambulance appear, blue lights flashing but no sirens. 'It looks like the paramedics are here. Do you want to go with her or will you stay with us?'

Conor appeared at that moment.

'They're here now, Ken, do you want…'

'She's being taken to Dublin, right?'

'Yes, to the hospital first where a death cert will be issued. If you have her medical files, you'll need to bring those to the hospital this evening when we get to Dublin. Then depending on what you want to do, burial or cremation here, or take her home…'

'I'm taking her home.'

'Ok, well then, the Embassy will issue you all the paperwork you need and they'll help you to get everything in order. It will take a few days though but I can extend your room in the hotel until you're ready to take Irene home.'

Ken let his wife's hand go gently, settling it back in her lap.

He allowed Conor to help him up.

'Thanks, Conor, I appreciate your help. I know Irene does, well, she would, too. I'll go back with your guys, and maybe take a taxi to the hospital then later. Her stuff is in my suitcase…I don't want to get in the medical guy's way.' Wearily he stood, patted Declan and Conor on the back as he passed, and went out to talk to the ambulance team. Conor shepherded everyone back to the café, so as to allow them to do their job without an audience, and they sat as a group, silently sipping teas and coffees that Conor had ordered but nobody really wanted. He needed some air; this was so hard, no matter how many times it happened. Given the age profile of those on tours, a few people died on them every year, but it was always hard for the guide.

Valentina fought tears as she stood outside having a cigarette.

Conor leaned on the wall beside her.

'She saved me, she and Lucia and Anastasia. If not she help I still…'

Conor drew her into a one-armed hug. 'I know, but she was glad to be able to do it. I said I'd handle the situation but she said no, she was determined to help you.' He spoke slowly and she seemed to understand.

'I don't thanks to you, Anastasia say it ok me sleep you house…'

'Its fine, no problem… We have space.'

She smiled a watery smile at him.

'Come on, come inside and have a coffee…we'll get going soon.'

The journey back to the hotel in Dublin was a subdued one, as everyone reminisced about the woman they'd known for such a short time. It always amazed Conor how close people became on tours; it was possibly one of the strangest social groupings imaginable. A group of strangers, united only by their desire to see a particular country, and yet they seemed to bond often on a much deeper level.

He settled everyone in to the Gresham Hotel on Dublin's O'Connell Street, the site of the fierce fighting during the 1916 Rising as the iconic classical General Post Office burned to the ground under sustained fire from the British, who were trying to expel the rebels holed up inside. On another day, he would have pointed out all the bullet holes on the buildings and the huge role the street played in Irish history but today was not a day for that.

The hotel was just what they needed, opulent and comfortable but away from the real buzz in the Temple Bar area of the city, with its all-night entertainment and music.

Declan left Lucia in the hotel with Elke, Zoe, and Valentina and accompanied Ken and Conor to the hospital. The doctor they spoke to was kind, and they did all that was necessary. Ken looked tired and Conor was anxious to get him back to the hotel.

'Would you fellas mind if we went for a drink? I think I could use one,' Ken asked.

'Of course, no problem. I know just the place.' Conor parked the bus up for the night and hailed a cab. 'Doheny and Nesbitts please.'

Within minutes they were inside the iconic old pub. Famous as a haunt of politicians and journalists, there was a gentle hum of conversation but no loud music or intrusive big screens.

Conor ordered three pints of Guinness and three drops of Jameson Irish Whiskey.

The barman dropped the creamy pints to their table and they sipped the warming whiskey as they waited for the pints to settle as Conor showed them.

'To Irene, Godspeed.' Conor raised a toast.

'To Irene,' the two men chorused and the three sat in silence.

'So, what's your story, Declan?' Ken asked. He seemed quite calm and Conor had remarked to Declan as much while they were waiting for Ken to fill out the paperwork.

'He's ready. That's why he's not devastated,' Declan explained. Though he was much younger than Conor, he had a lot more experience with death and those left behind. 'He's made his peace with her death a long time ago.'

Declan smiled and put down his pint. 'Well, if you're sure... It's a hardly believable tale but I assure you every word is true.'

Ken, Conor, and Declan sat in the pub for four hours, talking, telling stories, sometimes getting a little choked up, but it was good, cathartic for all three of them. Declan rang Lucia to tell her where he was at Conor's suggestion—he was still getting used to being part of a couple—and Conor left for twenty minutes to talk to Ana, but they talked and laughed and as they walked back to the hotel, they knew that whatever happened next, they were friends.

CHAPTER 30

*C*onor had dropped the others back at the airport the day the tour ended, but the deputation had come from Elke the night before.

'We are going to extend our flights, we have decided. Declan, Lucia, Valentina, me, and Zoe.'

'Ok. That's up to you of course.' Conor was a little confused.

'Well, Ken has decided to have Irene cremated here instead, and we want to be here with him for the service. Declan and Lucia can spare the time and Valentina needs to stay for the court case so...'

'Oh I see...right. Well, let's all get together and decide what's best to do in that case.'

They all met in the hotel bar and Ken explained he would take her ashes home but he felt like it was the right thing to do to have her service here. She loved Ireland and she hated fuss, which was what there would be if he brought her home. Initially he'd planned to, but after giving it some thought, he decided against a big funeral back in the states. People they weren't close to, long-lost family members and all of that—she wasn't into it.

'Well, it's up to you, Ken, whatever you want.'

'Well, is that possible, do you think?'

'I don't see why not. And do you want a service of some kind or just a cremation?'

'I was talking with Declan about that. I don't want a mass as such but a few prayers, maybe "Danny Boy," something like that might be nice? I don't know if someone could do that…what the situation here is with using churches if you're not…'

Conor and Declan exchanged a glance.

'I think we have just the man. There's a nondenominational chapel of rest in the crematorium in Glasnevin, it's nice there, and we can give her a lovely service.'

'Thanks, Conor. Should I call…'

'Not at all, I'll sort it out.'

EPILOGUE

*T*he day dawned bright and clear and the early morning mist was quickly being burned off by the sun. Ana went up on her tiptoes to fix her husband's tie.

'I just phoned to Mama and Tato, when you were in the shower, and Artie and Joe is fine.'

'Sure they will be. They'll have eejits made of them the same as the rest of us, but it's great we could get them over a few days earlier to take care of the boys. This is going to be hard and I need you beside me.'

'Always,' she whispered, and kissed him.

Lucia's hand was trembling as she pressed the green call button. Declan had convinced her and she eventually agreed, but now she wasn't sure. He had gone down to meet the others, and she was to follow him once she'd called. All she'd ever felt was rejection, and even after her mother's explanation, well, it wasn't as if you could just magically make all those feelings disappear.

'Hello, Lucia, is that you?' Emmanualla's voice was hesitant but hopeful.

'Yes, Emman... Mama, it's me.'

'Are you ok? I thought you might have had second thoughts. I don't deserve it, but I'm glad you did.'

'Me too.'

She told her about Irene and their plans to travel around Ireland for a little while on their own once everything was done.

'I have a really nice villa on the sea, I got it big enough for you and Declan and the baby if you want to visit, or stay or...'

Lucia thought about what that must cost, and felt a pang of disgust. No doubt her mother inherited all of the Sacco money, or whatever wasn't seized anyway, but she wasn't sure she could lounge around some villa being paid for by the misery of drugs or prostitution. It was as if her mother read her mind.

'I am only renting it, but it is my own money, not one penny of your father's. I have my own income, your father never knew about it, from my mother's side of the family. They have vineyards, so perfectly legitimate. All of your father's assets have been seized. If anything comes to me afterwards, and I doubt it will, I am going to give it to charity. Let his filthy money do some good for a change.'

The conversation flowed then. She told Lucia that the police had informed her that Paulie's funeral was that very day, and that she was glad neither of them was going to be there.

'So, will you two come? I could take care of you both, feed you up, introduce you to your family. They are all so looking forward to meeting you.'

Lucia thought for a moment, and suddenly being taken care of by her mother was very appealing indeed.

'Sure, we'd love that.'

There was a slight pause. 'Lucia, I have been thinking, perhaps I should not have told you all of the gruesome details. Your father was...well, he was a lot of things... But he loved you with all of his heart. I need you to know that, to believe it, because it is true. I didn't tell you before but one night, two or three days after you left with Declan, he came to my rooms. As you know, I had not seen him there since... Well, anyway, he begged me to tell him if I knew where you were. I told him that even if I did know, I would never tell him because he would hurt you and I will never forget how he looked. He cried, sobbed like a baby, And he asked me if I really thought that he would hurt you. He told me that he was sorry, for everything, and that you were the best thing that ever happened to him. He told me how you begged him to give it all up, and how he wished he had done as you asked. And I believed him, Lucia, he was truly sorry. For me, for all the death and destruction, for you. He even said he hoped that your disappearance had something to do with Declan because he was such a good man. I should have told you this the other night, but I just, I couldn't. I didn't want to ruin any chance we might have I suppose. I was being selfish, but now you know everything, the whole truth. He did repent, he did see the error of his ways, and it took losing you to do it.'

Tears of relief and love poured down Lucia's face. She would see him again. He had repented. God would be merciful.

She walked downstairs to meet the small group. Declan and Conor were already there, Declan looking very smart in a new suit. She caught a glimpse of herself in the large mirror in the lobby. She seemed to have gained some weight even in a week and looked healthy and happy in a red dress.

Conor hugged her and smiled. "'Tis a far cry from the sick little waif that landed here a fortnight ago you are now.'

'I know. I'm convinced it's Ana's magic potion, I take it every morning and now I eat like a horse. I ate all my own breakfast and half of Declan's this morning.'

'Well, you needed it, you both did. I like your dress by the way.'

'Thanks, I got it in Rome.' She smiled.

Elke had bought boutonnieres for each of them so she pinned the fresh flowers onto each of their lapels. Today was not a day for misery. Irene's life had ended exactly how she would have chosen. And so together they climbed into the coach. Conor assured them that the company had no need of it for another few days.

Father Eddie Shanahan led the service with his signature wit and compassion, and Valentina read a prayer; she'd been practicing it over and over with Ana to get it right. Ken gave a wonderful eulogy, full of love and funny anecdotes. And there was not a dry eye in the place while Laoise and Dylan played "Danny Boy" as Irene's coffin slid behind the curtain.

'Will you miss it?' Lucia whispered in Declan's ear.

'No, I've got too much to look forward to.' And he squeezed her hand.

After the service they all filed out into the sunshine again but Lucia held back.

Declan turned to see her standing in the chapel in her red dress,and he thought she'd never looked more beautiful. As he approached her, he saw she was crying.

'Lucia?'

'Pray with me, Declan,' she whispered. 'Just this once.'

'Of course, if you want to.' Declan was confused. Everyone else was outside, it was just the two of them.

'They buried my dad today.'

Declan nodded. He walked up onto the altar as she knelt in the pew.

'In the name of the Father, and of the Son, and of the Holy Spirit, amen. Eternal rest grant unto the soul of Paulie Sacco, O Lord, and may perpetual light shine upon him forever, may he rest in peace. May his soul and the souls of all the faithful departed, through the mercy of God, rest in peace. Amen.'

Declan turned to the cross on the wall behind the altar, placed there earlier by the management once Irene's status as a Christian was established. He bowed his head, then turned and walked off the altar for the last time, stood beside Lucia and took her hand, and together they went to join their friends.

The End

Thank you for reading my story. I really hope you enjoyed it. The series continues with *The Story of Grenville King, The Homecoming of Bubbles O'Leary* and *Finding Billie Romano*. You can get them here: author.to/JeanGraingerAuthor

If you did, I would be so grateful if you would consider leaving a review on Amazon.

If you would like a free book, please go to my website www.jeangrainger.com.

You can download the free novel and join my readers group. It is 100% free and it always will be!

ACKNOWLEDGMENTS

Writing a sequel is hard, and writing a sequel to your first ever book is probably harder, at least it is for me. I tried several times to write a sequel to *The Tour* but every attempt ended up in the bin, until one day the characters of Declan and Lucia popped into my head, fully formed and so I wrote this story. I really hope you enjoyed it.

As always, I have so many people around me that help me to get my books into a 'fit for human consumption' state. Thanks in spades to my editor Helen Falconer, without whom I doubt I would ever have had the guts to put a story out there. To Vivian Fitzgerald-Smith, proof-reader extraordinaire. To my cousin Jonathan who is exactly the person you would want in times of crisis. To the 10K Angels who are always on hand with advice, a laugh or a hand up from the depths of self-doubt. To my mentor and friend Jim Cooney who knows everything.

To my Advance Reader Team, thank you all so much for your support for my writing. You're scattered all over the globe but I value your input and I really appreciate your help.

I want to say a special word of thanks to my fellow author, dear friend and constant support, Joseph Birchall. As the other founder member of the Irish Indie Publishing Support Group, I have found not just a kind and fair critic of my work, but a comrade in words, we cheer each other's victories and give each other courage when the going gets tough. Thanks Joseph.

I am so lucky in my life, and grateful, for all the wonderful people with whom I share my spin on the merry-go-round. Thanks to Bethann, Pauline, Tracey, Eileen, Mary, Sandra, Liz, Karen, Ankie, Sylvia, Jess, for all the tea, wine, chats and craic. Thanks too, to the Natural Gas gang, the lads and the wags.

To my loud, funny, noisy, loving family, where stories are the life blood, thank you all.

As always, my finest achievements to date get a mention, Conor, Sorcha, Eadaoin and Siobhan. Ye drive me cracked but I adore you and I am so proud of you all.

And finally, to my husband Diarmuid. My greatest ally and my strongest support. Without whom there would be no books.

Jean Grainger,
Cork, Ireland.
June 2017

Made in the USA
Monee, IL
15 May 2020

31123450R00157